# A
# DRIFTLESS
# MURDER

# A
# DRIFTLESS
# MURDER

## JERRY MCGINLEY

The University of Wisconsin Press

The University of Wisconsin Press
728 State Street, Suite 443
Madison, Wisconsin 53706
uwpress.wisc.edu

Gray's Inn House, 127 Clerkenwell Road
London EC1R 5DB, United Kingdom
eurospanbookstore.com

Printed in the United States of America
This book may be available in a digital edition.

Library of Congress Cataloging-in-Publication Data
Names: McGinley, Jerry, 1948– author.
Title: A Driftless murder / Jerry McGinley.
Description: Madison, Wisconsin : The University of Wisconsin Press, [2022]
Identifiers: LCCN 2021007336 | ISBN 9780299332846 (paperback)
Subjects: LCSH: Murder—Investigation—Fiction. | Wisconsin—Fiction. |
    LCGFT: Fiction. | Detective and mystery fiction.
Classification: LCC PS3563.C363988 D75 2022 | DDC
    700/.54403578—dc23
LC record available at https://lccn.loc.gov/2021007336

This book is a work of fiction. Some places and businesses mentioned in the
story are real, but the characters and actions are completely fictional. The local
businesses are used to make the story realistic. None of the situations in the
book are based on actual events.

*For Gail*

*Not till we are lost, in other words,*
*not till we have lost the world,*
*do we begin to find ourselves,*
*and realize where we are and*
*the infinite extent of our relations.*

**HENRY DAVID THOREAU**

# A DRIFTLESS MURDER

# THREE YEARS EARLIER

THERE ARE FEW PEOPLE IN WISCONSIN OVER THIRTY YEARS OLD WHO HAVE never heard of Johnny Benetti. Father Giovanni Benetti was in his thirties when he was brutally murdered and then nailed to a crudely constructed wooden cross on a secluded back road in rural southwestern Wisconsin, a region of bluffs and rivers known as the Driftless because it was untouched by the glaciers that flattened the rest of the state. The murder took place on Halloween night almost fifteen years ago. His body was found by a deer hunter the next morning—All Saints Day in the Catholic Church.

Every year on the anniversary of the crime, every local television station and newspaper in the southern part of the state rehashed the details of the murder and the myriad of theories about who committed the horrendous, still unsolved crime.

Some area residents swore Father Johnny was the victim of a ritualistic sacrifice conducted by a satanic cult rumored to practice bizarre rites in that area. Supporters of this theory pointed to the killing of a goat just days earlier. Like Benetti, the goat was stabbed and then nailed to a wooden cross. Alleged cult members were questioned, but no one was charged or arrested.

A second theory claimed Father Johnny's death was the result of a jealous husband who suspected the charismatic priest of an affair with a female parishioner. Such stories were common during Father Benetti's seven years at St. Stephen's parish in the village of Lake Hope in Kickapoo County. These rumors were not surprising with a handsome, charming young man serving as spiritual advisor and trusted confidant in a community of hilly eighty-acre farms and struggling nickel-and-dime small businesses. Father Johnny was the closest thing to a celebrity in the region. From the days of the cavemen, jealousy has triggered more violence than any other motive— with the possible exception of religion.

Outside of Lake Hope, reporters focused on Father Benetti's role in bringing several pedophile cases to light within the Catholic Church. The outspoken priest pulled no punches when it came to disclosing the long-hidden crimes of his fellow clergymen. This was especially evident after the arrest and conviction of a well-known monsignor in a neighboring diocese. Father Benetti was a key witness in the investigation leading to the monsignor's plea agreement.

In spite of the numerous theories, authorities never made an arrest; in fact, no suspects were ever named. Word around the state was that citizens in the area knew who committed the murder, but for some reason refused to share information with law enforcement. This was idle speculation. In a strange revelation during a local press conference, Sheriff Thomas Welch admitted that his department was certain they knew who killed Father Johnny but lacked evidence to get an indictment. He assured local inhabitants that the crime was not random and local people were not in any apparent danger. The department was actively monitoring the movements and actions of the person of interest.

Whether or not the announcement was simply a red herring to reassure local folks, his words were apparently well received because life in the rural community went on just as it had before the sensational crime. This in spite of the fact that one of the state's most brutal murderers was probably walking freely about their town, eating in their diner, attending the high school football games on Friday night, shopping in their grocery store, and probably sharing a pew during Sunday worship.

Had anyone told me I'd be caught in the middle of this investigation fifteen years after it took place, I would have told them they were nuts. My involvement started with a phone call from a childhood friend. Diane Carey grew up a few houses from me on the north shore of Lake Mendota. As kids we were together constantly. After high school, our lives followed divergent paths—she became a nun while I spent my career in law enforcement. She left her chosen path much earlier than I did, and by the time we reconnected, we were both civilians. She called one late fall morning and asked if I'd be willing to meet her for dinner. She had a favor to ask.

When we finished our meals, I decided to drop the small talk and get down to business. "Okay, what is your request?"

"I wish I didn't have to ask, but I promised a friend on her deathbed." Diane paused for a sip of wine. She was energizing herself. I took the opportunity to swallow a much less dainty swig from my beer stein. I too was bracing for the storm.

"Before I left my," she stammered to find the right words, "my former occupation, I taught in a school near Milwaukee. I worked and lived with a woman called Sister Mary Sarah. We became friends. She eventually moved to Lake Hope where she taught at St. Stephen's School. She was principal there at the time of Father Benetti's death. She never mentioned the event in her letters. Recently, she was diagnosed with cancer and given just months to live. I visited her at a hospice center. She asked about my life. I mentioned I had a childhood friend who was an ex-homicide detective. When I said your name, she recognized it from media stories."

"Unfortunately, no one seems to forget."

"I returned to see her the morning she died. She was very weak, but she called me close and asked me to pray with her. I did. As I stepped away, she whispered, 'And ask your friend to solve Father Johnny's murder.'"

"Did she give you any hints as to how I should solve a crime after fifteen years?"

"She passed a couple minutes later."

"I'd like to help, but I wouldn't have a clue where to start. Local police and the State Division of Criminal Investigation handled that case. What could I find? Besides, the local sheriff's department wouldn't be thrilled to see an outsider stirring up old bones."

"I had to ask. But if it can't be done, it can't be done."

"Did your friend know who killed Father Johnny?"

"She never said anything—not till her last words."

"And she never gave any clues?"

"She asked if you could help, and then she just lay back on her pillow."

"She just asked for help and then died?"

"That's it. Though as she lay on her pillow, she did mumble the words 'Psalm 15' and 'James.' Then she gave a little wave and passed."

"I don't know Psalm 15," I confessed. "Do you think she was leaving a clue? Or was she just remembering a favorite piece of scripture?"

"I don't know. My guess is it's just something that stood out in her fading mind."

"I'll do a little research on Psalm 15. If I sense any hints into the case, I'll try to help you. If not, then I don't think there's anything I can do. Maybe James is a clue I can check into."

"Fair enough. I'll dig out my Bible and see if I can think of possible connections."

EVEN though my reading of Psalm 15 gave me no more insight than I had before I read it, I found myself checking into the Knotty Pine Motel in Lake Hope three days later. The motel had six units, all of which opened to the gravel parking lot. The interiors had seen no renovations since they were built in the forties. The walls were aged knotty pine paneling; the bathroom was small with a toilet, sink, and tiny shower; and the stench of old cigarette smoke, sweat, and wet dogs made it tough to breath. I was certain this was the place Hitchcock had in mind when he filmed Psycho.

My first stop, after dumping off my duffel bag in my motel room, was the sheriff's office. The department was small, only a handful of officers, so I figured I'd have a good chance of speaking directly to the sheriff. My concern was that he would be unwilling to open his files. I could argue that as a citizen I had a right to view public documents, but I knew that the courts had ruled that the only information law enforcement agencies had to release were the names of people arrested. Since no one was ever arrested in this case, I knew my appeal was futile. I did, however, want to introduce myself to the sheriff to give him a heads-up that I planned to investigate the case at the request of Sister Mary Sarah. Both of my assumptions were accurate: I did meet directly with Sheriff Phil Grimes, and he did refuse to provide any access to his files.

"There's no reason trying to solve a case that the sheriff's department and the state DCI haven't been able to resolve," he said. "Why open old sores that have finally started to heal?"

"I appreciate your concern, but I'm an experienced homicide detective, and as a licensed private investigator, I have a right to provide answers for my client," I responded.

"Your client is dead!"

"She knew she was dying when she asked me to get involved. She worked in the parish school at the time of Father Benetti's death and apparently believed I could crack the case."

"I've heard about you, Mr. Donegal. I want you to realize my department will watch every move you make. This is still an open case, so don't interfere with us."

"I have no intentions of violating laws or the legal rights of your citizens. If I decide I'm on a wild goose chase, I'll pack my bags and head home. My only reason for being here is because I was asked by a nun from her deathbed. I will not make a dime doing this job."

"Good publicity though. Stirring up this case should get you, and our county, plenty of notoriety in the press—good for you, not so good for us."

"The last thing I want is my name in the paper or my face on TV. I've had too much of both."

"I can't stop you from snooping around, but don't step over the line."

"Fair enough." I turned to leave but couldn't resist one more question. "You were a deputy when the murder occurred. Is that right?"

"Rookie patrolman. I'd worked the three-till-midnight shift the night of the crime. Chasing Halloween pranksters. I was home sleeping when I got the call saying they'd found a body. Being low man in the department, I stuck to patrol duties while the sheriff and his chief deputy handled the investigation."

"And the sheriff and chief deputy are no longer on the force?" I asked.

"Both left a year or so after it happened. It was a hard case on everybody—but especially for the guys who didn't find the killer."

"Are they still in law enforcement?"

"Hennie Duggan, the chief deputy, is still in the area. Heads security for the local utility company. The sheriff, he's somewhere up in Minnesota. Owns a hunting and fishing store. I haven't seen him since he left. But I see Hennie around. We work together if there's an issue at the utility company. Straight-up guy."

"One more thing, Sheriff. You know anyone named James who might be connected to the case?"

He thought awhile and said, "Can't think of anybody named James ever mentioned. Why do you ask?"

"Just a long shot. Dying words of the nun."

"No help to you there."

"I appreciate your willingness to talk to me, Sheriff, and I have no plan to cause any trouble. Fact is, I hope we can help each other."

"We got things under control here, but thanks for the offer."


HENNIE Duggan sounded like the next guy I should talk to. Straight-up guy, the sheriff called him. Maybe he'd share some details that weren't covered in the media.

I left messages on Duggan's home phone, which the sheriff had begrudgingly given me, but got no return call. I wasn't surprised. I put myself in his position—failed to even name a suspect in the most notorious murder in the state's recent history. Now an outsider comes to town snooping for answers. Of course, he knew my chances of finding a murderer after all these years were about as likely as buying a winning lottery ticket two weeks in a row. But even dragging up the story could put him in a bad spot. People remember Hennie Duggan working the case that never got solved. The former sheriff lived hundreds of miles away. But Hennie saw these people every day. Now he had to look them in the eye again. I knew better than to expect any cooperation from Duggan—even if he was considered a straight-up guy.

Duggan's address was a rural route. Drinking coffee at the only diner in town, I found out from the waitress that Duggan lived alone in a small farmhouse atop a ridge about nine miles from town. I got directions and decided to pay him a visit. As I left town before noon on Saturday, a mixture of freezing rain and sleet was falling. The roads were fine as I drove out, but it occurred to me that if the temperature fell just a few degrees, I would have a treacherous drive back on narrow, hilly roads. And based on how I guessed I'd be greeted by Hennie Duggan, I had no desire to get stranded at his place looking for help getting home. Considering the history of this crime, I was certain no one in the county wanted me sorting through their dirty laundry, and I was even more certain I would not be greeted with open arms by a man who was a key player in the failed investigation.

The road to Duggan's place was worse than I'd expected. Not much wider than a paved cow path, it wound through the hills and valleys like it had been laid out by a rattlesnake. The small farms I passed looked deserted. Apparently, Hennie Duggan liked his privacy. When I reached a house that still looked inhabited, I checked the mailbox. "Duggan" was crudely printed in red capital letters.

As I eased into the gravel driveway, I heard two gunshots. Thinking they might be directed at me, I hit the brakes and threw my truck into reverse. When the next volley erupted, I could tell by the muffled tone that they were further off—probably back in the woods. Deer hunting season was over, but there was plenty of other game. I shifted into drive and pulled all the way into the driveway. Ice was forming on the windshield now and a mix of rain and snow was starting to build up on grass. A white Ford Bronco was parked beside the house. Duggan was most likely in the woods collecting squirrels or rabbits for dinner. I got out of my truck and walked cautiously to the front door. I knocked but got no response. I went back to my truck, where I could at least stay dry while I waited. I hoped it was a short hunt because I did not want to drive back to town on ice.

Several minutes passed before I heard the next burst of gunfire. Two quick shots. Sounded more like a shotgun than a rifle. I was relieved to know Duggan's weapon had limited range if he decided to turn it on me. A few minutes later I saw him walk out of the woods carrying a turkey. A springer spaniel trotted at his side. Duggan took several steps in the clearing before he noticed my truck. When he saw me, he veered in my direction. His shotgun rested across his shoulder. From my days on the force, I remembered police officers liked to have people stay in their vehicles, so I rolled down my window and waited for Duggan to approach me.

As he stepped toward the truck, he held up the turkey, smiled, and said, "Supper!" He lowered the double-barrel shotgun and opened the breech. He held up the gun and said, "Got this old Browning from my grampa. He had it when he was young." Then he held up the turkey and added, "Still shoots."

"Nice-looking gun," I said, still not making any move to get out of my truck. Then I added, "My name is Pat Donegal. I was asked by a friend of mine to look into Father Benetti's death. I know it's a long shot, but it was the dying request of a Sister Mary Sarah who used to work at the local school here."

"I had a call from the sheriff yesterday. I figured you'd be stopping by. You're wasting everybody's time poking into this case again. But I knew Sister Mary Sarah, so if she requested this on her deathbed, I'll tell you what I can. The case is still open, so most of those details are closed to the public. Current sheriff is still responding to any leads that come in—not that there have been many in the last ten years. But technically he still has a deputy assigned to the case."

"I understand."

"Why don't we go up and sit on the porch? I got an electric heater there that throws out plenty of heat. I don't want to stand in this drizzle any longer. Plus, I can set down my supper and my shotgun."

"Sounds good. I'll only stay a few minutes. I don't like seeing that ice starting to build up on the roads."

We walked to the house and entered a three-season porch with rustic wooden furniture. Several deer heads adorned the wall. Now I knew why Hennie Duggan chose to live out here alone. He offered me a seat, set down the gun and turkey on a table in the corner, and then returned to the seat across from me.

"You were on duty when the call came in?" I asked, getting straight to the point.

"I thought it was a Halloween prank at first," he said. "Somebody calls and says there's a body hanging on a cross out on Sawmill Road. Hell, I figured some kids nailed up a mannequin or something. I couldn't believe it when I drove out and saw the priest hanging there. I taped off the whole area and waited for Sheriff Welch to arrive. The two of us scoured the area for clues. Then we called in the coroner— Doc Sullivan was coroner then. We took a lot of pictures and then took the body down from the makeshift cross. Body was stiff, so we knew he'd been dead for several hours."

"Did you call in the State DCI to help investigate?"

"Not right away. Sheriff called later. They didn't get there till the next day."

"Did anybody live up on Sawmill Road? Anyone see or hear anything?"

"No, it's mostly state land up there. There's public hunting, and the local sawmill owner has permission to clean out downed trees and thin out live ones if the state gives the okay. Kids used to have beer parties up there. But that ended after the murder. Nobody saw or heard anything. We figured Father Benetti was murdered elsewhere and then transported to the scene afterward. There were drag marks in the grass. But no tire prints, which probably means the killer was smart enough to keep his vehicle on the road. I'm sure you read all the articles. Lots of people had theories. We checked them all but couldn't find evidence to arrest anyone."

"Apparently Sheriff Welch made a statement that people in town knew the killer, but law enforcement couldn't find evidence for a conviction. He must have known something to make that statement."

"Ah, that statement was blown all of context. The sheriff was just trying to bait the killer. Make him think we knew who he was. He figured maybe somebody would panic and show his hand. Media made a big deal out of it, but nothing ever came of it."

"So, you didn't really have a strong suspect?"

"That was just media hype. We had suspects, and we investigated them all, but nothing turned up. We did a good job on this investigation, Mr. Donegal. You may think we're a bunch of hayseeds bumbling around over here in the hills, but we know how to do a job. If you think you can come here and make fools of us, you're wrong. We made a good investigation. Leave it alone."

"I have no intention of making anybody look bad. But under the circumstances, I feel like I have to see what I can find. And I really appreciate your willingness to talk to me. I heard you were a good man."

"Just so you know, Mr. Donegal, not everybody in the county is going to be as cooperative as I am. Folks are already talking. They're not happy about an outsider coming to dig up the past. This murder tore our county apart. Neighbors were suspicious of neighbors. Friends distrusted friends. Some families broke up because people saw things differently. I'd be careful if I were you. People won't want you here."

"I appreciate that, Mr. Duggan. I hope I don't ruffle too many feathers. And I don't plan to stay any longer than I have to. If there's nothing here, I'll leave. I spent my whole life in law enforcement. I know how people get when you start rooting around too close to home. I will be careful. And I understand why you decided to leave the department. There were plenty of times I wanted to do the same thing. And I heard Sheriff Welch opened a hunting and fishing business. Sounds like a good business to be in."

"We didn't walk away because we blew the investigation, if that's what you're suggesting. Just so happens we got chances to do something different. Not easy working for the public—too many bosses and not enough pay."

"I've been there. I know where you're coming from." I started to leave but then paused for one more question. "Ever come across the name James in your investigation?"

"Not that I recall. Why?"

"Just a name that popped up, but it's probably nothing. I appreciate your time."

Before I headed back to my truck, I shook Duggan's hand and again thanked him for taking the time to talk to me. I felt good about the visit. I concluded that the current sheriff was right—Hennie Duggan was a straight-up guy.

The trip back to town took over a half hour. The roads were slippery, but I made it back to the motel in one piece. I had bread, cheese, and summer sausage in my Coleman cooler in the room, so I made a sandwich before deciding on my next move. The motel owner kept a pot of coffee in the office and told me I was welcome to it whenever I wanted. I decided to accept the offer.

After lunch, I decided to visit a Wiccan coven who were rumored to have killed Father Benetti as part of a satanic sacrifice. Many people in the area linked the murder to the animal sacrifice found in a nearby rural area a few nights before Halloween. The sheriff's department investigated the connection but evidently found nothing to connect the group to the priest's death. According to what I read, there was still a group in the area practicing witchcraft. Since I knew little about these groups, I had more than a little apprehension about visiting them. But if I was going to satisfy Sister Mary Sarah's dying request, I knew I had to explore every possible connection.

Before leaving, I called my friend Detective Shea Sommers and updated her on my adventure. Shea served with the Madison Police Department, and we'd met years ago when I stuck my nose into an apparent drowning that I suspected was not as accidental as it appeared. We quickly learned we worked well together, and she occasionally called me in as a consultant for her cases. She had access to information I couldn't get, and I thought it might be wise to let someone know what I was up to out here.

"I'm sure the natives have rolled out the red carpet," she said.

"Not exactly, but no threats yet. The waitress at the diner smiled at me, the current sheriff was cordial, and the former deputy who investigated the case was friendly and helpful. So far so good."

"Are you armed?"

"I got my shotgun behind the seat in my truck, and my Smith and Wesson .40 caliber is in my duffel bag in the room."

"Your handgun won't do you much good in your motel. Put it in your coat pocket before you go chasing around."

"You're worried about me?"

"Things could get dicey over there. There's still a killer on the loose, and I'm sure he, or she, is not thrilled to have an experienced detective stoking an old fire. What's your next move?"

"I am going out to visit a Wiccan coven."

"I read about that group. Sounds innocent to me, but don't take chances. Somebody's hiding secrets they don't want uncovered. Watch yourself. If you come up with something good, I'm off next Tuesday. Maybe I can sneak over and give you a hand."

"If I find something, I will certainly welcome the help."

"Keep in touch, and don't do anything stupid."


BEFORE hanging up, Shea had looked up the property owned by the coven of witches. The coven was located in a remote, heavily wooded area about a dozen miles from Lake Hope. I was sure I would not be welcome there, but I headed out in the middle of the afternoon, not sure what to expect. The freezing rain had stopped, and the sky was clear. At least I didn't have to worry about slippery roads.

Using Shea's directions, I found the property nestled in a wooded valley surrounded by family farms. I expected a much more secluded site. From the road I could see one good-sized two-story cottage just off the road and four or five smaller cabins set further back at the edge of the woods. I didn't see anyone around but decided to drive in and take my chances.

As I approached the front door of the cottage, I noticed several symbolic-looking art pieces. On the front door was a large pentagram enclosed in a circle. On the wall next to the door was a painting of two crescents abutted against a full circle. Many smaller designs adorned the yard, shrubs, and trees. I was studying these symbols when the front door opened. A woman, probably in her late forties, wearing blue jeans and a brown flannel shirt, greeted me. I was surprised not only that someone came to the door before I knocked but also because I expected to be met by some exotic creature in a flowing black robe and high-peaked hat.

"Are you lost?" she asked without any formal greeting.

"No, I was told there was a coven of witches living here," I stammered. "My name is Pat Donegal. I'm a private investigator looking into the Father Benetti murder."

"Well, I am the *witch* you're looking for, but I'm afraid I'm not going to be able to help you much with your investigation. I was here fifteen years ago, and I answered all the sheriff's questions back then. What specifically are you wondering about?"

I proceeded to narrate the story of Sister Mary Sarah's odd deathbed wish. I explained I was just looking into the various theories that have been tossed around in the media over the years.

"Would you like to come in? I was just boiling a pot of water for an afternoon cup of tea. Would you like tea, Mr. Donegal?"

"I would, yes. And I appreciate your willingness to talk to me. People in the area have been more gracious than I expected."

"What were you expecting? A lost society out of a Stephen King novel?" She smiled. "You looked surprised when I opened the door. Who did you think would answer?"

"I'm sorry. I know very little about your group. I didn't expect you to be wearing jeans and a flannel shirt. I don't know what I expected."

"The water is boiling. Excuse me while I get the tea. Would you prefer regular tea or herbal? I have several flavors."

"Black tea if you have it. No sugar."

"Black tea, no sugar. Have a chair. I'll be right back."

I looked around the room. It appeared like any other cottage. On a small table next to my chair I noticed a book about Celtic folklore. In the corner was a bookshelf with probably a couple hundred neatly organized books. There was a sewing machine in the corner with a stack of various colored fabrics beside it.

My hostess returned promptly carrying a tray with two large mugs and a small plate of star-shaped sugar cookies. She slid the book across the table and set the tray in front of me.

"Help yourself, Mr. Donegal. Your tea is in the green mug. Have a cookie." She reached down and picked up the book. "Judging from your last name, I assume you are Irish. You might enjoy this book. The Irish have a very rich pagan heritage. Many of our beliefs and rituals go back to the ancient Celts."

"I don't know much about my ancestors. Are you Irish?"

"Little bit, which is how I got my name. But most of my ancestry goes back to Eastern Europe." She paused and smiled. "I'm sorry. I didn't introduce myself." She extended her hand. "I'm Raven Quinn. I have lived here for over twenty years. At one time we had probably thirty people staying out here. Now we have occasional guests—six are staying in the cabins this week. They are out walking in the woods. I suppose you heard all about the supposedly satanic animal mutilation that happened shortly before Father Benetti was killed. Not surprisingly, our group was blamed. Even though most of our neighbors know we are simple people who worship nature and follow ancient traditions, there are some people who assume because we practice a different religion, we must belong to some devil-worshipping cult. As I told the sheriff fifteen years ago, I am a vegetarian, as are most of the other members of our coven. We do not eat meat. We certainly would not kill an animal to celebrate our beliefs. We believe in the sanctity of all life—animal and plant. We respect the plants we eat. There is no way we would kill an animal or a human. Both the sacrificed animal and the priest were nailed to a cross. That is the ultimate Christian symbol. I believe your killer is someone involved with, perhaps unhappy with, the Christian religion."

"You make sense, Miss Quinn. I'm glad I came to see you. I learned a lot." I paused to consider my next question. "Did you ever meet Father Benetti?"

"Several times. In fact, he and I sat right here drinking tea and talking. He was an intelligent man, very curious. He wanted to learn about our beliefs. We had wonderful conversations. I liked him very much. I'm sure his parishioners would not be happy to hear that, but it's true. And I think he liked coming here as much as I enjoyed having him here. I was very sad when he died." She folded her hands in her lap as she finished. I thought she was going to cry. I felt bad for her. I would have enjoyed staying longer and learning more about her and about her beliefs, but I knew we both had things we needed to do. I finished my tea and rose slowly.

"I'm grateful for the tea and for your time. I enjoyed meeting you and listening to you," I said.

"I wish you well on your quixotic quest. Please be careful. There are people who do not want this horrible crime solved. Take care of yourself, Mr. Donegal. And please stop by again if you have a chance. We could talk and drink tea, and I could show you through the woods. There are many interesting things in our woods."

"Thank you. I hope I get a chance to accept that invitation."

WHEN I got back to town, it was too early for supper, and even though I knew I should call Diane to report on my progress, I decided to put off that call because I didn't really have any progress to report. Instead, I decided to drive out and look at the site of Father Johnny's crucifixion. It was several miles from town, but if I left right away, I'd have time to look it over before it got dark. I had no idea what I expected to find, but I knew I couldn't conduct an investigation without examining the crime scene.

It only took twenty minutes to get to Sawmill Road. The abandoned billboard where the crude cross was erected was easy to find. I pulled off the road and tramped along the ditch, not really looking for clues but more to get a feel for the place. The distance from the road to the billboard was about twenty feet. I stepped it off, trying to guess how long it took for the killer to drag the body to the pole holding up the sign, return to grab the two-by-six board and tools, nail the board to the billboard post, nail the body to the cross, and then get away without anyone driving past. The task would have taken close to thirty minutes. How could the killer be sure no one would drive by? I wondered if there was more than one person at the scene. I decided to wait to see how often cars used the road. After half an hour, I decided traffic would not have been a concern. Not one car drove past.

I returned to my truck, made a U-turn in the road, and headed back to Lake Hope. By this time, it was nearly dark. I hadn't traveled a mile when I noticed a black pickup backed into a logging trail. I hadn't noticed the truck earlier. Probably a hunter. I kept my eye on the rear-view mirror as I drove. When I was less than a quarter mile past the truck, I was sure I saw a black shadow move from the woods onto the road. Was someone following me without headlights? I pressed down on the accelerator till I was pushing seventy—too much speed for those narrow, crooked roads. I rolled down the window to listen for the sound of an approaching vehicle.

It wasn't long before I heard the roar of a V-8 barreling up behind me. If I was going seventy, he must've been doing eighty to catch me. My fight-or-flight juices were surging through my system. I wished I had placed my 12-gauge on the seat, where I'd have access if it came to a shootout. Navigating a tight curve with one hand on the wheel, I took my .40 caliber out of my pocket and set it beside my hip, glad I'd listened to Shea's advice. As I did so, I felt the spray of glass and heard the explosion of my rear window blowing out. I felt shards of glass and maybe shotgun pellets rip into my neck and shoulder. I leaned my head to the left to make myself less of a target in the rear window. If I accelerated, I'd probably wrap my truck around a tree or telephone pole. If I slowed down, I'd likely get rammed from behind—or shot. Neither option was appealing, so I slowed down just a little and looked for a side road or driveway I could try to pull into to give myself a fighting chance.

A second gunshot boomed behind me, but the aim was high this time, and I could hear BBs dig into the roof of my truck. I searched for some kind of escape route. My chance came when I saw narrow side road coming up on the right. I braced myself against the seat and tried to remember what I'd learned in driving school when I was a patrolman. It was time to act. About fifty feet before the intersection, I jammed on the brakes and cranked the steering wheel to control the swerve at a right angle. The truck leaned to the right. The driver's side wheels probably left the ground. It felt like I was going to roll, but just as the truck hit the gravel of the side road, I felt my rear left tire dig in. It was a rough couple hundred feet, but eventually the vehicle was under control. When the truck was stopped, I grabbed my pistol and jumped out. I was ready to fire when I hit the road running. But the other truck kept going straight. I was in the clear—at least for now. I took several deep breaths to get my system functioning again. Then I assessed my injuries and tried to determine how much the truck was damaged. In the dark it was difficult to tell. I decided to hop in, start her up, and try to make it back to town. There was little to worry about from my attacker since he had now lost the element of surprise. Still, I was certain I had not seen the last of the black pickup.

When I got to town, my first stop was the sheriff's department. I knew they wouldn't be any help in catching the person who shot at me, but I at least wanted it on the record that the incident occurred. I had a feeling this was not going to be the last time I was shot at, and I decided the next time I had better be prepared to return fire. I wanted the sheriff's department to know I was defending myself if I ended up shooting the son of a bitch that almost killed me.

When I walked into the office covered with blood, I was greeted by a shocked receptionist, who asked if I wanted her to call an ambulance. I told her I just wanted to report an incident. She quickly summoned a young deputy, who took me into a small office and found a clean towel to wrap around the back of my neck to stop the bleeding. He called out to the receptionist to phone Dr. Wright to see if he could stop by to look at my wounds. I didn't argue. Then the deputy took out a pad and wrote down my story, asking me to provide as many details as I could remember.

"It was a black pickup truck. That's all I know. I caught sight of it parked in a logging trail on Sawmill Road. It was getting dark, so I couldn't see much in the peripheral illumination of my headlights. After I passed, the truck followed me without headlights. Then he fired two blasts from a shotgun. That's all I know."

"Lot of black pickups and shotguns in the county."

"I don't expect you to find the guy. I just want it on the record that the attack happened."

After that he quizzed me about why I was in town and gave me the usual advice to just let sleeping dogs lie and leave the investigation to the department. I assured him I had no fear of sleeping dogs, but I told him I had no plans to break any laws during my investigation. By the time our chat was over, a man who looked to be in his eighties, carrying a black bag, walked into the office. Doc Wright cleaned the glass from my wounds, dabbed on antiseptic gel, and bandaged the cuts that were still bleeding. When he was finished, I told him I'd stop by his office on Monday to settle my account. "Don't worry about it," the doctor said. "This one's on the house. Just make sure there's not a second time. I have a feeling you may not be this lucky twice."

After leaving the sheriff's office, I headed to the small local hardware store. I bought a roll of clear plastic and two rolls of duct tape, so I could patch the rear window of my truck. I also bought two extra boxes of double-aught buckshot and a box of 12-gauge slugs. If my friend in the black truck decided to stop by the motel during the night, I planned to be prepared.

Once I had my hardware supplies, I drove to a tavern on the edge of town and had a couple beers and a frozen pizza. I called Shea to update her on my misadventures and to ask her another favor—something she might be getting tired of hearing. She was shocked when I told her about being shot at, and she told me I was crazy to stay in Lake Hope looking for a killer who'd probably never be found. I reminded her I had a history of taking cases that had little chance of turning out well. "I'm not known for my good judgement."

"I wish you'd throw in the towel on this one, Pat. Diane will certainly understand. By the way, have you told her what's going on?"

"I think I'll wait till it's resolved one way or the other. And as far as leaving town, I owe some son of a bitch a couple rounds of buckshot, and I'd hate to skip town without paying my debts."

"You any closer to finding a murderer?"

"If you call ruling out suspects making progress, then yes, I feel closer. The current sheriff seems decent enough—maybe not a great lawman, but I doubt he had any involvement in Father Benetti's death. He was a rookie patrolman. Plus, the former chief deputy I talked to—Hennie Duggan—seems like a solid guy. Works security here in town for the power and light company. The satanic theory is a joke. I talked to the witch who heads the coven here, and I found her to be quite enchanting."

"Enchanting? Did you just say *enchanting*? Sounds like a fairy tale. Did she give you a potion and cast a spell on you?"

"She did give me tea and cookies. Maybe they had magic in them. They were good."

"I never figured you for a tea-and-cookie man, Pat. Really? She was enchanting?"

"Let's change the subject, okay? The one guy I'd like to talk to is the ex-sheriff. He left town sort of suddenly and opened a hunting store in Minnesota. I hate to ask another favor, but maybe you could dig around a little. See if he looks suspicious. Name is Thomas Welch, but I don't know where he lives in Minnesota. Maybe you can find out if he had any silent money helping him out in his new business. It's a long shot, but you never know."

"It's a common name, but I should be able to track him down and find out where he got his money. I better also do some background checks on the witch. I'd hate to see you get mixed up with something demonic."

"Just worry about the sheriff. I can handle the witch."

"I'm glad you still have a sense of humor. And one more thing— I'm coming to visit Monday night. I got all day Tuesday and half of Wednesday to see if I can straighten out this mess. Sounds like some old man wandering around in a maze needs a real cop to help find his way out."

"I would certainly appreciate your help. But come armed and bring a sleeping bag. I don't think you're going to want to touch the sheets in this motel."

"I'm assuming there's more than one room there. I'm not big on sharing."

"I'm the only one in the place—you'll have your choice of five suites."

"Lovely. Call back if you have any good news—unless it involves an enchanting witch. I don't want to hear that."

"I owe you big-time, Shea."

"Don't worry. I'm keeping score."

I didn't sleep much Saturday night. I kept a vigil in case the black truck showed up. Since I was the only resident in the motel, I parked my truck in front of room five. I was staying in number two. If the shooter came looking, he'd make his attack on the wrong room. That'd give me time to make my counteroffensive. I checked every hour to make sure nobody else checked in to the Knotty Pine.

At around three thirty in the morning, I heard tires on gravel and jumped up to check. My loaded shotgun was in easy reach, so I was ready to open fire when I got to the window. Fortunately, it was just somebody in an SUV turning around in the parking lot, lost, and probably drunk. I stayed at the window for almost an hour to make sure.

IT was nearly ten o'clock when I woke up Sunday. I was stiff and sore. Though I was anxious to find my assailant, I decided to lay low for the day. I'd lick my wounds and put together a plan for Monday. When I went for my morning coffee with the motel manager, he surprised me with a plate of fresh apple cider donuts. I ate three. Then I went back, took a shower, and settled down to watch the Packers game on the seventeen-inch television. I dozed off frequently during the game— which was a one-sided drubbing of the Vikings. After the game, I headed down to the tavern and had a pair of quarter-pound cheeseburgers and two cans of beer—a nightmare for my physical health, but it did wonders for my psyche. On my way back to my motel room, I drove around the area looking for black pickups. I knew there would be several of them, and I'd have no way of knowing which was the right one. I spotted three black trucks, but all were parked along the street. Whoever attacked me would likely make an effort to stay hidden.

Monday morning when I went down for my coffee, I paid for two more nights for myself and also paid for a room for Shea for two nights. I was hoping by Wednesday morning we'd have the case closed. I knew in the back of my mind that if the ex-sheriff didn't turn out to be the killer, I'd eventually have to investigate Father Johnny's involvement in bringing other priests to justice for sexual abuse of minors. That was a nest of snakes I did not want to plow into. For two thousand years, better men than I have tried to break through the Church's iron wall of secrecy. If the search went in that direction, I was certain I'd never succeed.

My cell phone rang as I walked back to my room. It was Shea, and she was full of news. "Pat, are you at your motel, or did you spend the night in the magical forest?" she asked.

"Too early for enchanted forest humor. I just finished coffee in the motel lobby, and I'm ready to go solve a murder. What did you find out?"

"Plenty. You're going to like this. I may know who shot at you yesterday. How's that for a start?"

"That would make my day. What'd you find?"

"Did you tell me the former chief deputy is now in charge of security at the utility company?"

"That's right. Hennie Duggan. You think he's the guy?"

"He may be involved. I checked on Thomas Welch. He owns a sports shop in Pike Island, Minnesota. The financial backer when Welch bought the place—and currently a partner in the business—is Grant Collier."

"Should I know him?"

"You will soon. Turns out Collier is the owner of the utility company in Lake Hope. The company serves the entire region with electricity and natural gas. Collier is also the primary shareholder in the local bank, and—get this—for the past twenty-three years the parish president of St. Stephen's Church. How's that for doing my homework?"

"I'm speechless. You found out more from your office than I did chasing my own tail and getting shot at. I don't know what to say."

"But you're having more fun chasing your tail than I am sitting in front of a computer."

"Can't be a coincidence. In the middle of an investigation, this Collier character essentially buys out the two guys in charge of finding a murderer. Only one reason he'd do that."

"He doesn't want the killer caught. And if you can take more interesting news, I checked with the Minnesota motor vehicle department and guess what?"

"Thomas Welch owns a black pickup."

"Black 2014 Dodge Ram."

"I was just heading back to my room to plan out the day. I think you planned it for me. I don't know why they would murder a priest, but I'd bet they are involved in it somehow. You're a lifesaver, Shea. I don't know how to thank you."

"Thank me by not getting yourself killed before I get there. If these men brutally murdered a priest and nailed him to the cross, they won't stop at anything to keep their secret. They're dangerous men, Pat. And they're after you. Stay out of their way."

"Grant Collier is probably the brains behind this mess, and he doesn't have any idea I know he's involved. Men like him think they're too smart to get caught. I'm going to try to talk to him and suggest that I think Welch and Duggan committed the crime and then destroyed the evidence. Maybe I can get him to implicate the other two. I'll try to think of a way to trap all three of them."

"Wait till I get there. You can't do this alone. I'm on duty till four o'clock. I can be there by seven. You need backup." Shea wasn't suggesting. She was ordering.

"No, you've done too much already. I got myself into this jam. I'll figure a way out. Besides, this place is about 130 miles from your jurisdiction. If you get tangled up in this fiasco, you could end up losing your job. I think I can trust the current sheriff. I'll run things by him and see what kind of vibes I get."

"I'll be there by seven tonight. You're really close. Wait for me so we can do this right. We did the hard part—finding our suspects. Now we just have to bring them in. Don't blow it by trying to go lone wolf. Wait for me."

"Okay, nothing stupid," I lied. "But I am going to visit Collier and get a read on how he's involved. I'll also check around to see if there was bad blood between Collier and Father Johnny. A guy who serves twenty-plus years as parish president wants to control his church. Maybe the young priest was too popular and had too many new ideas."

"Could be the reason local people clammed up. They're afraid of Collier, or maybe they like him. Rich guy like that can do a lot of good for a small town. Talk to him, but don't let on you suspect him."

"All right. We'll do it your way. I'll be looking over my shoulder as I try to paste the pieces together."

"Oh, and one more thing, and you may think I'm crazy even suggesting it. You said Diane's friend mentioned Psalm 15 and James before she died."

"I read the Psalm but couldn't find a clue. Just about the good people who get into heaven. She was probably considering her next life," I said.

"Could be, but you also said she waved. What if she wasn't waving? What if she was holding up five fingers? Verse five of the Psalm refers to good people who lend money without charging interest. Collier is head of the bank—they charge plenty of interest. And chapter five of the Epistle of James blasts rich people and warns them of the terror that awaits them after death. It might be weird, but what if she was trying to give a direction to follow. A bit cryptic, but possible."

"Too weird to be a coincidence if Collier is our guy. And since when did you become a theological scholar?"

"Amazing what Google turns up." Shea chuckled on the other end of the line.

"I think you may have just solved the biggest enigma in state crime history."

"But now we have to prove it—without getting killed."

GETTING a meeting with Grant Collier was easier than I expected. I called his office after my conversation with Shea. His receptionist put me on hold for a few minutes and came back to tell me Mr. Collier was tied up in meetings all day but would be able to meet me at six o'clock in the warehouse behind his office. She said he had another meeting in the evening, so he could only spare a half hour for me. He was a busy man, but I still wondered about meeting in the warehouse. If he was behind Father Benetti's murder, a warehouse would be a convenient location to dispose of a nosey investigator getting too close to the truth. By accepting his invitation, I knew I was putting myself in danger, but I didn't want to risk any chance to confront him with what I knew.

I had almost eight hours to figure out a plan. My biggest problem was having no one I was certain I could trust for backup. Shea wouldn't arrive until at least seven. I considered calling Sheriff Grimes, but I wasn't positive I could trust him. If Collier got to the previous sheriff, there was a chance he controlled the current one as well. Hennie Duggan was another possibility, but he was on Collier's payroll at the utility company. I wasn't a hundred percent sure I could trust him. Essentially, it was going to be me against whoever showed up at the warehouse.

The one person I felt I could trust was Raven Quinn. I decided to drive out to talk to her, now that I had an idea of where my investigation was heading. She knew the priest. Perhaps he confided in her about problems in the parish. Without coming out and saying who I suspected, I could try to lead Raven to a discussion that might help confirm or deny what I suspected about Grant Collier and Thomas Welch.

When I arrived at the coven residence, the place seemed deserted. I tried the door of the main house as well as each of the cabins. I got no response. It occurred to me that maybe I was wrong. Maybe the witch coven had been involved and decided it was time to leave the area. Perhaps it was time to cut my losses and go back to Madison, or at least postpone the meeting with Collier until I had backup.

I was on my way to my truck when I heard voices either chanting or singing. I waited and saw five women and one man following Raven Quinn out of the woods. They stopped singing when they noticed my truck in the driveway. The group disassembled and headed to their respective cottages. Raven Quinn walked straight toward me.

"Mr. Donegal, back so soon?" She offered her hand and gave mine a firm grip. "Would you come in for tea?" She glanced at the bandages on my neck. "You've been injured. Please come inside. I can look at those wounds."

"I'll be fine—just a little skirmish with the local wildlife. Really, I was just out driving and thought maybe you could tell me more about Father Benetti. You said you talked."

"We did. He was a good person, a mystical one. We had much in common. But I refuse to converse in the driveway. Come inside."

"Thank you. But you have better things to do."

"I have nothing I'd rather do right now than help you solve Giovanni's murder."

Once inside, Raven moved quickly to the kitchen to start the tea. I took a seat at the small round table in the dining area. She returned and sat facing me.

"We can talk for five minutes till the water boils."

"Do you remember Father Benetti ever mentioning any problems in the church? Any conflicts?"

"He spoke very little about himself. He was curious about me and my lifestyle. He was never judgmental. He was very positive."

"Any money problems in the congregation that he might have mentioned?"

"Not that I recall. It was a long time ago. Maybe my mind chooses only to remember the good things we talked about. People are different that way. Some dwell on the dark memories while others focus on the positive. Don't you think that's true, Mr. Donegal?"

"Please call me Pat. I am retired from formalities. And, yes, I agree with what you said. Regretfully, I guess I'd say I belong to the first group."

"People can change."

"I hope that's true."

The teapot whistled and Raven walked to the kitchen. When she returned with the tea, I steered the talk back to Father Benetti.

"Father was a charming and handsome man from what I've heard. Do you think there might have been jealous husbands who may have wanted to get rid of him? Any divorces during this period that you remember?"

"I'm not involved in local gossip out here." She paused as if deciding whether she wanted to share a rumor she may have heard. "But I do recall the neighbors mentioning that Mrs. Collier left town shortly after the murder. They felt like it was odd that such a prominent member of their congregation would leave so abruptly. It drew attention for a while, but after a few weeks I suppose people forgot about it."

"From what I hear, Mr. Collier is a powerful man."

"And lets everyone know it. Always in the local paper, donating money for a skating rink or a shooting range. Makes sure he's right on the front page every time."

"Any idea why she left?"

"No." She leaned back in her chair and smiled. "I wish I could help you more, but at the same time I wish you'd leave this all alone. Somebody in town knows who killed Giovanni, and I worry that they'll be after you next."

"They've tried already. But I'm a pit bull. When I sink my teeth into something, I refuse to let loose. That will probably get me killed someday, but till I start focusing on the positive, I'll remain the proverbial old dog."

I finished my tea and stood to leave. Raven rose slowly. She followed me to the door without speaking. As I opened the truck door, she said, "Will you stop to say good-bye before you leave town?"

"I will," I said, hoping I would still be breathing when I left this town.

I returned to my motel room to make preparations for my meeting with Grant Collier. Carrying a shotgun into the warehouse was out of the question, but I did plan to have the Winchester loaded and ready on the front seat of my truck. I'd be carrying my .40 caliber handgun in a holster at the small of my back. Though not practical in a lot of situations, this setup provides good concealment and delivers an easy draw when needed. I assumed Collier would not be alone. Chances are Thomas Welch would be there to provide muscle. If they tried to search me for weapons, I'd trust my instincts to react to the situation. I planned to have a ten-shot magazine loaded in the Smith and Wesson and another one in my coat pocket. If I needed more than twenty shots, I was in big trouble.

As I was doing a final check of my weapons, my cell phone rang. It was Diane Carey wanting to know how the investigation was going. I gave her a thumbnail sketch leaving out the shooting incident on Sawmill Road and the planned meeting with Collier. She apologized for asking me to get involved and pleaded with me to drop the whole operation.

"It was foolish of me to even suggest you getting into this mess. I don't know what I was thinking. I pictured you coming over, snooping around for a couple days, and concluding there was nothing you could do. I should have known better. Pat Donegal doesn't walk away from a job till it's finished. You were that way when we were kids."

"I'm okay. And this isn't on you. I get a bit overzealous about unsolved cases. You know that from what you read in the press. I'm doing this because I need to see it finished. Whatever happens, it's not about you asking me to get involved. I'm close—real close. If the job isn't done by tomorrow night, I'll turn over everything I've found to authorities. Besides, Shea is coming over tonight to help me out. She's done more than her share already. We'll be okay."

"I talked to Shea today. She told me you're meeting with dangerous men tonight. She's worried you'll go alone. Don't do it, Pat. It's not worth it."

"It is to me. I got things under control. I'll call in the morning."

"I know I won't change your mind, so at least be careful."

With two hours to go before my rendezvous with Collier and Welch, I had one more stop to make to set things in motion. I also had time to stop at the tavern for a cheeseburger with fried onions and a beer. If this was going to be my last supper, I wanted to enjoy it.

At quarter to six, I made a slow drive around the power plant property, planning to see a black pickup and Collier's car. The parking lots were empty. They hid their vehicles so I wouldn't know how many to expect. Would Sheriff Grimes be there? Hennie Duggan? Other henchmen brought in for added security? Lights were on in the main storage building, and the garage-type door was open. This is where the drama would unfold.

An hour later, after a couple phone calls, I pulled into the parking lot. I parked my truck so that it was headed toward the street in case I needed a hasty exit. I also parked it so that there was a grassy field to my left. If Collier's men parked in front of me to block my retreat, I had a chance of escaping across the field. I checked my weapons before leaving the truck. It was do-or-die time.

When I entered the building, Collier was sitting on a reception desk facing me. Two goons stood one on each side of him, about ten feet in each direction. One, I assumed, was Thomas Welch, and the other was probably whoever wielded the shotgun while Welch tried to run me off the road. Neither man was openly armed, but I was certain they had guns within easy reach. I stepped to within ten feet of Collier.

"Mr. Collier, I appreciate your willingness to talk to me. As you know I have been investigating Father Benetti's murder as a favor to Sister Mary Sarah, who used to work in this parish."

"I know Sister. What do you want from me?"

"You were president of the church counsel. You must have known Father Benetti quite well. I was hoping you might know who wanted him dead."

"I told the real authorities everything I knew. They carried out a thorough investigation. What makes you think you can come here fifteen years after the murder, without access to any of the evidence, and solve a crime that experts have been unable to make head or tail of?"

Collier's tone sounded more annoyed than angry or scared. Maybe I was wrong.

"You do a lot for this town, I've heard. Even more for St. Stephen's parish. Were you close to the priest?"

"We worked well together, but we weren't buddies. And, yes, I do plenty for this town. There wouldn't be a Catholic school here if I hadn't provided over half the money to build it. But I've been fortunate. I'm glad to be able to help other people."

"I'm curious about Thomas Welch and Hennie Duggan. The sheriff and chief deputy in charge of the most publicized investigation in the state. Right in the heat of the battle, they both decide to take other jobs. Did you think that was strange, Mr. Collier?"

"Not at all. These men were under extreme pressure. Whoever committed the crime was a pro. I've heard the murder was related to Father Johnny's investigation of priests accused of molesting kids. Skeptics might say the Church brought in a hired assassin. Professionals don't leave clues. Sheriff Welch and Detective Duggan did everything possible to find the killer. When the investigation hit a brick wall, I was glad to help these officers out. I needed someone to head security here at the plant, so I offered it to Duggan. He has done one hell of a good job the past fifteen years."

"And the sheriff? You helped him start a business out of the state?"

"You've done your homework, Mr. Donegal. Yes, I loaned Tom start-up money. He's a good man."

"The investigation died once the two primary investigators left. A cynical person might think you were trying to steer them away from the case by providing them jobs outside the sheriff's department."

"Are you accusing me of killing Father Benetti? If you are, you better have something to back it up." Collier stood up and moved to about five feet from me.

"I'm just trying to put a puzzle together. Sister Mary Sarah, on her deathbed, mentioned two pieces of scripture. Both references are to wealthy people having a tough time getting into heaven. Why did she mention those two passages? Unless, she thought someone with a lot of wealth had something to do with the murder. I guess that's a long shot. Would never hold up in court."

"So, a dying nun mumbles Bible stories about rich people getting into heaven, and you conclude that the person with the most money must be the killer. Stellar police work, Donegal. Is that the kind of police work you did a few years back when you couldn't solve a case so you took the suspect out to the woods, and the suspect ended up dead? I read about that. I know how you solve crimes. That's why I asked a couple of friends to stop in to make sure the same thing didn't happen to me."

"It never happened that way. I'm not a vigilante."

"If you decide to play rough, it's three of us and one of you."

"I noticed. I expected it. I knew it wasn't you who shot out the window of my truck. No, that was your friend Mr. Welch in his black Dodge Ram truck. I assume one of these gentlemen is the former sheriff." The tall, bearded man to Collier's right tipped his hat and nodded.

"So, have you come to arrest me? Without any evidence?" Collier asked.

"I'm not a cop anymore. I told a friend I'd try to figure out what happened. If I wanted you arrested, I would have invited your current sheriff. You can see I came alone."

"I have a hard time seeing Phil Grimes put a case together. Does all right busting up beer parties, but I don't see him as a homicide detective." Collier stepped back and sat down on the desktop. "So, this is just a friendly chat?"

"I talked to one of your church members today. He told me Father Johnny used to get on his high horse about it being easier for a camel to climb through the eye of a needle than for a rich man to get into heaven. That must have bugged the shit out of you."

"He was young and idealistic, but he stuck his pious little paw out to me every time the church had a fundraiser. 'Oh, bless you, Mr. Collier, your generosity will be repaid by the Almighty.' He didn't even see the hypocrisy of it."

"Must've hurt though, sitting in your pew in the front row, in the pews that you had purchased, and knowing all those common folks were staring at the back of your head every time he mentioned his camel and eye of the needle story. That would have pissed me off. Probably upset your wife too." I paused to decide how to push him harder. "Did she get along with Father Johnny?"

"That's it. I'm willing to play your stupid games, but not when you bring my family into it. Either piss or get off the pot. Are you accusing me of murder because a priest hurt my feelings during a sermon? If that's what you got, call Sheriff Grimes. Tell him to cuff me and drag me to jail. Let's see how that works out."

I decided we'd had enough small talk. It was time to push toward the climax. Maybe I was wrong about Collier, but his demeanor told me he was a man who could explode if pushed too far. He'd danced around a lot of topics, but when I mentioned his wife, a new set of lights flashed. I knew I was putting my life on the line here, but I had to find out who killed Father Johnny.

"That local parishioner I talked to suggested maybe Father Benetti got too close to your wife. She left town shortly after his death. Do you think she might have been involved?"

Collier lunged toward me and stopped just inches from my face. No one had ever challenged him like this before—well, maybe one person had, and that was the priest at the center of this mess.

"You got balls coming in here and talking like that to me. This is my town." He reached into his coat pocket and pulled out a pistol. "I could shoot you and take you out to the woods and leave you for the turkey vultures and coyotes."

"Or you could nail me to a cross out on Sawmill Road."

"You're an idiot coming here. But you were right. It did bother me when the good priest came to me for handouts and then pontificated against the wealthy in his sermons. But I could handle that. And yes, my wife did spend a lot of time with Benetti. She was ten years older than he was, but she found him attractive and charismatic. I noticed. And I confronted him one night. I asked him straight out if anything was going on between him and my wife. He laughed at me. Like my wife was so far below him."

"I bet that bruised your ego." I spoke casually.

"You walk in here with some half-ass theory."

"I tend to be impulsive."

"I'm not. I had a plan for Father Johnny. That's why I got away with it. I told him I'd bought eighty acres of land and planned to build a retreat for members of the church. Planned to set up a summer camp for kids. I invited him to look at the property. That was Halloween afternoon. We walked around in the woods. I had a hunting knife, and I left him lying in the forest. Tom came up with the crucifixion idea. He'd investigated a goat sacrifice. Bunch of kids having a beer party thought it'd be clever to offer up a sacrifice and blame it on the witches. Perfect plan for us. A priest on Halloween offered up as part of a satanic ritual."

"Then you had the sheriff destroy evidence and lead the investigation. Almost a perfect crime." By this time Collier had returned to his perch on the desk. His gun hung relaxed in his hand. He was deciding how to get rid of me.

"Almost perfect?" He laughed. "Where's the flaw?"

"Your problem is I'm not the only one who just heard what happened. You see, the whole time we've been talking, my cell phone has been connected to two real law enforcement people. Sort of a little conference call. You use conference calls, don't you, Mr. Collier?"

"You're bluffing. You're not that clever."

"It's even being recorded."

"Bullshit! Take him out to the woods, Tom. I'll meet you when it's finished."

"Why not do it right here?" Tom Welch spoke up. "You got two witnesses. It's self-defense."

"No, do it in the woods. And get rid of the evidence."

"You're the boss," Tom said as he picked up a shotgun that had been leaning against the wall behind him. The other goon followed his lead, also grabbing a shotgun and stepping toward me.

It was then I heard the footsteps behind me entering the warehouse. Collier looked up surprised.

"Drop the guns! I heard the whole conversation." It was Hennie

Duggan. I thought it was a long shot when I called him in the late afternoon to fill him in on my plan. He worked for Collier, and if my instincts were wrong, the odds would be four against one.

In a flash, Tom Welch raised his shotgun, but before he touched the trigger, a blast boomed to my left. The explosion lifted Welch off the floor and threw him back. I pulled my handgun and aimed at Collier, who stood bewildered. In another instant, the man Collier called Lee raised his gun and aimed in my direction, but before he fired, three loud pistol shots echoed. Lee collapsed in a heap. I expected to see Shea Sommers step out of the shadows, but instead it was Sheriff Grimes. Collier dropped his gun, opting for his chances in court rather than feeling the sting of burning lead.

When the echoes cleared, Hennie Duggan and Sheriff Grimes stepped forward. Grimes handcuffed Collier and told him to sit in a chair behind the desk. As he passed me, the sheriff gave me an odd smile and said, "That was either the bravest stand ever taken by a lawman or the dumbest."

"I'd be dead if you two hadn't trusted me."

The next couple hours were a muddle of sounds and lights. Two patrolmen from the sheriff's department walked in and started taping off the area to protect the crime scene. They'd have a busy night recording witness statements and putting together reports. That was part of the job I didn't miss.

I found a folding chair and carried it to a dark corner, away from the chaos. I sat down, put my elbows on my knees and my head in my hands, and closed my eyes. I muttered to myself, "Holy fucking shit!" I had trouble catching my breath. Because of me, two men were dead. They were bad men, but it could just as easily have been the sheriff and former deputy. Could have been me. I remembered Shea Sommers. I couldn't think straight. Shea was driving here. She was recording the open phone call. Where was she? I knew I needed to talk to Hennie and Sheriff Grimes, to thank them, but my mind couldn't put together coherent thoughts.

Then I remembered I had told Shea to mute her phone before I walked into the building to meet Collier. I didn't want to take a chance of tipping him off about the phone connection. Shea was hearing the whole episode without being able to respond.

I took my phone from my shirt pocket. "Shea, you still there?"

"Jesus, Pat, I've been having a heart attack listening to you try to get yourself killed. I didn't know who was shooting and who was getting shot. Plus, I hit a goddamn deer."

"Sorry, Shea, I'm not sure what happened myself." I paused to get my bearings. "Are you okay?"

"Physically, I'm fine. Mentally, I'm a fuckin' basket case."

"Where are you?"

"Main Street. I see flashing lights in an alley. I'll be there in a few minutes."

I resumed my pose with my head in my hands. I could hear voices outside the building. A crowd of gawkers was gathering. I tried to breathe deeply to gain focus. After several minutes, I heard a familiar voice.

"You crazy son of a bitch, don't you ever do that to me again."

I looked up and saw Shea silhouetted in the bright lights. I stood up and embraced her. "I promise," I said. "Thank you for being here."

On my last day in Lake Hope, Grant Collier saved the county a great deal of money and unneeded turmoil by hanging himself with a bedsheet in his cell. Even with the best lawyers, he had little hope of avoiding a conviction, and his reputation and influence were already obliterated. With Collier's death, the front-page story would soon turn into tabloid filler. Lake Hope could return to bucolic obscurity. Sheriff Grimes and his new chief deputy, Hennie Duggan, could focus on underage beer parties and domestic disturbances. And I could return to my two-room boathouse apartment overlooking Lake Mendota, hopefully never to see Kickapoo County again. But life makes some funny turns.

# / 1 /

I STARED AT MY PHONE, DEBATING IF I SHOULD DIAL. I WAS NERVOUS about calling Pat Donegal to ask for help, but I had just been handed the strangest case of my career, and I needed a brain like Pat's to help me wade through the bizarre details. Though he swore he'd never be back to Lake Hope after his eventful first visit, Pat returned as a consultant to the county sheriff's department and ended up staying after he began a relationship with the local Wiccan priestess, Raven Quinn. Pat was living with Raven at her retreat several miles outside of Lake Hope.

In most ways, Pat and Raven could have been cast in a new version of the Odd Couple. Raven was a nonviolent vegetarian who practiced the ancient rituals handed down from the Druids. Pat was a retired detective who tended to break all the rules. He was not a man you wanted as an enemy. He was not opposed to using his gun when his or someone else's safety was threatened.

It had been several months since I had talked to Pat. Over the past couple years, we had worked a few cases together, but I never felt comfortable asking him or anyone else for help. Pat's a tough guy—friendly if you're on his good side, but also intimidating. I hesitated because it was possible there was no case at all. How rare could it be to find a pile of fresh guts on a remote bluff in rural southwestern

Wisconsin during hunting season? But what if the entrails turned out to be human? It took me twenty minutes to work up the courage to hit the call button. As the phone rang on the other end, I secretly hoped no one would answer.

"Donegal."

"Pat, it's Hennie. I hope it's not too early to call."

"Hennie, how are you? I've been up long enough to guzzle down a couple mugs of coffee. What's up?"

"I was going to ask if I could buy you a cup of coffee, but it sounds like I'm too late. Sorry. I can call another time." I was ready to hang up when I heard him respond.

"If you're buying, I can force down another cup."

"I appreciate that. No big surprise, I really need your help on a case. I know you're getting away from police work, but I thought you might be itching to get back in the game. Though if it's going to cause a rift between you and Raven, forget I called."

"That situation is a bit complicated. I'll explain when I see you." Pat paused. "And you're right. There are itches you need to scratch. I can be there in a half hour."

"I'll look forward to seeing you. And I'm sorry to hear things aren't going well."


I hardly recognized Pat when he entered the diner. He had sprouted several weeks' gray stubble on his face and looked like he could be pushing a grocery cart along State Street in downtown Madison. That surprised me since he typically took care of himself due to his prior battle with lung cancer. He wore a faded Packers sweatshirt that looked like he had slept in it a few nights. The bottoms of his jeans and his shoes were coated with dry mud. He looked like a different man from the one I'd seen just a few months earlier.

"Pat, I'm glad you could stop in," I said as I stood to greet him.

"It's time to get back to the real world. Things have been weird. I won't bother you with the details." He shrugged his shoulders and looked embarrassed.

"Is Raven okay?"

"As far as I know." He sat down and looked unsure about what to say. "She's living in Minnesota. I haven't seen her in four weeks. But that's not what we came to talk about. What's your case?"

"Hey, if it's a bad time to get involved, just tell me. I don't want to screw things up. I know Raven doesn't like the work we do."

"Don't worry, Hennie. It's a perfect time to jump back in."

I hesitated. "You're sure?"

"I'm ready to go. Shoot me the details." Pat winked and nodded.

"Okay, last night we got a call just after dark. A local man was bow-hunting for deer on Ibsen Ridge, highest point in the county. It's a remote area that overlooks the Mississippi River. Hard to get to up there unless you take a four-wheel ATV. Anyway, this guy claims he would have called from the scene, but he couldn't get a phone signal. He said he was hunting and spotted a gut pile."

"Got to be quite common this time of year."

"Sure, but there's a twist. The hunter said they weren't deer or wild pig guts. He said they were human."

"Jesus Christ, who the hell studies a pile of guts that close?"

"The guy said he did two tours in Afghanistan as an army medic. He saw plenty of human entrails. These were fresh, hardly touched by wild animals. He guessed a day old, two at most."

"Do you know this guy? Is he right in the head?" Pat signaled the waitress and pointed to my coffee cup and then at himself. She understood and nodded.

"I know about him," I said. "Name is Zach Layman. Does volunteer work for veteran groups. Plus, he freelances some construction work around the area."

"So, he left the goddamn guts up there overnight?"

"He had to. Didn't want to tamper with evidence."

"You believe him?" Pat scratched his head.

"Till I find out different," I said. "We got two patrolmen heading up to tape off the scene right now, and the state Division of Criminal Investigation agents are on the way. They won't waste time getting here once they hear this story. Should have results as soon as they gather samples. At least enough to tell us if they're human remains."

"How about bear guts? Hunters shoot bear around here, don't they?"

"Bear hunting is out of season."

"Some son of a bitch is willing to kill a human and gut him, I don't think he'd worry about shooting a bear out of season." Pat was covering all the bases, like he always did.

"Good point. I never gutted a bear or a human, so I don't know if they look alike or not."

"What's your plan?"

"I thought we could drive up to Ibsen Ridge and look around. By the time we get there the patrolmen should be done with their four-wheelers, so we can switch vehicles and keep the ATVs and the trailer. We'll have our own look around. Layman said there were ATV tire tracks around the scene. He also said there were remains of a fresh campfire, and there might be drag marks in the leaves where the carcass—body, I guess I should say—was pulled from the gut pile to the fire ring. But I guess that could've been a different hunter."

"The shooter might have cooked some of the meat?" Pat paused to consider what he just said. "That's awful damn gruesome if it was a human body."

"Not something I want to think about," I said. "More likely, he loaded the body on the four-wheeler to haul it home. Either way, it's a damn grisly story. I've never worked a cannibalism case before—not looking forward to starting now."

"Maybe I should have turned off my phone this morning."

"You don't have to go with me, you know. Whatever happened up there isn't going to make a pleasant way to start the week."

"Shit, I wouldn't miss this one for the world. I'll just run back to the farm and get some different boots and warmer clothes."

"Raven's place is almost on the way. I can pick you up in forty-five minutes. I'll just swing by the office to pick up the gear we'll need." I took a deep breath before finishing. "And, Pat, you know I appreciate your help. I just hope I don't get you into something we will both regret."

"I've made a shitload of decisions I've later regretted. I can handle it."


AS we started the drive up to Ibsen Ridge, Pat was quiet, unusual for him. I thought maybe he had second thoughts about getting back into the harness. But from the way he looked, I figured he could be nursing a hangover—though I'd never known Pat to drink more than a few beers. We rode in silence for a few miles. Then I decided to dig into what was going on.

"Want to talk about what's going on with Raven?"

"Nope."

Simple as that. He just sat staring out the side window, watching the sheer sandstone rock formations. This entire Driftless region had been bypassed by the glaciers during the last ice age, tens of thousands of years ago. Cold water rivers had slashed the area into a maze of steep hills and jagged river valleys. In spring, the snowmelt and rain combine to turn these streams and rivers into raging beasts.

"Want to talk about anything?"

"Sure. I always wondered why your town is called Lake Hope when there isn't a lake within ten miles."

"You're asking that now? You really do want to avoid talking about your life."

"Hey, a couple years ago, I kept looking around for the lake when I was driving your winding country roads working the Father Johnny case. After a while, I was embarrassed to ask. I thought maybe I missed something."

"We're going out to study the scene of a horrific murder and mutilation, and you want to know why there's no lake in Lake Hope?"

"You asked if I wanted to talk about something, so I asked a simple question. If you don't want to tell me, fine."

"All right, if you want to dodge the other subjects, I'll tell you about Lake Hope."

"I'm all ears."

"A hundred years ago, the state decided to build a dam on the

Kickapoo River. All the towns wanted the dam—be good for commerce, provide cheap electricity, and help control the spring floods. So, the village here, it was called Fargus Ferry back then, decided to put together some money to entice politicians to give them the dam. Even changed the name of the town to Lake Hope."

"Aren't you glad I asked?" Pat grunted.

"It'll make the trip go faster," I said. "So, the village sent an envoy with a sack of cash to visit the governor."

"My guess is the governor got a bigger sack of cash from some other town. Otherwise, you'd at least have a mill pond."

"You guessed it. So, we got a town called Lake Hope without a lake."

"Are we there yet?"

"Not even halfway. Hey, speaking of names, how'd you get the name Donegal? I thought that was a town."

"Town and county in northeast Ireland. Based on family lore, when my great-grandfather came over during the famine—along with half the population of the country—his name was M-a-c-D-o-n-n-a-g-h-a-i-l-e." Pat spelled it out. "The agent at Ellis Island told him he'd never get a job with that name because nobody could spell it or pronounce it. Since his place of origin was Donegal County, the agent told my great-grandfather his new name was Donegal, pronounced in a way an American would pronounce it *donn'-eh-gul*, and that's the way it stuck. Simple, eh?"

"Want to hear about my name?"

"Not really. Wake me up when we get close." Pat slid down in the seat and closed his eyes.

"What the hell's up with you? You look like a mess, and I'm guessing you haven't had a shower in a week. What's going on?" I shocked myself by being so blunt. I hated to stir up trouble when I asked him to help me, but I knew if we were getting into a bizarre investigation, I was going to have to count on Pat to cover my back.

"That's how you're going to treat me after I agree to climb bluffs to help look at a pile of guts?" Pat sat up straighter in the seat. He flashed a wry smile. "Okay, so I've been living alone for a month, ten miles from town, not talking to anybody, trimming trees. What've I got to dress up for?"

"I need to make sure you're up to the job. Who knows what we're going to find up there?"

"Don't worry about me." He paused and rubbed the whiskers on his chin, then spoke again. "Let me give you the *Reader's Digest* version. Okay, Raven and I hit a rough patch. Don't have a lot in common. We did the best we could, but it was hard. Sometimes we'd go days without talking. Then she told me she was going to Red Wing, Minnesota, for a few days. To clear her head, she said. When she came back, she tells me she's taking a job in Red Wing. People she knew were opening some sort of new age healing center. Wanted her to be a counselor. She's got degrees in psychology, and with all her knowledge about natural remedies and whatnot, they said she'd be a perfect fit. She liked the idea. Said it had nothing to do with us. Claimed she still wanted to stay friends but just needed to try a new environment. The funny thing is—she asked if I'd consider living at her place to keep an eye on things. Said it was up to me, but if I could keep things going till spring, she'd appreciate it. Told me she'd be back on weekends when she could get away, and we could spend time together." He paused to take a deep breath. "But Raven hasn't been back since she left."

"So, you hanging in there all right?"

"I started drinking a little more. Well, quite a bit more. Not beer. There were times in the past that I had a few run-ins with the gin bottle. I can handle a few beers without any problems, but put the juniper juice in front of me and I start yowling at the moon. It started before Raven left. She pretended not to notice, but she knew something was wrong. It got worse, I guess, after she left."

"Are you still drinking?" I asked.

"Not today yet."

"Listen, Pat, I really want you to help me on this case, but I can't have you working if you're not sober. I know you bend a lot of rules, but drinking on the job can't be one of them. If you can't promise you'll stay away from the booze, then I have to send you home with the patrolmen. Do you want to drink or help me solve this case?"

"I need to get back in the saddle, Hennie. Put some purpose back in my life. I can be good. Give me a breathalyzer test every morning if you doubt me."

"Don't think I won't. We've been in some tight scrapes together. My guess is we're going to have more—maybe soon. Can I count on you?"

"Got my word."

# / 2 /

PAT AND I RODE A FEW MILES WITHOUT SPEAKING. HE WAS PROBABLY weighing his options: stick with me and get involved in a bizarre case with a disemboweled, mutilated, probably sexually assaulted victim whose body was hauled off by some fiend whose crime would clearly surpass any experience either of us had ever imagined, or ride home with the patrolmen, curl up on a soft couch, and drink himself into oblivion. I had to admit opting for the latter might be Pat's wisest decision. While he pondered his options, I sat wondering how confident I felt working with a man known for his tendencies to sidestep protocol every chance he got.

I'm a rule follower. I don't like to push boundaries. Pat got results, but I worried about what means he would use to find the monster that could commit a crime like the one we were going to confront. I realized even though I had enjoyed working with him on three or four previous cases, I really didn't know Pat very well. Was there a dark side I hadn't seen? Was I sure I could count on him when the chips were down?

Pat broke the silence. "What's our plan?"

"We'll relieve the two patrolmen and wait for the state investigators. Once they start their work, we'll scour the perimeter looking for clues. Whatever happened up there, the killer must have left some evidence or clues behind. If we're lucky, the forensics guys will tell us the entrails are not human. Then we'll call the game warden and be on our way back to Lake Hope."

"I got a feeling we'll be looking for clues," Pat said with a slow sigh. "I shouldn't make conjectures before we see the scene, but I'd say this has sexual predator written all over it. And if someone does something this heinous once, there's a good chance he's done it before and will do it again. You probably got a new Ed Gein or Jeffrey Dahmer to deal with."

"Let's wait till we see the scene."

As we drove through the rolling hills, I noticed Pat perking up a bit, studying the landscape.

"Nice hills, eh?" I questioned.

"And a lot of them."

"They're called the Ocooch Mountains. Beautiful area. Never touched by the glaciers."

"I didn't know Wisconsin had mountains. Good thing I came. I get a free geography lesson."

"Technically they're not mountains according to geologists or whoever makes the rules about what's a mountain and what's a hill, but folks around here have called them the Ocooch Mountains for a hundred years. Named after an Indian tribe."

"Very educational field trip. Are there still Ocooch Indians around?"

"I doubt it."

"Check into that for me, will you, Hennie? Who knows? Maybe my great-, great-, great-grandmother was an Ocooch."

"Odds of that are mighty slim. But I'll ask around."

"Thanks," Pat mumbled as we pulled into a small parking area at the foot of a ridge.

**AFTER** trading vehicles with the patrol team, Pat and I made our trek to the top of the bluff. We followed deer trails that sometimes looked more like rabbit trails. I'm not sure how much experience Pat had riding a four-wheel ATV. There were a few times I wasn't sure he was going to see the top. His apparent hangover could've had something to do with his poor driving.

Once at the top, we used the time waiting for the DCI team to make our own observations. Unfortunately, there wasn't much to go on. The gut pile, which still looked basically untouched by scavengers, was the only obvious evidence that a crime had been committed. There were tire tracks from an ATV, but that could have been any hunter in the area. Next to the mound of entrails, there appeared to be drag marks in the leaves where a body could have been moved. That could've been a dead deer or wild pig. I had to chuckle when Pat first walked over to check out the gut pile. He casually walked off several feet, discreetly puked his guts out, and then walked back as if nothing had happened. I didn't let on I'd seen him, unsure if it was the gory sight or the gin the night before. Probably a combination.

When he casually strolled back, he mumbled, "That is frickin' ghoulish. Human entrails in the middle of nowhere."

"Sorry you came?"

"Shit, no. Let's find this bastard before he hits again."

"If he hasn't already."

After checking the taped-off crime scene, we sat on a fallen oak tree and waited for the state lab crew. The ground was littered with leaves, mostly dull-brown oak and bright-yellow hickory, with some paper birch and mountain ash mixed in. Finding shell casings would be a challenge.

Pat was quiet for a while, then he stood up, walked over to a patch of blackberry bushes, and took a leak. When he returned, he asked, "You're a hunter, aren't you, Hennie?"

"I hunt," I said. "Mostly pheasants and grouse. Turkeys and deer, maybe a rabbit once in a while."

"So, you're not a trophy hunter, huh?"

"No, though I got a couple of old deer heads mounted on my porch. Do you hunt?"

"Never got into it. I don't blame guys who do, but I can't figure out why anybody'd want to shoot an elephant or lion just to pose for a picture."

"Prove their manhood, I guess. Teddy Roosevelt did it, and Hemingway. Something to show off."

Pat sat back. He seemed to be reflecting on what we were getting into. He took a container of water from his jacket pocket and took a long slow drink of water. At least, I was hoping it was water. Then he gave me a wry smile.

"So, the first time I met you, out at your farm"—Pat paused to choose his words—"you'd been turkey hunting. You made me a little nervous when you walked out of the woods carrying a shotgun."

"I didn't know who you were. I wanted to make you nervous."

"You were holding a turkey, and your dog was beside you. Do I remember that right?"

"Well, if I was in the woods, you can bet my dog was with me. Why do you ask?"

"Just curious." He paused and rubbed his grizzled chin. "I didn't think it was legal to hunt turkeys with a dog." The sly smile widened through Pat's gray stubble.

"What the hell? Are you a game warden now?"

"No, no, I'm just making conversation." Now he couldn't hide the grin.

"I went out to shoot a pheasant, and a turkey flew up. Instinct took over, so I shot. I was hunting on my own land. It was actually a fine shot, bringing down a big tom with number 6 shot." I paused to let him savor the moment. "Are you going to turn me in?"

"Oh no, I've been known to bend a rule or two."

"Is this payback for what I said before about your drinking?"

"I'm just filling the time while we wait." He stood up and walked toward the path we'd come up. "I hear the forensics team."

From a distance we watched the crime scene investigators dismount their all-terrain vehicles and begin unloading equipment. There were four agents, three men and one woman. They each had large duffel bags with equipment for the investigation. One male agent quickly showed his alpha status by addressing the other agents, using vivid hand gestures. He was out of range for us to hear him. Once they were organized, he scoured the area looking for us. I stood up and walked toward him. Pat followed.

The Division of Criminal Investigation leader wasn't very friendly. Without even introducing himself, he said, "I hope you guys haven't stomped all over the crime scene. Wish you would have waited for us to analyze the scene before traipsing around up here." He never made eye contact as he spoke.

"This could be a brutal crime scene. It's our jurisdiction. We have been very careful, but we need to investigate." I tried not to sound too defensive. "And we didn't touch the gut pile." I pointed at a small group of pines where the entrails were located.

"For all we know it's a dead deer or wild pig. Now, I'd appreciate it if you'd give us space to do our work." He seemed bored and irritated to have to speak to us.

"I hope they're not human, but I've been told otherwise." I thought of saying more but decided not to stir up trouble. I was glad Pat held his tongue.

We watched as the team spread out to start their work. The alpha and the female agent headed toward the gut pile. They put on masks, gloves, and coverings over their shoes. They knelt down in front of the entrails and began their study. Then the leader stood up, walked to his bag, and took out a camera. For several minutes he took dozens of photos of the scene. The other two agents were on their hands and knees scrutinizing a forty-foot radius of the remains. The agents occasionally placed small yellow number tags on the ground to designate possible evidence. They jotted notes in small tablets. If they spoke to each other, it was in low tones that I could not detect. They obviously knew their jobs and were anxious to get to the task.

Pat and I wandered further from the crime scene looking through the brush and leaves for shell casings or anything that could be potential evidence. I used a metal detector, but I didn't have much luck. I collected a couple beer cans and spent shotgun shell casings, but nothing that looked fresh. The shells were faded and covered with dirt. They looked like they'd been here for more than a few days. But I bagged everything I found. After thirty minutes of digging through leaves, I told the DCI leader that we'd leave them to their work. He looked relieved to see us go. He spoke again without looking up. "We'll let you know what we find," he said. That was it. I didn't bother responding. I felt like a third grader, the way he talked down to me. But we needed their help, so best to just let it go.

Pat slept most of the trip back to Lake Hope. When I dropped him off at Raven's place, he insisted I call him as soon as results came back. I told him it might be a day or two, but I'd let him know as soon as I got a report. He must've decided he wanted in on the case. I was glad to have him on board.

When I'd worked investigations with Pat in the past, he often called in his friend Shea Sommers, a detective with the Madison Police Department, to help us. Shea was a good cop. The two of them worked great together even though they frequently wrangled back and forth like tiger cubs. I envied their relationship. They were both tough, smart, and at times almost comical. I generally felt like a third wheel when we worked together.

# / 3 /

AFTER DROPPING OFF PAT, I WENT BACK TO THE STATION AND STARTED searching law enforcement databases for missing persons in Wisconsin and surrounding states. However, without knowing what I was looking for, or even if the remains were human, I was basically just spinning my tires. But if I found someone in the area reported missing in the last few days, I'd be ready to jump-start an investigation as soon as I heard from the DCI forensics team. Statewide, there was a missing teenage girl in Kenosha County, assumed to be a runaway. A seventy-nine-year-old man walked away from a memory care unit at a nursing home in Green Bay, and a fisherman from New Albin, Iowa, was reported missing while fishing in the Mississippi River three days earlier. His empty boat was located on the Wisconsin side of the river, no more than ten miles upstream from Lake Hope. I jotted down the details regarding the fisherman. He was the most likely connection at this point, though I had no idea how his entrails could have climbed to the top of a bluff. But it was a start.

I was heading toward the parking lot on my way home at about seven o'clock when Millie, our new dispatcher, came running out to tell me the state investigator was on the phone. I followed her back into the office.

"Chief Deputy Duggan here. What have you got?"

"Not a lot of details yet. We'll need to run DNA tests, but I can tell you that your department has a homicide to solve. Won't know any more for at least twenty-four to thirty-six hours, but we'll push this one, considering the unusual nature of the case."

"I appreciate you letting me know. I'm already checking for missing persons, but without knowing what we were looking for, I can't do much."

"As soon as we run the early tests, we'll be able to give you an idea about gender, age, ancestry, eye color. Enough to get you started. Based on the volume of the remains, I'd guess we're looking at an adult, which is a hell of a lot better than dealing with a child."

"That's some consolation," I said.

"One more thing. I can say with some certainty that whoever cut out these remains had some medical training. Organs and intestines were neatly removed with surgeon-like precision. Almost no tissue damage."

"That could be useful information. Thank you."

"We'll push as quickly as possible. Crimes like this are what horror movies are made from. You need to catch this butcher fast."

I waited till about nine o'clock to call Pat. I did it partly because I was hungry and wanted to get home to fix supper, and partly because I wanted to find out if Pat was still sober at nine o'clock. I was relieved that he sounded perfectly lucid. Maybe he was taking my threat seriously. He told me he would contact Madison Police Detective Shea Sommers, who was a wizard on databases and the internet. If someone was missing, Shea would know about it by morning. I was always a little nervous around Shea, partly because she was a very good-looking woman, and I've always been shy around females. But I was glad to get her help.

Next morning, I got to my office early, hoping there would be news from the crime lab. I knew the lab couldn't possibly work that fast. Still, I wanted to be ready when news arrived. I continued to comb law enforcement sites for recent reports of missing adults.

Nothing new. Our Iowa fisherman was our most likely candidate, but how could he fall into the Mississippi River and end up on top of the tallest bluff in the county? I poured coffee from my thermos and wondered if Shea Sommers would have better luck. At seven thirty, I called Pat to see if he wanted to return to the scene to search for leads. He was already on his way to town when I reached him. He said he'd packed warm clothes and two quarts of coffee. I was glad he was enthusiastic. I was certain I was going to need him.

We trailered the four-wheelers back to the ridge. Pat was still unshaven, but his demeanor showed renewed excitement about getting back to catching bad guys, as he put it.

"You say the DCI claims the assailant had medical training." Pat pondered his next question. "So, does that make you want to look closer at the ex-army medic who reported the remains?"

"That sounds like the next logical step, but everything I hear about Layman tells me there's no way he did it."

"Soldiers who go through two tours of combat patching wounded GIs back together have to come home with baggage. Post-traumatic stress causes a lot of guys to do things nobody would ever expect. He was up there and didn't call in till the next morning. I'm just saying, we got to consider the possibility."

"Oh, I thought about that all night when I couldn't sleep. But it makes sense his phone wouldn't get a signal that far from town."

"Your phone worked the other day when you called the office." Pat quickly added, "I know different carriers have different dead zones, but the top of a bluff seems like a place to get good reception."

"We'll check his phone," I said. "But why would he shoot somebody, gut him, remove the body, and then call us the next day? That doesn't make a lot of sense."

"He could've been hunting, like he said, maybe saw another hunter, had some kind of flashback, and responded instinctively. Who knows how a guy who's been through hell and back reacts under certain conditions? Maybe he took the body with him and disposed of it somewhere." Pat loved to play devil's advocate.

"So, if it was another hunter, why haven't we heard he's missing?"

"Maybe a loner who lives out in the boonies all by himself. That sound like anybody you know?" Pat flashed his sly grin.

"Yeah, me. Makes sense, I guess." I didn't have a better theory to throw out. "Course, if the case is that simple, why did I need you to help solve it?"

"Maybe it wouldn't have been so simple if I hadn't been here to suggest the obvious."

"Okay. You're the expert. We'll check it out."

"Let me tell you something, Hennie. The older I get, the more I realize I'm not an expert on jack-shit. I used to think I had all the answers—not so much anymore. I guess the wisdom of old age is learning you're not as smart as you thought you were."

"Sounds like this business with Raven has got you down."

"Let's focus on our gutted victim—his or her problems are much worse than mine."

About that time, we arrived at the base of the bluff. We unloaded the four-wheelers and headed to the top. We expanded our search radius with metal detectors, but we came up empty. We checked the ashes in the fire pit—nothing but ashes.

"We're wasting our time up here," I said to Pat. "Maybe the killer used a bow and arrow. Makes sense a hunter would be bowhunting this time of year."

"We could check for blood traces on the trees and bushes," Pat said. "There's a chance the killer could have cut himself while gutting the victim and got blood on his hands. I'm sure the state crew already looked, but it may be worth a shot."

We both got down on our hands and knees and crawled around examining trees and leaves for blood. Again, we came up empty.

"I think it's time to head back to town and wait for the crime lab to give us a call," I said. "Maybe you can snoop around to see if you can dig something up on Zach Layman."

"We have to start somewhere."

By the end of my shift, there was still no more information from the DCI. I told Millie to call my cell if any news came in. I thought about calling Pat to see what he'd found out, but I decided to give him time to explore.

On my way home, I drove past the address given by Zach Layman. I hated to think Pat's theory could be right—primarily because my impression of Layman was positive. He served two tours of combat, seemed to have a great reputation around town, and from what I'd learned during a quick background check, he had a squeaky-clean record before and after his time in the service. Plus, I dreaded an investigation that would possibly dredge up dirt about a veteran who'd earned medals for his service. But it troubled me that from the few cases I'd worked with Pat, his instincts were uncannily accurate.

From what I'd learned, Layman lived with his wife and young son in a small house in one of the oldest neighborhoods in Lake Hope. He was working odd jobs as a carpenter and handyman while he finished an online college degree in nursing. When I reached his house, the lights were on, and I could see Zach and his wife sitting at a table eating supper. I felt positive Pat was off base this time. Jumping to conclusions based on stereotypes of troubled vets bringing the violence they'd experienced in battle home with them was lazy police work. Maybe that's why Pat's career had a trainload of questions trailing behind it. And now if he was drinking, it only made sense that his thinking was misguided. I decided I'd be smart to go home and make a real list of probable explanations for the bloody case that would likely haunt me through the coming weeks.

Late the next afternoon, I got the call I'd been waiting for. A supervisor from the DCI lab told me the evidence had passed through a preliminary battery of tests, and the team was able to put together a profile that would help our investigation. According to lab results, our victim was a male, probably in his forties, and most likely of Northern European ancestry, with possible traces of American Indian blood. A more detailed profile would be available within a week to ten days. That information would be required for a definitive identification, but for the sake of our investigation, this report gave us what we needed to get started.

My first move was to secure details of the missing fisherman from Iowa. I called the police department in New Albin and spoke to a Lieutenant Flynn. I explained the nature of our case, and he was happy to share the details he had.

"The missing man is Guy Hansen. White male, fifty-six years old, lives alone in a cabin about a mile from the Mississippi River. A loner from what we know. His sister who lives here in New Albin filed the report. She checks on him every few days. Said she can't be sure exactly what day he went out fishing, but it would have been between this past Saturday and Tuesday. His body could've washed up on the Wisconsin side of the river Thursday morning, so that timing makes sense. Anything else I can provide?"

"We got an early DNA profile. Sounds like it could be a match. Do you know, was he a big man?"

"Heavyset. Not very tall."

"Hansen sounds Norwegian or Swedish. Crime lab said he was likely of Northern European ancestry."

"Mostly Norwegians around here. Some Germans, a few Irish."

"Any idea if there was any Native American blood in the family?" I asked.

"I don't know much about his family. I could give you his sister's number. She could tell you more."

"That'd be great. You've been very helpful, and I'll keep you in the loop if I find out this Hansen fella is our victim."

"I'd appreciate that," he said. "Let me look up that number."


HANSEN'S sister, Margie Gorman, was cooperative, doing all she could to find her brother—or at least find his remains. I didn't want to tell her about the gruesome evidence we were working with. I just said we had a possible homicide victim.

"Homicide? Can't imagine nobody wanting to hurt Guy. He minded his own business and didn't have a pot to piss in. So, no reason for somebody to hurt him or rob him. I figure Guy just fell out of his boat. Maybe he finally caught that monster catfish he's always talked about, and it pulled him overboard. I'll admit he tended to drink when he went out on the river. Wouldn't have taken much to swamp his fishin' boat if a big wave came along. Maybe one of them big old barges came past and didn't see him. Guy liked to fish at night." She paused to gather her thoughts. "Ain't much of a surprise, but it's still awful sad. He didn't have much of a life, but he never complained."

"I appreciate you talking to me. I know it's not easy at a time like this. And I sure hope they find your brother real soon. He sounds like a good man."

"I'm not sure if he was a good man or not, but he was a damn fine brother. I'm gonna miss him." There was a poignant sigh before the final sentence.

"One other thing I'd like to ask, do you know if there's any Native American blood in your family?" I was hesitant to ask.

"Why would you want to know that?" She sounded surprised. "I don't know much about our ancestors, but as far as I know my people are all blond-haired and blue-eyed. Never heard about any Indians in the mix."

"It was just something I had to inquire about," I said. "I wish you the best, Mrs. Gorman. And I'll let you know if I hear anything on my side of the river."

I called Pat and told him what I'd heard. He told me Shea hadn't come up with any new missing persons. Said he'd dug around through files regarding Zach Layman. Just like what I had found—impeccable military records, no arrests, not even a speeding ticket.

"We still have to keep him as a person of interest till we find other leads," I said, "but I don't think he's our killer."

"Like I told you yesterday, I'm probably not the expert you and Shea give me credit for," Pat said. "And this time, I hope to hell I was off base."

"If we don't get any more missing persons, I better get a DNA sample from the missing fisherman's sister to try to see if he's our victim. According to what the crime lab said, this Guy Hansen is fairly close to their preliminary profile, about the right age and Northern European. Though there was a possibility of Indian blood, and his sister didn't think that was very likely, but who the hell really knows about great-grandparents and back even further?"

"He's the only lead we got right now. Though there are a lot of loners out there who could go missing and nobody'd ever notice. May be a drifter got picked up by some psychopath and lured up into the woods. You hear about all kinds of shit going on around the country, no reason it can't happen here."

"Well, let's not let any of this leak out," I said. "I've been telling everybody to treat the details as top secret, so as not to start a panic. I knew I didn't have to tell you."

"No, we better keep this to ourselves. One thing, whoever did this probably doesn't even realize he left evidence behind. What are the odds a random gut pile found in remote woods would ever be recognized as human remains? You were lucky to have your medic up there hunting."

"That's one way of looking at it," I said. "But I don't know how lucky I feel getting this case dropped in my lap."

"Good point. If it gets too gruesome, I can always head to Madison and help Shea chase drug dealers and teenage car thieves."

"I wouldn't blame you if you left, but I know you're not going to walk away from a case this bizarre."

"You know me well, Hennie."


FIVE days passed with no new developments. I went to Iowa to talk to Margie Gorman. Without giving too many details about our investigation, I convinced her to give me a saliva swab to compare to DNA evidence we had found. I don't think she understood why I was asking for the sample, but since there was still no sign of her brother either alive or dead, she was willing to do whatever she could to try to find closure. For me, finding out one way or the other whether our victim was Guy Hansen would determine the direction of our search. I was doing some paperwork before leaving the office for the day when my phone rang. It was the DCI. The lab technician was direct and to the point: "Based on a comparison of Mrs. Gorman's sample with that of the victim, the crime lab is certain the victim is not Mrs. Gorman's brother." This sent us back to the starting line. No new missing person reports had been filed. We widened to scope of our search, first to neighboring states and then to the entire Midwest. No one fitting our description had been reported missing.

The big break came when I got a call from Shea Sommers, who had been using her free time to track down any information that could help our investigation. She called my cell while I was at home watching TV.

"Hennie, I hope I'm not bothering you. I might have found a break in your case."

"Great. I can use all the help I can get," I stammered. I was always a bit shy around women, and probably even more so with Shea.

"I was just searching through recent missing person files and one pops up in the Milwaukee area. He might be your victim."

"Let's hear it," I said, shutting off the TV and turning my full attention to Shea.

"A male named David Swalheim. Forty-six years old. His wife reported he went hunting nine days ago and hasn't been heard from since."

"Nine days? She doesn't report he's missing for nine days?"

"According to the report, she claims he often went hunting for a week or more without checking in," Shea said.

"Interesting marriage. But who am I to judge?"

"Wife claims he sometimes hunts in remote areas of the state. Camps and hunts deer, turkeys, whatever is in season."

"Sounds promising."

"The name sounds Scandinavian. No kids, but he may have brothers or sisters for DNA matches. Maybe a hairbrush."

"I'll call the wife tomorrow. See how cooperative she wants to be."

"Always the spouse, right?" Shea chuckled as she spoke.

"It happens." I was embarrassed about prejudging the wife.

"Hey, Hennie, before I let you go, I was wondering how Pat's doing. Is he helping much on the case?"

"He's been good. He's rooting around for clues. I'll give him a call to pass on your info." I paused, not sure how much to say about Pat's situation. "You probably heard Raven's living in Minnesota. She took a job up there."

"I heard things were dicey. Pat and I went fishing in late September. Rained like a bastard all weekend, and we never caught a fish."

"Sleep in a tent?" Why would I ask such a stupid question?

"Oh, God no. We rented a cabin—two bedrooms! So anyway, Pat filled me in on a few of the details. I didn't ask many questions. Too bad. She was good for him." Shea paused like she had more to say. I was debating asking her about his drinking, but mercifully, she beat me to the topic. "Did you notice he's been drinking?"

"I noticed it the first day we went to the crime scene. He looked like hell. I told him if he wanted to work for the department, he had to be sober. He's been good when I've seen him since then. How did you know?"

"The last night we were up north, he got all pissed up. Must have been sneaking it all day. It wasn't pretty. I'm glad you put him back to work."

"I hope it's for the best. I'll keep in touch, and thanks for all your help. But don't you ever sleep?" I asked.

"Once in a while, but I think it's overrated."

"Not me. I'm gonna turn in now and see if I can arrange a trip to Milwaukee in the morning."

"Be sure to take Pat."

"I'll give him a heads-up before I go to bed. Take it easy, Shea."

"Any way I can get it, right?"


**KELLY** Swalheim looked to be in her late thirties, maybe forty. We met her at their big house on a lake in the Milwaukee suburbs. She was attractive, dressed in a tan blazer over a white shirt, and tall black boots. She had long black hair worn loose over her shoulder and back. When she opened the door to greet me and Pat, she looked disappointed, like she was expecting someone better. When we introduced ourselves and explained why we were there, she appeared stoic, revealing little concern about her husband's absence.

She didn't invite us into the house, so we stood in the foyer.

"He's gone more than he's here. He sells drugs—pharmaceuticals, not crack cocaine. His region covers four states. We're not a really romantic couple. He's good-looking and spends three or four nights a week in hotels. He likes to drink too much. Carries a lot of cash. It doesn't take a brain surgeon to figure out he does a lot of screwing around when he travels. And I mean that literally. And if he isn't working, he's hunting or golfing. Leaves for several days. If I ask where he's going, he'll say, 'Wherever there's something legal to shoot.' He's gone more than he's here."

"So that's why you didn't report him missing earlier?" I asked.

"He was supposed to be back for his nephew's wedding on Saturday. When he didn't show up, I called his cell. Left messages. He never got back to me, so I called the company he works for. They hadn't heard from him all week. I figure he's probably shacked up with some nineteen-year-old bimbo. But after a couple days, I reported it to the cops. They considered him a missing person and filed the report."

"Could he have been hunting this past week when you thought he was working?"

"Sure, though I didn't see him loading any guns into his car. He may have said he was working, but I don't pay much attention. David makes a ton of money and is gone most of the time. A lot of women call that a perfect husband."

"So, you are not worried that he's missing?"

"Like I say, he could be working, or hunting, or porking some cutie in any town between here and Omaha. He does what he does. Maybe he'll show up tomorrow. What can I tell you?"

Pat spoke for the first time. "Does he have a gun case we could look at to see if any of his guns are missing? We're from a rural area, popular with hunters."

"So, you call and tell me you want to ask some questions about my missing husband. You don't even tell me why you're interested. Did you find a body or something?"

"Not exactly," I responded slowly, "but it's possible there was an incident in our county a week or so ago. We're checking missing person reports."

"Did David shoot somebody or what? Nothing he did would surprise me."

"No, we don't think that happened, but it would help us if we knew if he was planning to go hunting."

"He keeps his guns locked in a closet. I sure to hell don't have a key. Besides, don't you need a warrant or something?"

"I'm sorry, Mrs. Swalheim, but your husband's missing. We're trying to find him. I hate to bother you. We're just asking questions. And we don't really need a warrant to look through a victim's possessions."

"So, David is the victim?"

"We don't know," I said.

"Listen"—she looked irritated—"I have someplace I'm supposed to be. I don't think I can help you until you decide to tell me what's going on."

"Like I said, we're just asking questions, trying to locate a person reported missing. If you don't want to help us, that's up to you." I could feel my face flush as I spoke.

"Well, I don't have a key for his gun closet, so why don't you come back when you know what you're looking for." She opened the door as she finished speaking. Pat and I took the hint and headed toward the car.

"Now that was a delightful woman," Pat mumbled as we walked to the car.

"Reminds me why I never got married," I said.

"Think she'll help us get a DNA sample to match our intestines?"

"I wouldn't count on any cooperation from Mrs. Swalheim."

"We'll find other means," Pat said. I didn't feel comfortable about the way Pat said that. Pat's idea of gathering evidence was different from mine.

It didn't take much research to find David Swalheim's brother, Daniel. He taught at a small career college in Madison. Shea Sommers agreed to meet with him and convince him to give her a cheek swab.

Shea can be very persuasive. It turns out Daniel had very little contact with his younger brother, but he wasn't surprised to hear David was missing. He commented that David was not an easy person to like. He had no qualms about giving Shea the sample. Two days later the crime lab called with the results—a nearly perfect match. We knew our victim. All we needed to learn now was where his body was, how his guts ended up on top of a bluff in Kickapoo County, and more importantly, who was responsible for those guts being separated from the rest of his body.

So far, we had two persons of interest: Zach Layman, the medic who discovered the remains, and the victim's wife, Kelly Swalheim. Layman seemed like a long shot to me though he was the first one to find the remains, and he did have the medical background to perform the gruesome but skillfully performed removal of intestines. The victim's wife showed little concern about her husband's disappearance, plus she was unwilling to cooperate with our efforts to find him. I decided I would call the Waukesha County sheriff's department to assist in convincing Mrs. Swalheim to let us look through their house for clues to help us track David Swalheim's movements in the days leading to his apparent murder.

The local sheriff's deputy also agreed to inform Mrs. Swalheim that we had strong evidence indicating her husband had been a victim of foul play. Without releasing the delicate yet gruesome evidence we'd found on Ibsen Ridge, they assured her that there was a very good chance her husband had been killed. They also explained that authorities in the area of the incident felt there was a strong cause to believe he had been murdered. According to the deputy I talked to, Mrs. Swalheim showed little grief or surprise at the news. Shock can cause people to react in unexpected ways. She made it clear during our recent visit that she and her husband had less than a loving relationship. Still, it was foolish to jump to conclusions without carrying out a full investigation. Unlike Pat, I like going through proper channels.

PAT and I hit the road early the next morning, heading for another meeting with Mrs. Swalheim. The Waukesha sheriff had secured the needed paperwork to gain access to the property in case Mrs. Swalheim continued to refuse to cooperate. His approach was to list the wife as a possible suspect. That way she had to let us into the house and other buildings on the property. As expected, she did resist our request for permission to enter her home. Having the local deputies on our side convinced her that she could be arrested if she refused to let us in. Finally, after digesting her lack of options, she begrudgingly opened the door and let us in. The local deputies stood by to make sure Mrs. Swalheim behaved herself while Pat and I conducted the search.

The primary area of interest for me was the gun closet. Naturally, the door was locked, and Mrs. Swalheim said she didn't have a key. I hoped with a little coaxing, I could jog her memory.

"Mrs. Swalheim, we spoke a couple days ago," I began.

"Yes, I remember."

"Let me start by saying how sorry I am about your loss. I don't want to trouble you more than necessary, but—" She cut me off mid-sentence.

"Yeah, I watch cop shows on TV. I know you guys are just dripping with remorse when you come to interrogate the families of a crime victim. You know you can't wait to rip through this house trying to find evidence that I killed my husband."

"That's not true. I do feel sorry for your loss," I said.

"Doesn't change anything. I don't know what happened to David. He left here almost two weeks ago. He was fine. Now you say he's probably dead. I have no clue what happened. If you have evidence, why don't you tell me what happened?"

"We are just starting our investigation. We need you to tell us everything you know so that we can piece together what happened."

"I don't know shit about what happened. I don't even know why you think he's dead. Did you find his body?"

"No, not exactly. But—"

"I have nothing to tell you or show you. Come back when you can tell me what happened."

"We need to check that gun closet to find out whether your husband was on a hunting trip, or whether he was in Kickapoo County for some other reason," I explained.

"I can't give you a key if I don't have a key, can I?"

"Then our only option," Pat said, "is to get a crowbar from the car and rip the door off its hinges. If you'd prefer that, I'll be glad to go out to the car." He started walking toward the front door.

"Wait, it might be in his top dresser drawer, where he keeps his personal things." She spoke without expression. "Wait here."

After several minutes, she returned without the key. "I called my lawyer. She told me she wanted to read your warrant before I agreed to any further searches."

"You're welcome to have your lawyer here, Mrs. Swalheim," said the lead Waukesha County deputy, "but there is nothing she can do to stop the search. It is a legal document signed by a county judge. Either you give us a key for the gun closet, or we'll open the door by force."

"Her office is only five minutes away," Mrs. Swalheim pleaded. "Can't you wait five minutes before you destroy my house?"

"We can wait five minutes," I said. "But your lawyer being here is not going to stop us from conducting an authorized search."

"Well, let's wait till she arrives." She spoke sullenly.

It was less than ten minutes before the lawyer—a stern, physically fit woman about fifty years old wearing a navy-blue suit, plenty of makeup, and her straight black hair pulled into a tight bun—arrived and swiftly walked toward Mrs. Swalheim.

She took her client by the forearm and walked her several steps away, out of our hearing range. They spoke back and forth quickly, somewhat unpleasantly, and then returned to the small circle of investigators. She extended her hand toward me, since I had stepped forward to greet her. Her handshake was swift and surprisingly firm. "I am Clyda McCabe, attorney for the Swalheims. I have been advised that you believe David has been the victim of a possible homicide. Without knowing the details of your case, I will accept your theory. But given that this news has been a terrible shock to Mrs. Swalheim, I firmly request you postpone your search of this property until the victim's wife has had time to assimilate the dreadful news. I can assure you, my client has played no role in whatever happened to her husband."

"I realize this is a difficult time, but David Swalheim has been missing almost two weeks, and the sheriff's department can't waste time as we try to solve this mystery. If someone did harm to your client, then I think it's in all our interests for my department to figure out what happened. And to be completely honest, I get a feeling Mrs. Swalheim is trying to prevent us from doing our work."

"That's ridiculous. My only concern is protecting the rights of both my clients. You've told us nothing about the evidence you have that a crime has even occurred. What exactly do you have, Officer Duggan?"

"Okay, I'll tell you what we have. We found human remains in our county."

"A body?"

"Not exactly." I hesitated, trying to decide how much I wanted to reveal. I could feel sweat trickling down my back. Then I decided to hit them with the facts and see how they'd react. "Okay, here's what we know. Several days ago, a hunter discovered partial remains, intestines and organs, to be exact, which turned out to be human. We checked missing person reports and cleared, using DNA tests, the first three reports we examined. The fourth person was David Swalheim. We compared DNA at the scene with a saliva swab from Mr. Swalheim's brother, Daniel. Those tests conclusively proved to be a match. So, yes, we're quite convinced that David is our victim."

"Do you know how he died? Or where he died?"

"That's what we're trying to understand. That's why we need to look through Mr. Swalheim's possessions, to make sense out of this terrible situation."

"I can give you financial details, but I'll need to get them from his office."

"Thank you. That will be very helpful, but we also need to look at his clothes, the tools in his garage, everything. Including the contents of his gun closet. If he was on a hunting trip, maybe this was an accident. We have been asking Mrs. Swalheim for permission to search the house."

"Do you consider her a suspect?" Clyda McCabe was all business.

"I didn't when I came here, but, honestly, by her actions in blocking our attempt to solve this case, we now consider her a person of interest. That is why the search warrant was authorized, because your client refused to cooperate with our inquiry." I handed the lawyer the warrant, and she studied it for a few minutes.

"I believe my client found the key earlier, when she called me."

"I appreciate your cooperation."

Kelly Swalheim stepped forward and slammed the key into my hand. I thanked her.

"Closet's in the basement." She scowled.

Pat and I headed downstairs. Pat sighed as we opened door. "Whoa, there must be twenty weapons in here—none of them cheap. He could arm a militia."

"Maybe he has," I said. "Who knows what he's into? Somebody killed him and gutted him."

"Good point," Pat said as he knelt down to look more closely at the weapons. "All organized by caliber—starts with a Winchester .22 and builds all the way to a Barrett .50 semiautomatic."

"A couple guns are missing down toward the big game end. Probably deer rifles."

Pat looked closely at the guns on each side of the gap. "Well, there's a .30-06 Springfield on one side and a Marlin .444 on the other. Whatever guns are missing are not for shooting squirrels. If Swalheim was hunting, he was after big game—maybe bear or elk."

I examined the carpeting in the closet. "Something heavy's been recently moved," I said.

Pat looked at the rug. "Probably a safe or filing cabinet. It's been moved in the last couple days I'd guess." He crawled along the carpet running from the closet to the sliding glass doors leading out to a patio. "See these tracks?" He ran his finger along the carpet. "Looks like wheels of an appliance dolly. I'd guess someone moved a heavy cabinet across the rug since the last time it was vacuumed."

"And Swalheim's been missing about two weeks. What are the chances a house like this goes two weeks without vacuuming?" I asked.

"My guess is Mrs. Swalheim has a cleaning service at least once a week. I can't picture her pushing a Hoover across the floor."

"So, it probably wasn't her husband who did the moving. And I can't picture her wrestling an object that heavy out of the house." I looked at Pat, who was back focusing on the pressed-down carpet where the safe or cabinet had stood in the closet.

"Whatever it was, it must've weighed damn near two hundred pounds. My guess is a safe. Where did she move it, and why?"

"We got some work to do. I'd be surprised if Clyda McCabe will let her client answer any questions today—not without us charging her with something, which I'm certainly not prepared to do. So, we'll hold off for now. Maybe it's time to find out what our drug salesman did in his spare time."


THE next couple days I spent clearing up paperwork in the office. I was also running background checks on everyone we'd encountered so far. Zach Layman, our army medic who'd discovered the remains, still looked squeaky clean. I hoped we could soon cross him off the suspect list. Conversely, the Swalheims sent red flares in every direction. They seemed to have too much money for the income he earned. Their house was valued at well over a million bucks. She drove a new BMW, and he owned a top-of-the-line pickup truck. They rented a boat slip for a thirty-foot sailboat at a marina on Lake Michigan, and they retained one of the most expensive lawyers in Wisconsin. But how could Kelly Swalheim kill her husband and somehow transfer his entrails to the top of a bluff in Kickapoo County? If she did it, she didn't act alone. I would ask Pat to do some secret surveillance to see who was a likely accomplice for the *grieving* wife.

# / 4 /

I HAVE TO ADMIT ONE JOB I LOVED WHEN I WAS A FULL-TIME COP WAS SUR-
veillance. Sitting in the dark, drinking coffee, and eating Slim Jims,
waiting for some perp to step into my trap and solve a case where I
had few leads. Sometimes you get nothing. Other times the golden
goose falls into your snare and the crime solves itself. So, when
Hennie asked me to keep an eye on Kelly Swalheim's house for a
few nights, I was ecstatic. I used my magnetic sign on the door of my
truck that read Picasso Painting Contractor, a trick I picked up years
ago. Then I parked a few doors down from the Swalheim home with
my binoculars and camera and waited for something to happen. First
night I got zilch. Kelly stayed home and had no company. I waited
till about one, then retreated to my room at the Motel 6. I slept till
six. After a visit to Dunkin' Donuts, I was parked on the other end of
Kelly's street. At eight thirty-five, Kelly left the garage, and I followed
her to an apartment building on Bluemound Road in Brookfield. She
went inside and stayed till almost noon. Then she came out with a
muscular man, probably in his forties. They had an animated conversation—I assumed an argument—then hopped into their respective cars. I tossed a mental coin and decided to follow the boyfriend.
Black Lexus with tinted windows. I jotted down the plate number and

followed at a safe distance. I followed the Lexus down Bluemound to Highway 100. Couple blocks later, the Lexus pulled into a big shopping mall and the driver headed inside. I considered following him in but decided to stay with his car. I phoned in the plate number to the Kickapoo sheriff's department. Hennie wasn't in his office, but another deputy ran the number. Came back to a 2017 Lexus owned by Harley Januss.

Rather than doing my own research, I decided to call Shea. She had mastery over every database available to law enforcement. If there was anything on file about Harley Januss, Shea would find it.

"Madison Police, Detective Sommers, how can I help you?"

"Shea, it's Pat. Glad to catch you in the office."

"Won't be for long. I'm just cleaning up some paperwork. What's up?"

"You heard about the murder case we're working on?"

"Hennie called a few days ago. I helped get the brother's DNA. How do you get to investigate all the fun shit?"

"Just living right, I guess. Neatly disemboweled entrails with no other body parts. Out in the middle of nowhere. How can you beat that?"

"You're not calling because you miss me, so what do you need?"

"Harsh! Actually, I do miss you. I'm ready to move back to Madison. Do you think I can still rent that boathouse your rich buddy owns?"

"I don't know if he got somebody else to watch his place for the winter or not. Thought you were all settled in at your witch's retreat."

"Things change. I think I mentioned Raven took a job in Minnesota."

"Sorry, Pat, I forgot. Didn't mean to make a joke."

"It's all right. I'm fine. I'm just ready to get back to the city."

"You doing okay?"

"Fine, in spite of what Hennie probably told you. Guess he never saw my darker side—little binge drinking is all. He said he was going to test my blood if he thought I was coming to work drunk. But I'm behaving. Few beers once in a while."

"Good. So, what do you need?"

"The wife of the victim is hard to figure out. Not what you'd call grief-stricken. She wouldn't talk to us till her lawyer showed up. This morning I followed her to some guy's apartment. She goes inside, stays a couple hours, comes out to parking lot, they argue, then go their separate ways."

"Interesting. Maybe she thinks this guy killed her husband."

"Maybe, or maybe he's a boyfriend." I paused before getting to my real reason for calling. "Anyway, I ran his plate number. Car belongs to Harley Januss, J-A-N-U-S-S. Lives in Brookfield. I followed him to a mall. Maybe he works here. I'm wondering if you have time to do your magic."

"Always find time for you, Pat, especially if you say you're coming back to work with me instead of Hennie. I probably can't beat the case you're working on now, but I'll do my best."

"I'd say getting stoned by religious fanatics tops this case for excitement—though I can't say I want to do it again. I still got scars."

"That was ugly." Shea sighed before continuing. "Keep an eye on your guy, and I'll call soon as I find something."

I waited in the parking lot an hour then gave up and headed back to the Swalheim house. The house looked all dark, so I returned to the motel for a nap. When doing surveillance, it's smart to catch a snooze anytime you can.

SHEA called about three thirty. I was having a burger at a dive bar within walking distance of the motel. Fortunately, there was nobody else in the tavern, so I just ducked into a corner booth to hear Shea's news.

"I found a few items of interest. Harley Januss, forty-three, no felony convictions, but several arrests. Disorderly conducts, assault and battery, one sexual assault, none ever went to trial. Victims chose not to press charges, or there wasn't sufficient evidence. He worked as a bouncer, fitness instructor, and currently co-owns a restaurant at the mall in Brookfield. Milwaukee police suspect he does some muscle work for the Sangiovese family. He seems like a nice guy to console the grieving widow."

"Or threaten her." I tried to figure out if that made sense. "It sounds like you hit the jackpot. Gee, the guy works for the Sangioveses, I wonder who his partner is in the restaurant. We may have a new suspect."

"Know anything about the Sangiovese family?"

"Oh, yeah, plenty. Crossed paths several times when I worked for Lakeshore County. Tough bunch."

"Hope you're not thinking about meeting with them by yourself."

"Remember how I looked after the antiabortion zealots got through with me? Or the bikers at the bar in Madison? I'd look ten times worse if I tangled with the Sangioveses."

"Don't do something stupid!"

"You doubt my judgment?"

"Do I need to answer that?"

"But"—I paused to build the suspense—"I do get along with the youngest brother, Sammy. I helped him out of a couple jams when he was eighteen or nineteen. I don't think he has much to do with the family business. He owns a used car lot. I've talked to him a few times. Long as I avoid his family's business, he might help me out. Who knows? Maybe Swalheim was into something dirty. Seemed to have a shitload of money, and I'd guess his wife liked to spend it."

"I hope you don't get beat up or killed. I'm not crazy about wasting a vacation day to attend your funeral."

"You're going to feel really rotten if something does happen."

"You know I'm kidding."

"I will keep you informed. And keep those vacation days just in case I need help."

"Have I ever let you down?"

"I must say, of all the people I've met in my life, you are the first one I'd call on if I was in trouble," I said.

"God, don't get mushy on me. You're going to make me feel guilty about all the horrible things I've said about you behind your back."

"Where did I go wrong in my life to deserve you?"

"If we started that discussion, it'd take all night, and neither of us would get any work done. Take care of yourself, Pat."

"And you!"

SAMMY Sangiovese acted happy to see me. Actually, I'd say he was shocked to see me.

"Pat Donegal, Jesus, where did you come from? Barely recognized you. You're retired, right?"

"Retired from the sheriff's department several years ago, but you know how it is. Old cop like me can't keep his nose out of other people's business for long. So, I do some consulting for a couple departments. Nothing big, just enough to keep my juices flowing."

"I was hoping you stopped to buy a vehicle. I got a nice Toyota Tundra here. Less than twenty thousand miles. Four doors, long bed, four-wheel drive, all the bells and whistles. Only 29K. Clean title and everything."

"I'm on a cop's pension. How do I afford a truck like that?"

"Don't tell me you're here on police business."

"Not about the family, I promise. Just want to throw out a couple names. Harley Januss and David Swalheim. You know them?"

Sammy shrugged. "Can't say I do. Though I heard the name Swalheim. Big-time trophy hunter. Not a sport I respect much."

"That's the guy. Know anything else about him?"

"He has a lot of money."

"Pharmaceutical sales. Big business, I guess."

"You think he's into something besides selling medicine?" Sammy watched me closely, trying to figure out why I was asking him these questions.

"He owns a big house, nice cars, good-looking wife."

"He's also a country club guy. Belongs to Bay Shore Country Club. Membership is probably 30K a year. Lot of money for a salesman."

"Do you belong there?"

"No way. I sell cars for a living, but I got customers who've taken me there to play golf. I heard Swalheim is a low handicapper. So, he must not spend all his time hunting."

"Lot of gambling out there?"

"Does a bear excrete feces in the forest? Country clubs are full of alpha dogs with bundles of money. Some of those guys bet more on a golf game than we make in a year."

"That may explain his standard of living," I said.

"Not unless he moves around. Members quit betting if somebody cleans them continually."

"I can tell you, if you keep it to yourself, there's good chance Swalheim met with foul play. I can't tell any details, but we got reason to think he's dead." I spoke quietly.

"If I hear something, I'll give a jingle. Got a card with your number?"

I handed Sammy my card. "So how about this Januss character, know anything about him?"

"No, but I'll ask around." Sammy smiled and put his hand on my shoulder. "But think about this Tundra. Your truck looks like it's seen its better days. Lot of room in this one. Big V-6. Four-wheel drive. Important man like you needs a good vehicle."

"You're a good salesman, Sammy. Maybe if I solve this case, we can do business."

"Listen, I make it a policy to stay away from police investigations. I ain't involved in anything illegal. And I try to avoid contact with people who are. You been good to me over the years, so I'll let you know anything I hear about Swalheim. Off the record, of course."

"I'll appreciate anything you can give me. And who knows? My truck's been shot at, broken into, run off the road—maybe a bigger, faster truck could keep me out of trouble."

"You'd look really good behind that steering wheel." He pointed at the Tundra.

I had no doubt Sammy planned to call one of his brothers as soon as I left the lot. By the time I got back to my motel, my phone was ringing. It was Sammy.

"You car salesmen work fast," I said. "Got something for me, or are you still pitching that Tundra?"

"Little bird told me something you might be interested in. You already know Swalheim is a big-time hunter. My guess is you found his body in the woods somewhere. From what my source tells me, Swalheim had some bizarre ideas about what was included under the term hunting." Sammy paused for my response.

"I can't wait to hear this."

"Apparently, your victim belonged to a club, maybe started by some famous writer, according to my source. You know, the little bird."

"Birds get around. See lots of strange things," I said.

"Well, this club is a hunting club where the prey is other hunters. The little bird tells me it's all real hush-hush. One guy contacts another member, probably on a throwaway phone, and schedules a hunt. They exchange GPS coordinates and set a time. Guess it's all done with code names, so nobody knows who they're hunting."

"They actually hunt each other with guns?"

"They ain't playing paintball, Pat."

"So, guys meet at a designated place and try to shoot each other?"

"That's what the little bird tells me, and I consider him a reliable birdie."

"Wow! I appreciate the info, Sammy. Now I think my next move is to track down the throwaway phone used for the arrangement. It's a start."

"My little bird might be able to help you there too."

"That is some useful bird. I better get a sack of sunflower seeds to pay him back."

"What I hear is Swalheim has a hunting lodge and maybe eighty acres of hunting land not too far from here. May be a good place to start looking."

"Must have it under a false name. We checked his name for properties other than his house. Came up empty."

"Just a thought, but my birdie told me the land was probably registered in his wife's maiden name. You know, some folks like to keep secrets."

"My guess is Mrs. Swalheim is not going to tell me anything about a hunting lodge, but I got my sources too. I really appreciate the leads. What do I owe you?"

"Listen, Pat, you helped me out of tight situations more than once. Helped me become a respectable member of society. I'm glad to repay a favor." Sammy paused, and I heard a quiet chuckle. "But I want you to remember I sell reliable vehicles. And I know how to sharpen a pencil when dealing with old friends."

"I may take you up on that. I'll be in touch, Sammy."

"I hear anything else, I got your number."

"Thanks."


WITH the new information from Sammy, my investigation had new energy. I called Hennie several times to bring him up to date, but my calls went directly to voicemail. I left several messages, but he never called back. After two days, I decided to call Hennie's boss, Sheriff Phil Grimes. I worked some cases for him in the past, and he saved my bacon during the investigation of a local priest's murder a couple years earlier. I felt I could trust him to figure out what was going on. The second time I called his office, I was able to talk to Sheriff Grimes.

"Sheriff Grimes, it's Pat Donegal. I've been helping Hennie with the homicide on Ibsen Ridge."

"Pat, glad to hear from you. You having any luck?"

"Stumbled on a couple leads. I've tried to contact Hennie to update him, but all I get is his voicemail, and no call backs. What's up?"

"Not sure. Hennie said he was going to meet with the victim's wife, and all of a sudden, he calls in sick. Says he needs a couple days off. I haven't heard a word since. I tried to call but no response. Did he tell you anything that might give us a clue?"

"We haven't talked much. He put me on my own. He told me to put a tail on Swalheim's wife to see what turned up. But that was a few days ago. She seems to be less than the grieving widow. I followed her to what appears to have been a rendezvous with a guy named Harley Januss, who my source tells me is not the most upstanding citizen in Waukesha County."

"You got sources down there already?" Grimes asked.

"Hey, this is close to my old stomping grounds. I worked in Lakeshore County, right next door, for thirty years. I know people." I paused to change direction. "But back to Hennie, I haven't got a clue. I'll admit he wasn't very happy the morning he took me out to check the murder scene. I was a little hungover, and he was worried he couldn't trust me on the job."

"Does he have reason to worry?" Grimes asked.

"I'd been staying alone out at Raven Quinn's place, and I admit I was drinking, but I told him if I'm working a case, I stay sober. I've been behaving ever since."

"Not like him to just take off during a big case."

"I think something happened. Maybe he found out something the killer wanted to be kept secret," I suggested. "Could have had to do with his talk with Swalheim's wife. Maybe we should put out a search."

"I sent our young deputy out to his place, but there's no sign of him," Grimes said. "The deputy talked to Hennie's neighbor who watches his dog when he's out of town. Neighbor said Hennie stopped a couple nights ago, almost midnight, and picked up the dog. Said he needed some time away, and he'd be back in a few days."

"Who takes off in the middle of a case?"

"Never know." Grimes spoke slowly making sure he chose his words carefully. "I don't want to say too much here, but you know what happened eighteen years ago when the priest was killed. Hennie quit in the middle of the investigation. I'm not accusing anybody, but, well, we may have to proceed without him. I'll be happy to help with the case when I can, but I can't be away from the county too much."

"Understood," I replied. "I know where you're coming from, but it puts me in a tough spot. As a part-time consultant, I don't have a lot of clout in Waukesha County. I need someone with a real badge to run the investigation."

"Either that, or you need a real badge." Sheriff Grimes paused to let me figure out what he was planning to say. "I can swear you in as a deputy, and with your years of experience, I'll give you the official title of homicide detective. That way you've got full power to run this investigation. With all you've done for the county the last couple years, there won't be any problem getting it authorized by the board. You willing?"

"Shit, Phil, I got to think about this. That was not on my radar when I woke up this morning. It's been a long time since I've been in the chain of command. And I'll level with you. I'm not the easiest guy to have on your force."

"I heard the stories, Pat. But we're in a bind here. Small department. Brutal murder and my lead investigator deserts me." There was an uncomfortable pause. "We can't let this case get away from us. Somebody gutted a man in our county. There's a good chance he'll do it again, if he hasn't already. I need you to take charge."

"Let me chew on this idea tonight. I'll call you first thing when I get up. I won't abandon the investigation, but let me try to figure out if there might be a better way."

"I'm counting on you, buddy. Maybe Hennie will get his head screwed on right and come back to work, though I worry about a guy who'd walk away from a case like this. It's not the first time he abandoned ship."

"Hennie's a good man. I wish I could talk to him and see what happened." I took a deep breath and then said, "We'll come up with a way to make this work, Phil. I know we can count on Shea Sommers to use a few vacation days to help us out if we need her—more accurately, when we need her. We'll get it done one way or another."

"Thanks, Pat."

In a way I was flattered with the offer to carry a detective's shield again. My final case as a detective in Lakeshore County ended with mixed reviews. I succeeded in ending the reign of a serial killer. Unfortunately, many people questioned my methods. Now whoever murdered and disemboweled David Swalheim needed to be caught and locked up. With Hennie gone AWOL, it depended on me to figure out who did it. I told Phil I'd give him an answer in the morning, so I decided I'd head down to my new favorite watering hole, have a couple beers, get something to eat, and weigh my pros and cons.

I could have walked to the Wagon Wheel Bar. It was only four blocks from my motel, but I decided to take my truck just in case I needed to get somewhere in a hurry if there was a break in the case. I was on my second beer and finishing a platter of fried perch when I noticed two women stroll into the bar who looked as out of place as two toy poodles at a fox hunt. I immediately recognized Clyda McCabe, Swalheim's high-priced attorney. Coincidence that she and her friend show up in a dive bar near my hotel? Or was she here to dissuade me from questioning her client's involvement in a brutal murder? Most cops put an unhappy spouse at the top of any investigation, and with Kelly Swalheim's total lack of cooperation, I had plenty of suspicions about her role in her husband's death.

Since I had chosen a small booth in a dark corner, I decided to keep my head down and remain unnoticed. This worked for about five minutes until Clyda McCabe, whose eyes were constantly scanning the small dark tavern, noticed me and headed to my table.

"Mr. Donegal," she said with sly smile, "what are the odds of running into you at this quaint little bar?"

"Depends if you were looking to run into me. It's not the kind of place I'd expect to see you. But who am I to judge?" I took my last swig of beer and wiped my napkin across my lips.

"You flatter yourself. Why would I come looking for you?"

"Maybe you have a juicy bit of information you want to share. Something your client would prefer to keep secret."

"I'm afraid I wouldn't be earning so much if I violated my clients' trust—especially clients who haven't been accused of breaking any laws."

Clyda took a dainty sip of her cocktail, then studied me before speaking. "Actually, the friend I came in with asked me to meet her here. She is a real estate agent selling a commercial property just up the street. She just took a call about an offer. She had to leave but should be back in thirty minutes."

"Not much time to make a real estate deal."

"The buyer's been dickering about the price. He's not willing to bite the bullet and meet the asking price."

"Would you like to sit down?" I offered.

"No, you're eating dinner. I shouldn't bother you. I just saw you sitting here and thought I'd say hello."

"No bother," I said. "I'm done eating. They have good fish if you're hungry."

"Had a late lunch, but I'll buy a drink if you don't mind me joining you."

"That's not necessary." I stacked my dirty dishes to make room at the table. "Let me get rid of these plates." I juggled a plate, coleslaw bowl, silverware, and empty beer steins, and headed to find a bussing table. When I returned, Clyda was still standing next to the booth.

"Now, what can I get you to drink? Another beer?" she asked in her all-business lawyer voice.

"What are you drinking?" I mumbled, as if that should determine what I ordered.

"I am having a vodka gimlet. I worked hard today, so I think I earned a second one."

"Well, I'm full of beer, so why don't you get me a gin and tonic, light on the tonic and heavy on the gin. But I'll buy."

"It's not 1950, Pat. Women can pay for drinks now."

"I didn't mean it that way," I stammered, but Clyda was already on her way to the bar and never heard what I said.

Not surprisingly, Clyda's friend never came back. It was a setup. I should have been smarter than to switch to gin. Once the rounds started coming, the evening got fuzzy. Clyda kept up with me, but in hindsight I'm guessing when it was her turn to go to the bar for drinks, she probably ordered her gimlets with water instead of vodka. I'm sure she played me for a stooge, filling me with liquor and then pumping me for information about the case. To be honest, I'm not sure how much I told her. She asked why Hennie Duggan hadn't been around, and I probably told her about his strange disappearance. I'm certain I also told her I'd be taking over the case, though my memory is foggy. I don't remember details. Clyda was clever, and I stupidly became tangled into her web. I do remember early in the conversation her offering me a job as an investigator for her firm. Flattery works well on drunks. I also remember that at the end of the night, she offered to give me a ride back to my hotel. She had a car service on call when she decided she'd had enough. Like any drunk, I insisted I was okay to drive four blocks. She persisted until I agreed to take a ride. She probably saved me from an arrest for drunk driving, which wouldn't have looked good on the eve of my accepting a position with the Kickapoo County sheriff's department.

Dry mouth and drunkard's remorse woke me up well before dawn. I tried to piece together the missing events of the night. I did remember one tidbit of information Clyda shared with me. More than once, as I recall, which suggests it was a primary reason for the *accidental* encounter at the dive bar, she told me to look into a group called the Kilimanjaro Society. Said it could be a key lead in the case. Probably a red herring she dragged across my trail to try to divert attention from her client. But maybe it'd help the case. I would ask Shea to look into it. It was probably the bizarre hunting group Sammy told me about. And if two sources were telling the same story, then it probably had merit.

Drunks regret things they say while binging on booze, but actions are worse. For me, admitting to myself that I took Clyda McCabe to my hotel room was what really haunted me in those sleepless predawn hours. I don't remember what we did or when she left, probably as soon as I passed out, but my brain was clear enough to fully comprehend that I hadn't lured Clyda into bed with my charm and good looks. She was sacrificing herself to serve her client. Had I been smart, I would have called Sheriff Phil Grimes and turned down his offer to deputize me as a detective and put me in charge of this crazy murder investigation. But nobody ever accused me of making rational decisions, so when I called the sheriff's office at seven thirty that morning, I accepted his offer and decided to do my damnedest not to let anybody find out about my imprudent rendezvous with the attorney for our primary suspect. What do they say about idiots who make foolish choices time after time and somehow believe the outcomes will change?

I figured calling Sheriff Grimes with the news that I was officially onboard with the investigation would earn me a pat on the back and a blank check to go catch a murderer. Unfortunately, a little red tape was required first. Should I have been surprised?

"You'll need to fill out an official application and some other paperwork about benefits and employee expectations. Usual bullshit. Also, we need to register any weapons you'll be using while working with our department. Nothing exciting, but things to cover our backsides—yours as well as mine."

"Christ, Phil, a round trip from Milwaukee to Lake Hope and back will waste most of the day. Can't we just fax this stuff?"

"I'd rather get it done right. Regulations, you know. Plus, neither of us wants to be liable for red-tape infractions. Humor me, Pat."

"Can we meet halfway? Madison maybe?"

"Can't. I got to meet with the county board members and the county attorney to get their formal blessing about hiring you."

"How about a deputy?"

"Can't spare anyone. With Hennie missing, I need the little manpower we got."

"How 'bout Millie?"

"She doesn't start work till four o'clock."

"Offer her some overtime. She's single."

"Let me give her a call at home. If she's willing, I'll come up with overtime money or maybe a vacation day. You start driving, and I'll let you know if I can shorten your trip."

After a quick stop for coffee and a couple long johns from Dunkin Donuts, I headed toward Madison. Five minutes later, my phone rang. I picked up without checking caller ID.

"Tell me you convinced Millie to meet me in Madison," I said.

"Who's Millie? Ex-wife? Girlfriend? Murder suspect? What am I missing here?"

"Clyda," I stammered, "I thought it was the sheriff calling me. I was expecting—"

"Sorry, I figured you'd be glad to hear from me."

"Well, I am. I'm just surprised. What's up?"

"I won't keep you since you're waiting for a call." She paused, probably sipping a latte. "First off, I had a good time last night. I wasn't stalking you. I honestly did just swing by the Wagon Wheel for a quick drink with a good friend. I'm actually glad she didn't come back."

"I enjoyed myself too. Though next time I'll stick with beer. Probably made a fool of myself."

"You were fine. Quite good actually." She gave a slight chuckle. "By mentioning next time, are you asking me to get together again?"

"Well, my guess is you could find someone more exciting to be with."

"Don't underrate yourself, Pat. You performed admirably. I had a good time. But, actually, that's why I wanted to call this morning. I have to ask this. Would it be okay with you if we kept our meeting just between the two of us? I'm not sure my client would be thrilled to hear I was colluding with the authorities investigating her husband's murder. It may sound stupid to even ask, but I'd feel better keeping it hushed."

"That idea works for me. Truth is, I'm on my way to Madison right now to sign papers to become a detective for the Kickapoo sheriff's department. I may be leading the investigation."

"Congratulations. What happened to the other officer? Was his name Duggan?"

"Hennie Duggan." I paused to choose my words. "Something came up, making Hennie temporarily unavailable. I'm sure he'll be back soon, but till then I'll be heading the investigation."

"Sorry to hear about Mr. Duggan, but I'm sure you're up to the task. Does that mean you'll be pestering my client again? Or is this Millie your new suspect?" She forced a laugh, though it was a serious question.

"No suspects yet."

"Oh, that's right, now you just call them persons of interest. First day back on the job and you already have the lingo. So, will our next meeting be official?"

"Hard to say. It's my first day."

"I'll let you go. Boss is probably spitting nails waiting for you to get off the phone. I hope to talk soon—and not as a lawyer and a cop."

"That'd be great."

After I hung up the phone, I wondered if this was another red herring. Telling me to keep our rendezvous confidential to cover the fact that she was fully acting in the role of an attorney the previous night. Well, whatever the reason, I was more than willing to keep things quiet.

I hadn't driven five miles when my phone rang again. I assumed it was the sheriff, but again I was wrong.

"Sorry, Pat, I know you're expecting a call, but one quick question. Where is David Swalheim's body?" Now I was sure Clyda was playing me. Our secret tryst had been a setup to pump me for information—and probably to put me in a precarious situation where I might reveal details to prevent certain events from leaking out. I wasn't sure whether to confront her directly or to try to turn the situation to my own advantage. After an uncomfortable pause, I chose the latter.

"Sorry, Clyda, I can't talk about that right now. But as soon as I'm officially in charge of the investigation, I may have more information."

"No problem. And again, sorry to bother you." Click.

What the hell had I gotten into now?

I was halfway to Madison when the phone rang again. I hesitated answering, afraid it was Clyda again, but when I did answer, I heard a new voice.

"Hello, Pat, this is Millie from the sheriff's office."

"Millie, nice to hear from you. I hope you called to tell me I don't have to drive all the way to Lake Hope."

"Then you'll be happy. I'm forty minutes from Madison, but I'm afraid there's more than one paper to sign."

"I can handle that! Where should we meet?"

"I don't know Madison at all. Think of a place that's easy to find."

"Okay. You'll be coming in on Highway 14, so let's meet in

Middleton. There's a diner on the right just as you get to town. Called the Cardinal Coffee Cup. There's a stoplight and a Kwik Trip gas station there. You can't miss it. I'll be there in forty-five minutes."

"I'll find it. If I get lost, I'll call."

Millie was waiting when I got there. She looked to be in her thirties, petite, with red hair. She seemed friendly, but a bit shy. We grabbed a booth and Millie immediately pulled out the paperwork. I ordered coffee, eggs, and toast—an early lunch. Millie said she'd just have a cup of tea, but I insisted she eat something before driving back to Lake Hope. She agreed to a blueberry scone. Our business was done by the time the food arrived. Millie seemed nervous, and I wondered if Hennie had told her any dark stories about me.

"Hennie said you're new in the office, but I gathered from his comments that he enjoyed having you on the staff." Stupid thing to say.

"Deputy Duggan is very nice. Everybody in the office is friendly and helpful." She made little eye contact when she spoke.

"Do you work evenings?"

"Four till midnight. Office work mostly, but I'm also the night dispatcher. That's interesting. Small county, but it seems like there's always something happening. Mostly minor accidents or break-ins or lost dogs." She smiled.

"Minor events are good. I have been involved in too many serious crimes."

"Hennie said you're famous. Solved lots of murders and stuff."

"I don't know if I'm famous, but I'm old, so I've seen a lot of action. Being a cop is more glamorous on TV than in real life. Lot of long hours."

"I heard about your new case. That's weird."

"A real puzzle so far. I never saw one like this." I paused to take a few bites of eggs and a long swallow of coffee. "Have you heard anything from Hennie?"

Millie picked nervously at her scone without looking up. "Not really." She paused. "I did talk to him before he left. He came back to town to pick up his dog. A neighbor watches the dog when Hennie's out of town."

"Did he mention where he was going?"

"He just said he was heading up north to clear his head. I didn't ask questions."

"I'd like to talk to him about the case, but he doesn't answer his phone. I hope he's all right."

"He told me he was going to turn off his phone." She sipped her tea. "This case bothered him a lot."

"I understand that. We're not making much progress."

"I don't think he's coming back very soon." She made eye contact when she spoke this time. "He gave me a key to his house. Said I could stay there if I had to leave my grandma's place." She ate some of the scone and sipped her tea. "I was taking care of my grandmother for the last year. But she passed away. The house she was renting has been sold, so I'll need to find my own place."

"Sorry to hear about your grandma."

"She was ill a long time. I could move back home, but I like my job. Anyway, Hennie gave me a key, which makes me think he'll be gone a while. I'm not sure if I'll stay in his house or not. I'll wait to see what happens with my grandma's place."

"Well, I hope you get everything settled. And I look forward to talking again."

"I hope you solve the case." She smiled. "If I hear from Hennie, I'll let you know. Maybe he'll deal with whatever's bothering him. Did something happen to him?"

"Not that I know of. I've been doing surveillance, so we haven't spent much time together." I drained the last dregs of coffee. "This case would be a lot easier if we could work as a team like on old investigations."

AFTER leaving Millie, I wondered what could've happened to pull Hennie off the case. Did he get a hot lead he was afraid to follow? That'd make no sense. Hennie was a good lawman—even if he had walked away from that case when the priest was murdered. He was new on the job then. But I needed to forget about Hennie and figure out who killed David Swalheim. And where was the body? As I drove, I couldn't help replaying my previous night with Clyda. Was she playing me for a sucker, trying to figure out what I knew? Would she go to a hotel with a cop to help get her client out of a jam? Lawyers have done worse things. Two things particularly vexed me. Was she serious about hiring me to work for her firm? And was the tip about the Kilimanjaro Society intended to help the investigation or create a fishy diversion to lead me away from her client? I decided it was time to bring Shea into the mix. She'd helped me already, and I had no reason to think she wouldn't get more involved. I headed back to the hotel to figure out what to do next.

It was midafternoon when I called Shea's cell. Since I'd worked occasionally as a department consultant for the Madison Police Department, her superiors were only slightly irritated when I called her at work. Shea was a wizard finding cyber net clues, so she'd saved me countless hours tracking down evidence and suspects. Sometimes I wondered why she took my calls, since I generally put her in danger and ate up her vacation hours.

"Shea Sommers, how can I help you?"

"Let me count the ways," I said.

"Pat, I've been screening my calls, but I'm driving so you slipped through my defenses. What's up?"

"Makes my heart flutter to know how happy you are to hear from me."

"Enough bullshit. What do you need?"

"List is too long to go into over the phone, so let me give you the condensed version. Basically, everything is going to hell on this investigation. Now Hennie disappeared."

"Abducted?"

"He just took off—to clear his head, he told a woman who works at the department."

"How can I help?"

"The one lead that keeps popping up involves a hunting club where rich guys apparently hunt each other."

"Hunt as in try to kill?"

"Sounds that way. All these movies about the collapse of civilization—they're not science fiction anymore."

"So, someone hunts, kills, and guts another human for sport. Then what happens?" Shea was struggling with the puzzle pieces. "I remember a story like that in middle school English. Only in that one, it was a rich guy who captured shipwrecked sailors, released them on his island, and then hunted them down for fun. But this group you're talking about sounds like they are hunting someone who can shoot back. At least both sides have a sporting chance. But it's still very weird."

"Since we haven't found a body, my guess is the winner takes the body home as a trophy."

"And you want to drag me into this dystopia?"

"Sorry. It feels like I'm dogpaddling through a tsunami. Now Hennie bails out."

"What can I do?"

"For starters, try to track down this group called the Kilimanjaro Hunting Society. I googled but found nothing but ads for expensive safari vacations. You have better resources."

"It's called the dark web, and you're better off not knowing how to get there. It's demoralizing finding out what's really going on in the world. But I'll find your little boys club."

"Thanks. I'm a lone wolf on this case, and I am flying by the seat of my pants. I will be calling again."

"I got vacation to burn, and no interest in taking a safari. If you give me a couple days' notice, I can back you up—again!"

"That is the first encouraging thing I have heard since we found that pile of guts. You know I appreciate it."

"I'll get even someday. Count on it."


WHILE Shea worked on tracking down the hunting club, I decided to focus on the lodge. Finding Kelly Swalheim's maiden name and then discovering land registered in that name was an internet search even I could handle. Within an hour I'd found eighty acres of land, some of it bordering Lake Michigan in Lakeshore County. It was registered to K. A. Sullivan. The wife's maiden name was Kelly Anne Sullivan—too perfect to be coincidence. Now my problem was gaining access to the lodge without warning the suspect and giving her time to clear evidence.

Since I'd worked for Lakeshore County for years, I should have had instant cooperation. Unfortunately, the higher-ups in the department were not my biggest fans. Help was unlikely. The other option was to visit the property without a warrant and do a little unofficial search. This plan presented plenty of drawbacks. First, if caught, I'd jeopardize any chance of building a case for trial. Secondly, a hunting lodge, especially one related to a guy who had an arsenal that could arm a third world country, would probably be inhabited by people with weapons and expertise in using them. The third drawback, as if I needed another one, was that I was sixty years old with one functioning lung. Odds were not high I'd succeed in this mission. I could ask Shea to back me up, but that would endanger her career and her life. I wasn't willing to take that risk. So, without even giving Lakeshore County a heads-up about the lodge, I got out my camouflage coveralls, loaded my .40 caliber Smith & Wesson and 12-gauge Winchester, and found directions to Kelly's property. My first official day on the job and I was breaking every law in the book.

I ate an early supper at the Wagon Wheel then headed north on I-43. Once in Lakeshore County, I was familiar with every back road and cow path from my days on the job. Kelly's property was only a few miles off the highway, but the area was surprisingly desolate considering how close it was to Lake Michigan and Milwaukee. Owning eighty acres of prime real estate meant it was either inherited or purchased by someone who had money to launder. Either way, it was going to make an eventful night. I had no trouble finding the property. The perimeter was enclosed by a seven-foot fence. The main entrance had a security gate and no doubt closed circuit cameras. The property was adjacent to a state park, which allowed me access away from the front gate.

I parked on a gravel road that led to a rustic public campground that was closed for the season. There was little chance anyone would spot the truck, and if someone did, they'd assume I was a hiker or maybe a couple of teenagers exploring all the secrets of nature—not necessarily the flora and fauna. In addition to my coveralls, I wore a ski mask and gloves. I carried a backpack containing standard burglar's tools as well as backup ammo. Once I reached the fence enclosing the Swalheim property, I walked a quarter mile before finding a concealed grove of white pines that provided cover for me to cut a hole in the fence to enter the property. With luck I could find my way back to this spot when my mission ended. The moon was in gibbous phase—just over half visible. Though there were scattered clouds, there was plenty of light to allow me to find deer paths to lead me through the thick brush cover. I followed a creek until it led to a paved road wide enough for two cars to meet if each drove partially on the shoulder. I stayed off the road, sticking to the tree-lined shoulder. If a car appeared, I could easily find cover.

It took fifteen minutes of cautious stalking before I spotted the house, a log cabin on steroids. In the moonlight, the silhouette of the lodge looked like a castle. Though there were security lights surrounding it, the house itself looked dark. I was relieved by the silence, which meant there probably wasn't a watchdog on duty. I guessed the place would be inhabited by caretakers. But there was no sign of life. I stayed in the wooded cover as I circled the house. As I crept around the lodge, I spotted a large garage or storage shed. It jutted out from a side entrance. Since the closest yard light was on the other side of the garage, I decided to use the dark side as my approach to the house. Rather than entering the house through a broken window or door, I decided to gain access through the shed. If the building was protected by a monitored alarm system, I'd probably find myself either shot or in jail. What I was doing was foolish, but what was new about that? I knew if I used the crowbar in my backpack to pry open that back door to the shed, I was committing a felony, and if I got caught, I'd lose my new position with the sheriff's department, jeopardize a murder investigation, and very likely land in prison. If I was smart, I'd go through proper channels and get a warrant to search the property. But warrants take time and also alert suspects. In a matter of one second, I would make a decision with lifelong consequences.

# / 5 /

AFTER ENDING THE CALL FROM PAT, I RECEIVED A DISPATCH OF POSSIBLE
gunshots with injuries at an apartment complex on the north side of
Madison. These shootings were becoming too common, and several
had recently proven fatal. Most were related to gang disputes, generally drug turf battles. I flipped on the siren and flashing lights and
raced to the scene. This time the injuries were minor. A man claimed
he was walking home from work when he received a gunshot wound
in his thigh. He said the shots came from a dark sedan. He didn't recognize the vehicle or shooter and swore he had no gang affiliation.
The victim was treated at the scene and chose not to go to the hospital. I took his statement as uniformed officers canvassed the neighborhood. As usual, no one heard or saw anything. I headed back to
the station, filled out my report, talked to the uniform team, and filed
it as an open investigation—certain the case would never be closed.
Such is the life of a cop.

I waited till I got home to search for info on Pat's Kilimanjaro
Society. My home computer had access to ScareKrow Browser, an
encrypted server that allows clients to maintain anonymity. These
sites cannot be indexed and are not available through traditional web
browsers. Many of the sites found through ScareKrow can link the
user to illegal services. Other sites simply provide privacy for users

who want to avoid public scrutiny. I guessed that if the hunting club existed, it could be found on the dark web.

It didn't take long to track links to the hunting club. When I opened the site, I was greeted by a quotation from Ernest Hemingway that confirmed the mission of the society—even though the site itself never clearly defined the nature of the group or the procedure required to gain access to information about joining. Clearly, prospective hunters had to be nominated by current members in order to participate.

Hemingway's quote was taken from an article he wrote for *Esquire* magazine. He stated: *"There is no hunting like the hunting of man, and those who have hunted armed men long enough and liked it, never care for anything else thereafter."* So, this was the "sport" that possibly led to the disembowelment on Ibsen Ridge. The reason a body wasn't found is because the so-called hunter probably kept it for a trophy. Now the challenge was to find a way to gain access to the secret society.

It was almost midnight when I ended my search, so rather than calling Pat, I sent a text. If he was still awake, I told him to call me. I waited an hour for a response before I decided to go to sleep. At six thirty I woke and checked my phone. No response. I called Pat's number, but the call went immediately to voicemail. Apparently, his phone was turned off. I tried several more times between my shower, the early MSNBC news, and three cups of coffee. Still no answer. Knowing Pat was working this case alone, I decided to take a couple of vacation days to head to Milwaukee to provide backup. My boss wasn't thrilled when I requested days off without warning, but Pat had provided our department valuable help as a consultant on several cases, so permission was granted. I headed home and packed an overnight bag, plus weapons and enough ammo to start a minor revolution. As usual, I hoped I wouldn't use it but was certain I would.

On my drive to Milwaukee, I called Phil Grimes, the Kickapoo sheriff.

"Sheriff Grimes," I said, "this is Shea Sommers, Madison Police Department. We met a few times when I was helping Pat and Hennie."

"Shea, good of you to call. Did you hear about Pat?"

"I tried to call him, left several messages, but got no response."

"We're in a real bind here. Tough murder case to solve, Hennie ditches, now this deal with Pat."

"What deal?"

"Lakeshore County authorities are questioning Pat about a murder."

"What the hell? Who died?"

"Man named Harley Januss. Kelly Swalheim's boyfriend."

"Pat called the other day to see what I could dig up on Januss. He seemed like a questionable character. Maybe worked for the mob. How's Pat involved?"

"Januss was shot on property owned by Mrs. Swalheim. A hunting lodge up in Lakeshore County. Eighty acres with limited access. Authorities up there got an anonymous call from an unregistered phone, saying there was a man killed. So, they went out and found Januss and no obvious clues. When they checked security cameras near the front gate, they saw Pat's truck driving past. First heading north, then ninety minutes later heading south. Deputies found a hole cut in the security fence."

"They think Pat was the anonymous caller?"

"They're thinking Pat was the shooter. Timing works. Obviously, Pat was in the area. And he'd been tailing Januss a couple days ago. You know Donegal worked for Lakeshore County for almost thirty years. You'd think that'd help him, but I guess he rubbed officials the wrong way."

"Pat's very good at that. He rubs most people the wrong way."

"So I've heard, but I haven't seen that side of him." He paused to phrase the next question. "So, Shea, can you help us out? Our department's so damn small, and with Hennie wandering around with his head up his ass, and now Pat finding a way to get himself in a jam, I'm painted into a corner. Lakeshore County's chief deputy is keeping me up to date, but meanwhile our case is going nowhere."

"I got vacation time, and I'm approved to be away from the job for a few days, so I'll head to Lakeshore County to see if I can rescue Pat. Then we'll see what happens."

"Thanks, Shea, you're a lifesaver."

"Don't thank me till I do something."

"The county will pay for your time."

"Well, we'll hope for the best. I'll be in touch."

When I got to Milwaukee, I headed north on I-43, trying to put some kind of plan together. I was starting to think the better I got to know Pat, the more concerns I had. He was a hell of a cop, but he sure worked in some screwy ways. I was certain he hadn't killed Januss, but who cared what I thought? The damn guy just had a natural talent for complicating every situation. I told myself if I was smart, I'd turn around and drive back to Madison, either do my own job or actually take some time off and do something fun. Hell of it is, I don't really know how to have fun.

As I drove, I again tried Pat's cell phone, but it went straight to voicemail. Must still be in custody, and Lakeshore County was serious enough about Pat as a suspect that they'd taken his phone. I used Siri to get directions to the sheriff's department. I wondered how to approach the officers questioning Pat. Even though I was a police detective myself, I really had no legal standing as far as representing a suspect in another jurisdiction. You'd think law enforcement departments would be glad to cooperate with each other, but my experience taught me that when one cop confronted another cop, a major pissing contest ensued. And outlying counties did not typically hold Madison in high esteem. I also knew that Pat's departure from Lakeshore County took place under a thick mass of charcoal-colored cumulonimbus clouds. Though it grated me like fingernails on a chalkboard, I decided to try my female charms. What the hell? I'm still in my thirties, attractive, and smart enough to know what happens when a woman undoes the top two buttons of her blouse, rolls her eyes, and pretends to be as naïve as a high school sophomore. Over the hill, pot-bellied patrol sergeants, confined to desk duty, fall all over themselves trying to be helpful. However, if Lakeshore County employed a female desk sergeant or young buck who followed procedure and was only concerned with building a résumé and earning a detective's shield, my plan would totally flop. Then I'd come up with Plan B.

Plan B it was. As I explained my situation to the bored-looking twenty-something-year-old receptionist at the desk, she made no effort to make eye contact, instead scrutinizing her meticulously manicured purple fingernails. When I finished explaining who I was and why I was there, she casually scrolled through files on her computer screen before announcing, "I'm afraid Mr. Donegal was released forty minutes ago."

"Could I speak with the officer who interviewed him?"

"Not sure who that officer was."

"Could you check?"

Without answering, she again scrolled through her computer files. "That would be Detective Blackmoor, but he left to get lunch. Would you like me to call him?"

"No, I think you've been helpful enough already." She never looked up, and I'm certain my sarcasm drifted well over her head.

In the parking lot, I sent Pat a fairly blunt text: "Goddamn it, Pat, call me now!"

I was halfway back to Milwaukee when my phone rang. "Detective Sommers." My irritation was obvious in my tone.

"Shea, hey, this is Pat. Got your message. Where are you?"

"I just left the Lakeshore County sheriff's department. What the hell is going on?"

"Misunderstanding. I worked it out."

"Why didn't you return my calls? I took time off work to help with your case, but let me make this very clear, if you're pulling some of your usual bullshit again, I'm going to turn around and go back to Madison. I put my reputation on the line to help you out, and then I hear from Sheriff Grimes that you're being questioned for a murder. I'm not going to ruin my career to help a maverick ex-cop break all the rules."

"Take a breath, Shea. I appreciate you coming down to help. I need you here. And I'm not pulling any bullshit. I'm working the case. I had nothing to do with killing Januss. Listen, I'm on my way to talk to a guy who might know what's going on. I got a room at the Motel 6 on Rawley Avenue in Brookfield. They got plenty of vacancies. Why don't you get a room? Sheriff Grimes will be happy to foot the bill. Get yourself settled in, and I'll meet you at five or so at the Wagon Wheel Bar. It's only a few blocks down Rawley. I'll buy you a beer and dinner and fill you in."

"Motel 6? You guys travel first class." I paused to get my thoughts together. "But, Pat, I'm not going to put up with any crap. You're working a case with Hennie, and he all of a sudden bails out. Now you're questioned about killing one of your suspects. I got no interest in getting involved in something that's going to cost me my job. Don't drag me into something I'm going to regret."

"Shea, I don't blame you for not trusting me. I screw up sometimes, but this investigation is legit. Let's have dinner, and I'll explain things. If you don't like what I say, then you shouldn't get involved. I got no desire to ruin your career."

"See you at five," I said and hung up. When I first met Pat a couple years ago, I'd heard and read stories about his unorthodox techniques, but after working a couple cases, I thought he was the best cop I knew. Now I was starting to have doubts. Hennie had told me about Pat's drinking. Then Hennie disappears, apparently quits his job. I don't know what happened, but it made me wonder if I really wanted to get involved. Maybe Hennie learned something he didn't want to know. Maybe it was about Pat.


DONEGAL was in a booth drinking beer when I entered the Wagon Wheel Bar. He was looking through notes in a spiral notebook and didn't see me approach. He looked surprised when he spotted me. Maybe he was expecting someone else, or he was surprised that I hadn't taken the option of heading back to Madison and keeping my life simple. He started to slide down the bench to make room for me, but I waved him off and slid into the bench opposite his. He closed the notebook and shoved it to the other end of the table.

"I wasn't sure you'd show up." He forced a smile.

"Neither was I," I said.

"Listen, I had nothing to do with shooting Harley Januss. He was killed with a high-powered rifle. I have two handguns and a shotgun. Lakeshore County sheriff said I was in the clear."

"But I heard you were seen on CCTV coming and leaving the property."

"I was seen driving past the gate." His back and shoulders straightened as he spoke, a defensive posture.

"Phil Grimes said they had you on CCTV twice, ninety minutes apart."

"Are you working for Lakeshore County, or are you going to help me solve the Swalheim murder?"

"I just want to know what I'm getting into."

"Listen, it wasn't my idea to take the lead on this investigation. Grimes damn near begged me to take over after Hennie left. If you don't want to get mixed up in this, I understand. Hell, we don't even have a body—just guts and organs. Not a hell of a lot to try to build a case on."

"You have no idea where Hennie is?" I asked.

"He just took off. A woman who works as a dispatcher in his office said he came back to Lake Hope, talked to a neighbor, picked up his dog, and vanished. I guess I'd be shocked, if it weren't for the fact that he quit his job eighteen years ago when that priest was murdered. Hennie seemed like a good cop, but maybe he hasn't got what it takes."

"You think he might have shot Januss? Hennie's a hunter."

"No way. Why would he shoot a suspect before we even build a case?"

"Who knows? You were out there, maybe Hennie was too."

"I went out alone. I found out the Swalheims owned a hunting lodge and eighty acres of land registered in the wife's name. When we went through Swalheim's house, there were signs of a safe or filing cabinet having been recently removed. I figured whatever was moved was probably at the lodge, and it probably had something to do with Swalheim's death. I was just driving out there to get an idea of what was there. I had to figure out a way to get a warrant to search the place."

"Why not go contact your old buddies at the Lakeshore County sheriff's department and have them get a warrant?"

"I don't have a lot of buddies in that department. Most of them threw confetti when I left. The detective who was my partner got pushed out a couple years ago. Apparently, they didn't like the way he handled his cases."

"So, you didn't cut a hole in the fence and break into the house?" It seemed strange to be interrogating a guy I worked tough cases with, drank beer with, and even went on a fishing trip with, but I had to find out what was really going on.

"No, I was just driving—"

"Goddamn it, Pat, stop lying. If I can't trust you, I can't work with you. And I'm damn close to walking out that door and leaving you floundering."

"Okay, I did enter the property."

"You cut through the fence and then broke into the house? Without a warrant?"

"I entered the house through the garage. I didn't see or hear anybody. I looked through some rooms and found the cabinet I was looking for. It was unlocked, so I took a look. I found some hunting brochures, couple throwaway cell phones, a bunch of cheap thumb drives, and a shitload of ammo."

"Did you take anything?"

"I took the two phones and a couple of thumb drives. I figured the phones could give me an idea who Swalheim had been talking to before he died. The flash drives could be computer files. It's not like I was taking evidence. It was the victim's property."

"Or his wife's property," I cut in. I spoke quietly even though no one else was in earshot. "Isn't she your primary suspect?"

"I guess."

"And she's listed as the owner of the land and hunting lodge?" I gave Pat time to respond, but he remained silent. "Good lawyer could argue you illegally entered property owned by the suspect and illegally confiscated evidence. That would get any case thrown out of court."

"I planned to take it back. I just needed some kind of lead to get headed in the right direction." Pat leaned across the table and spoke softly. "I was finished checking the house and went out the back door to avoid a yard light. That's when I stumbled over the body. The guy had been dead less than an hour, judging from the temperature of the corpse. I didn't even check for ID or anything, though I was sure I recognized Januss. Anyway, I didn't disturb anything, went back to my truck, and headed home. I went about twenty miles and used one of the burner phones to call 911."

"You put yourself in a real fucking mess. A murder 150 miles away, no corpse, a suspect killed, evidence tampered with, and the cop in charge out in the wind somewhere. I don't see how you can straighten this out. I'm not too sure I want to be part of it." I stood up, deciding whether to walk out and head back to Madison or to walk to the bar and order a beer. Without saying anymore, I headed to the restroom, then went to the bar. I thought about buying a beer for Pat but decided not to. I wanted to let him know that things had changed between us.

By the time I returned to the booth, Pat had company. An attractive woman, about fifty, her hair pulled back in an elegant fishtail bun, was sitting in my seat. When Pat saw me approach, he slid down to make room next to him. I opted to remain standing.

"Oh, I'm sorry, Pat. I didn't know you had company." The woman winked as she spoke. "I just popped in to meet a friend, but she's not here, so I'm going to head home."

"Please don't leave on my account," I said. "I'm having one beer and taking off." I still hadn't decided if I meant to go home to Madison or back to the Motel 6.

"Sit down, Shea." Pat awkwardly gestured toward the seat next to him. "This is Clyda McCabe, an attorney representing Kelly Swalheim." Then he pointed at me and said, "And Clyda, this is Shea Sommers, best detective in Madison, maybe all of Wisconsin."

"Madison?" Clyda looked surprised. "How does a Madison detective get involved in this case?"

"Shea and I work together a lot. I do some consulting work in

Madison, and when I need help on cases outside of Madison, I usually end up letting her do all the work. We've been a good team."

"So, Detective Sommers, are you working the Swalheim case or the Januss murder?"

"Not sure I'll work either. I just stopped to touch base with Pat to see how things were going."

"I didn't mean to interrupt anything." Clyda started to slide out of the booth. "I saw Pat sitting here alone and decided to say hello. But I need to get going."

"No, sit down," Pat said. "You stopped to meet a friend for a drink, so have one with us. Let me get it." Pat nearly pushed me out of the way to climb out of the booth. He was a big man and clamoring out of a tight space was not something he did gracefully. "I need a beer anyway. What can I get you?"

"I feel like a third wheel here. I should take off." Clyda got to her feet and gathered her purse and sweater.

"No," I said. "Sit down. Have a drink."

"If you're sure I'm not interrupting," Clyda said. "Then I guess I still drink vodka gimlets if you want to get me one."

Sounded to me like Pat and Clyda had had drinks together before, which added one more element to this strange case. Why would the lead detective and the lawyer for the primary suspect be meeting in a bar for drinks? How could a prosecutor possibly build a case against anybody? I was sorry I even thought about getting involved in this brewing fuck-fest.

For the next twenty minutes, we tried to make small talk and to avoid the obvious questions we all had about confusing relationships. Nothing was said about the murder case until Clyda finished her gimlet and set down her glass.

"I probably shouldn't bring up this topic, but I'll blame it on the vodka," she said. "I've been wondering, Pat, was the body of the victim ever found?"

"Not yet," Pat said. "Sheriff Grimes has hired a team of cadaver dogs to search the area, but, far as I know, they haven't found anything."

"Too bad," Clyda said slowly. "I was also wondering about the guy who found the remains. Is he a suspect? A guy goes hunting out in the middle of nowhere, finds a gut pile, and recognizes it as human entrails."

"Medic in Afghanistan. He saw plenty of human remains."

"I heard he was a veteran. Must've seen horrible things in combat." Clyda was still speaking slowly.

"I'm sure he did." Pat was abrupt.

"A lot a GIs come home with a ton of baggage—PTSD and what not. Ever think he could have snapped? Maybe saw another hunter and, you know, maybe overreacted? People in war go through a lot."

"Talking about details of the case is not a good idea, under the circumstances." I tried to steer the conversation in a different direction.

"No, no, don't take me wrong." Clyda stood quickly and clumsily slid from the booth. "I was just talking. I should have known better than to discuss an ongoing investigation. Sorry. I'll leave you two alone."

Clyda turned stiffly and spoke over her shoulder. "Nice meeting you, Detective Sommers, and always nice seeing you, Pat." I assumed that last comment was aimed at me. If she thought Pat and I might be romantically linked, she wanted to make sure I knew they had met socially before tonight. Little did she know that was the absolute least of my concerns.

THE next morning, I went to the hotel lobby around seven. Pat was already there looking through notes in a spiral notebook. He looked up and smiled.

"I hope last night wasn't too weird," he said.

"This whole case is too weird. I agreed to come here because I thought I could help solve this murder and gather evidence for a conviction, but the more I consider the details, the more certain I am that this whole investigation is hopeless."

"You're giving up before we start working together?" He sounded surprised.

"Honestly, Pat, I don't think I can work with you on this case."

"Okay." He set down his notebook and leaned forward. "I know things aren't going very smoothly right now, but we've worked tough cases before."

"Tough cases? You have a pile of guts without a body. The lead cop on the case disappears. A primary witness is killed. The new cop in charge finds the dead body while breaking into the other primary suspect's house to steal evidence. That same new cop in charge may have alcohol issues and has apparently been socializing with the main suspect's lawyer."

"Oh, that part's nothing. We just happened to bump into each other in a bar. No harm in trying to get information to help build the case."

"I assume you're talking about her, because she's the only one who can benefit from pumping the lead cop for information."

"I'm not stupid, Shea. I know how to handle a case. We've worked together many times. I did all right then, didn't I? And don't forget that evidence I took belonged to the victim. Therefore, I had a right to take it."

"Not when you break into and enter a property owned by the primary suspect." I paused to take a breath. I wanted to sound composed, which I wasn't. "Listen, I know you get results, but I think this one's out of control. You've been through a lot the last year. Honestly, I don't think you're ready to take charge of an investigation."

"Fine." He leaned back in his chair. His angry tone revealed a dark side I'd never seen. "Go back to Madison. Hennie obviously doesn't want to work with me and now you don't, so I'll do it myself."

"I told Phil Grimes I'd help with the case, but I don't think we're going to get much done working together, so I'm heading over to Kickapoo County. I'll work the crime scene again and try to track any leads I can. I want to make sure the medic who found the body can be ruled out as a suspect. I'll also dig into that hunting club. There might be something with that."

"That sounds like a plan. Let me know if you find anything." He attempted to sound calm but there was still an edge to his voice. "And the reason I took the phone from the hunting lodge is because if

Swalheim was involved with the man-hunting, then he no doubt used a throwaway phone to make connections. I wrote down the three numbers listed in his recent call list." He took a slip of paper from his notebook and handed it to me. "And there are a few notes, maybe passwords or some sort of code. You may want to start there."

I took the slip of paper and stuck into my jacket pocket. "Thanks, I'll check into it."

I had already moved my overnight bag to the car, so without more conversation, I turned and headed toward the door. Pat said, "Here, take the key to Raven's place. Beats the hell out of that Bates Motel. And take this phone." He tossed me the burner phone. "Try calling the numbers. See what you come up with."

I took the key and phone, nodded a thank you, and headed out the door. It wasn't until I was halfway to Lake Hope that I realized I was now in possession of property stolen from the suspect's house. Was that Pat's scheme? To get me involved in his bullshit? If the answer was yes, then this was the end our of collaboration.

**WHEN** I arrived in Lake Hope, Sheriff Grimes was more surprised to see me than I was with the fact that I'd left Pat on his own with his investigation. But I genuinely believed I could accomplish more working the case myself than I could teaming up with him. I might have been wrong, but it seemed like Pat had let the investigation spiral wildly into some unexplored sixth dimension. I didn't want to get dragged into his quagmire, and I felt that looking at the case from a fresh perspective could possibly turn the investigation in a new direction. Grimes admitted he was confused by my decision but said he would trust my instincts and would support me any way he could. My first question was about progress finding the rest of Swalheim's remains.

"We've had the DCI team working the bluff for days," Grimes explained. "Plus, cadaver dogs have scoured the area. No leads. Our best guess is the victim was killed elsewhere and the entrails were transported to the top of the bluff—probably by an all-terrain vehicle. We have no idea about motive."

"And the medic who discovered the guts—you feel certain he didn't do it?"

"Zach Layman is squeaky clean. Not a blemish on his civilian or military records. He's cooperative, and there's nothing to make me think he had anything to do with the murder. There's no apparent connection to the victim."

"Well, I'd still like to talk to him," I said. "Maybe he could have seen something or somebody when he was hunting."

"We've asked," said Grimes, "but he claims there was nothing suspicious. No hunters, no vehicles. It was a weekday, just nothing going on out there. But feel free to talk to him. I'm sure he'll cooperate."

"I'll call him tomorrow. I'm staying at Raven Quinn's place for now. Apparently, she's in Minnesota and Pat was living there alone. He offered me the key and said I could stay there. I'll give it a try."

"Otherwise, there's a hotel in town, but I guess you stayed there last time. I don't blame you for not wanting to go back. Everybody complains about it, though there has never been any trouble out there that I heard about."

"I'll try Raven's. Maybe the fresh air and wide-open spaces will clear my head. And I'll stop in the morning and let you know my plans. I got a couple ideas."

"I appreciate any help you can give us. We need all we can get the way things have gone so far."

I figured one of the reasons Pat offered me Raven's house was to show me he hadn't turned into some kind of madman since I'd seen him last. He no doubt figured that Hennie had told me about the drinking and unusual behavior. Truth is, I did want to snoop around the place to see for myself whether Pat had gone off the deep end. I wouldn't blame him if he had. He worked through some strange cases during his stays in Lake Hope, and now with Raven moving out of state, he had issues to deal with.

ONCE I'd settled into Raven's house and set up my laptop on the dining room table, I decided to try my luck with the numbers Pat had given me. Yet, I knew that if Swalheim was using a throwaway phone to arrange a hunting date, then whoever he was calling was doing the same.

I was not surprised when I couldn't find links to the numbers. The obvious thing would be to call the numbers and see who answered. If the phone was a connection to the human hunting club, then it could be the killer on the other end of the line. But what would I say if I did get an answer? Could I pretend to be a hunter seeking new prey? Would they believe a woman would play their insane game? Why not? Maybe I could use my gender to lure the hunter into a new challenge.

Before trying a phone call, I studied the notes Pat had given me. They were handwritten and a bit hard to decipher. As clearly as I could figure, the notes said: "Answers Francis Macomber, responds Robert Wilson." Strange password. I googled "Francis Macomber," hoping to possibly find the club's organizer. What I found was a story by Ernest Hemingway, "The Short Happy Life of Francis Macomber." After reading a synopsis of the story, which was apparently one of Hemingway's most highly acclaimed, I decided to read the story, which I found online. I found the story quite bizarre. Macomber, a wimpy sort of man, attempts to prove his manhood to his wife, Margot, by going on a safari to shoot lions and water buffalo. His first attempts to show his machismo backfire, and Margot ends up in the sack with their hunting guide, Robert Wilson. When Francis finally stands up to a charging buffalo and actually kills the beast, he is, perhaps accidentally, shot in the head by Margot. Using the names from this story for passwords would make perfect sense. My guess was that all calls and participants remain anonymous, therefore the secret code. The person receiving the calls responds, "Francis Macomber," and the caller says, "Robert Wilson." Connection made. What's the worst that could happen by trying the code—other than getting into a shootout with a big game hunter? I assumed once a link was made with a fellow hunter, a time and place were agreed to, and the game was on.

I should have told either Pat or Sheriff Grimes about my scheme to connect with a man-hunter. But why? If the idea worked, I'd let them know. If it flopped, no one needed to find out. So, with my notes in front of me, I punched in the first number. After four rings, I got a message that the number was no longer in service. No surprise. I dialed the second number. It rang several times.

"Hello, this is Francis Macomber." The slow, flat voice seemed hesitant.

"This is Robert Wilson," I said firmly. I waited for Macomber to make the next move.

"You don't sound like a Robert Wilson," he said. "Are you sure you've called the right number?"

"If you're Francis Macomber, then I'm Robert Wilson."

"This call concerns me in two ways. First, you sound like a woman. And second, this same number called me a few weeks ago to establish a meeting. But when I reached the designated location, no one showed up. Is this some sort of trap or scam to uncover my identity for some type of extortion scheme?"

"No extortion scheme, Mr. Macomber. I assume that earlier call was from my husband. I should say my *late* husband. He met with an unfortunate hunting accident."

"That sounds mysterious. Perhaps I should call you Margot." The previously reluctant voice became lighter and a bit playful.

"Yes, I get it." I laughed. "Margot might be a better code name for me. My husband was weak. He found out about my flirtation with members of the Kilimanjaro Society, and he wanted to play the game also. Unfortunately, he didn't last long."

"And you, I'll call you Margot, are serious about setting a date?"

"I didn't call to discuss literature."

"But I've never tried hunting a woman."

"That's surprising. I find misogyny runs rampant among type A macho men."

"Is that what I am? A macho man?" He chuckled.

"You're willing to put your life on the line for sport. You trust your abilities and your courage. Grace under pressure. Sounds macho to me."

"And what about you, Margot? How do you describe yourself?"

"I'm a real ball-busting bitch who likes to see men beg for their lives."

"You do realize that many of these contests often end in death."

"I fully understand the rules, and, you will notice, I am still alive."

"I have to respect your guts, Margot, so let's set a time and place."

"Ibsen Ridge in Kickapoo County, Wisconsin."

"That's where I was supposed to meet your husband. Are you sure this isn't a setup?" The caller sounded wary of proceeding.

"I assume you still have the coordinates from your last visit. I don't know where you live, so I'll let you set the time. Unless you're wary of hunting a woman."

"Oh, I can get there in a few days. How about this Friday night? Hunt starts at midnight. Arrive early if you want to study the terrain, though I assume you're quite familiar with the layout."

"If you want a new location, that's fine."

"I've been there. I know the area."

"Midnight Friday works for me."

"You do understand that there are no rules involved here, other than abiding by the starting time. Naturally, honor is the key to Hemingway's code of behavior, so we must hunt fairly. No automatic weapons. No assistance from other hunters. And, please understand, to the winner goes the spoils, all the spoils, if you catch my drift."

"I understand completely, Francis. And I look forward to our meeting."

When I hung up, I felt nauseous. Here was an apparently rational human being making plans to try to kill a woman he'd never met. And making it quite clear that he would feel free to do anything he wanted to do before he killed her. *The spoils of battle.* Yet he spoke of honor and a code of conduct. It honestly made me want to go to Ibsen Ridge on Friday night and hunt down and shoot the son of a bitch. What troubled me was that he acted as if he had nothing to do with Swalheim's death. Either he was a good actor, or he simply wanted a chance to kill the wife of the man he'd already shot and gutted. Maybe he wanted a mounted couple to display in his trophy room.

My next decision was to figure out how I was going to take an experienced hunter alive when he'd be doing everything in his power to kill me—and worse.

I decided to keep this conversation to myself until I knew if I wanted to involve Pat or Sheriff Grimes. I wished Hennie Duggan was still around since he was the experienced hunter in the group. Although, I knew Pat had plenty of experience hunting down criminals and, when necessary, shooting them. And I certainly was not squeamish about using my weapon to defend myself or other innocent people. But this was different. This was hunting another person for sport. This was going to take some thinking.

Though unsettled by my earlier phone conversation, I did have a feeling I'd actually made progress. There was a reasonable chance I just spoke to our killer. Now I had to decide how to use this connection to solve the case. I felt like taking a walk to clear my head, but late-October evenings come early. I realized it was the last day of the month—Halloween. Strange when I thought about the talk I'd had with "Francis Macomber" on All Hallows Eve. Yes, ghouls actually do exist.

I decided to treat myself to a burger and a beer, so I headed into town to Murphy's Bar, basically the only place to get a beer in Lake Hope. It was a good crowd for a Tuesday—others like me with no kids to take trick-or-treating and no desire to sit home handing out candy to miniature Star Wars villains and little princesses. I sat at the bar to allow for better mingling. Small-town taverns are havens for folks willing to share local secrets with strangers. When I caught the bartender's attention, he approached with a smile, probably glad to see a new face in his establishment, but probably even happier to see a young woman alone without a ring on her finger.

He placed a cardboard Green Bay Packers coaster in front of me. "What'll it be, ma'am?"

"Ma'am? Really? I'm old enough to be called ma'am when I enter a bar?"

"Sorry, just trying to be polite."

"Have you still got that IPA called Jungle something?"

"Nope. They quit making it. But I got a good local IPA from Driftless Brewery."

"Perfect. I'll have that. Is your grill turned on?"

"Yup. I can make you a burger. Or I can throw in a frozen pizza. Emil's. They're good."

"Cheeseburger with fried onions," I said. "Do you have fries?"

"No fries. Chips, or I got a pot of chili in the kitchen. Goes good with burgers."

"That works."

"Cup or bowl?"

"Bowl. And can you chop up some raw onions?"

"Sweetheart, where have you been all my life? Cold beer, burger with fried onions, and chili with raw. Where were you twenty-five years ago when I was young and single?"

"Still in middle school, so it's best we didn't meet."

"Sorry. I was just making a joke."

"I know. I'm kidding you back. Now stop talking and get me my beer."

"Yes, ma'am!" He grinned sheepishly.

For a fifty-year-old bar owner, Murphy kept himself in good shape. Probably was quite a catch twenty-five years ago.

The beer was good, and the crowd was keeping Murph on his toes. I sipped my beer until my food came. The burger and chili were good, and I scarfed them down like I hadn't eaten in a week. I figured the heartburn would set in about the time I hit the hay, but, hell, it would be worth it.

I decided if I wanted conversation, I was going to have to mingle with the clientele. I'd almost finished my beer when my first subject appeared. He looked early fifties, black hair that was badly cut like a self-shorn mullet, a bit flabby, but not too bad. Looked like he could have Native American blood.

"I see your Halloween costume conceals your identity," he said as he slid onto the stool next to me.

"Excuse me?"

"Your jeans and sweatshirt. I wouldn't have pegged you for a detective."

"Have we met?" I asked.

"We have, but I generally don't make an impression that folks remember." He smiled, a bit embarrassed.

"I've only been in this town a couple times, so you must've met me after one of the cases I worked." I was scrambling through my mental hard drive trying to place the face, or maybe the voice.

"The Father Johnny case. You and Mr. Donegal were scurrying through the crowd trying to get to your hotel room."

"Rooms," I corrected. "That was a hectic evening."

"I asked you a question when you passed. But you ignored me and kept walking."

"Sorry. It had been a long day." I tried to remember him but had no luck. "Were you with a TV news crew?"

"Newspaper." He extended his hand, which felt like a soft wet fish. "Joe Flaherty, publisher, editor, reporter, photographer of the local paper. Can I buy you a drink?"

I looked at my nearly drained beer glass. "Thank you, yes, I'll have Driftless IPA."

He awkwardly signaled Murph. "Two IPAs, please."

"So, you're the entire staff at the local paper?"

"Yes. Rather boring really. Some weeks our lead story is announcing who won the booby prize at the local euchre tournament. Not a lot happens here."

"But three major cases last year. You must've been thinking about a Pulitzer Prize."

"It was amazing—murders, a kidnapping, missing persons. But I'm afraid my stories didn't get much traction."

"And now another bizarre case."

Our beers arrived, and Joe produced his wallet and paid for our drinks.

"Thanks," I said. "I owe you one."

"One is usually my limit." Again, the gawky embarrassed smile.

"If not tonight, then another night." I smiled back, thinking the local journalist might have some insights into the case of the gutted hunter.

"I can't get any details from the sheriff. Either they don't know anything, or they're just keeping it hushed." Joe paused to sample the beer. He grimaced a bit at the hoppy bite. "You must be working the case, so you know more than I do."

"Not really. I just got brought in as a consultant. First day, so I don't know much either."

I had to decide quickly how to keep the conversation flowing. I couldn't reveal too much, but if I didn't say enough, then I had little chance of pumping Joe for info. "An ex-army medic was hunting up at Ibsen Ridge and stumbled onto a gut pile. Normally no big deal, but this guy, being a medic, recognized the guts as human remains."

"Yeah, I heard that part. Zach Layman. Everybody likes him. Two tours in Afghanistan. Can't imagine he had anything to do with it. But, you never know."

"Doesn't sound like the type. Any other gossip around town?"

"Nobody would tell me. Afraid they might get their name in the paper. Plus, I'm not very sociable."

"You're out tonight."

"Halloween. This place beats sitting home handing out Tootsie Rolls."

"You must live alone," I said without thinking. Other than trying to keep a conversation going there was no good reason for such a stupid comment. At best, he might think I was hitting on him, and at worst, he could think I was pegging him for a loser, or maybe a suspect. "Sorry. Dumb thing to say."

"It's all right." A warm glow flushed across his face, something I thought people outgrew after puberty. "I sort of live alone."

"None of my business, Joe." I took a long slow drink of beer. Joe aped my movement. We both drank slowly thinking of the next direction in our conversation.

He spoke first. "So, is that your job? Police consultant?"

"I'm a detective in Madison. But Pat Donegal helps me out on cases, so I try to repay him when I can."

"Donegal's not a real cop anymore is he? I thought he was a consultant."

"He's retired, but he helps here in Kickapoo County when they need him. He has a lot of experience."

"I've heard some stories about him." Joe blushed again.

"Well, you know. People talk."

"I didn't mean anything, you know." He gulped down the rest of his beer and appeared to repress a belch before speaking. "I better go. I got a couple stories I need to proofread yet tonight. I need to have the paper ready to print by noon tomorrow."

"I enjoyed meeting you, Joe." I reached in my jeans pocket and pulled out a card. "And if you get any leads, I'd appreciate a call. My cell number is on the bottom of the card."

"I'll do that, and you do the same. A good story sells papers. Good sales mean more advertising."

"If something breaks, I know where to contact you."

He flashed his awkward forced smile. "Oh, and I guess you said I had a beer coming. Maybe we can meet here another night."

"I'm sure I'll be back. There are not a lot of places to go in the evening in Lake Hope."

"I'll look forward to seeing you again." He suppressed a giggle.

I assumed Joe was attempting to make a pass. I too forced an awkward smile. He slid off the stool and headed for the door. He never spoke or made eye contact with any of the other patrons. He seemed like an odd personality for a guy running a local business. But who ever said I was Cleopatra?

After Joe left, I nursed my beer for a while hoping somebody else would sidle up next to me to enlighten me about this seemingly unsolvable case. After ten minutes, I decided to finish my beer, buy a six-pack of Driftless to take back to Raven's, and curl up with the internet for the evening. It was the dullest Halloween I ever suffered through.


ZACH Layman worked as a self-employed handyman and took nursing classes online. When I called the next morning to ask if we could meet, his wife answered. She sounded very friendly and told me her husband would be home for supper at around five thirty. She would have him call me. He called around six and said he'd be happy to talk, even though he had already explained everything to Hennie Duggan. I said I was being brought in as an extra set of eyes and ears and that I'd like to hear the story from him. He agreed to meet the next morning at the local diner.

Zach Layman looked like what I expected: clean-cut, physically fit, cropped haircut, and casually dressed. He stood up when I introduced myself and waited till I was seated before he sat down.

"I appreciate your meeting me, Mr. Layman. I know you've talked to Hennie."

"No problem, Detective. Not much to say other than I was bow-hunting, saw a pile of guts, and checked it out of curiosity."

"Then you realized the remains were human?"

"Not right away, but when I saw the liver, I did a sort of double take. I've seen deer livers and human livers. I can tell the difference."

"You must have been shocked realizing you were looking at human entrails."

"I'll admit, Detective, it made me a little sick, kind of flashed me back to a place and time I prefer not to go back to."

"I understand. I was never in the military, but I imagine it's painful to deal with an experience like you went through."

"Most of the time I'm fine. But something like this, well, it shakes a guy a little."

"So you called 911?"

"I tried, but I couldn't get a signal. It was getting dark, and I had to hike down the bluff while there was still light, so I waited to call."

"So, you called when you got a signal?"

"It was dark by the time I got home, so I figured I might as well wait till morning. Nobody was going out there in the dark to look at a pile of guts."

"That makes sense." I wanted to show Zach I was not questioning what he did. "See any cars or people as you were leaving? Or maybe when you got there."

"No, it's quite isolated, generally nobody around."

"Do you go there often?"

"Maybe once a week during hunting season. If I don't have jobs, I like to traipse around the woods. Good therapy."

"Any luck? With the hunting, I mean."

"I saw a couple does this fall, but no bucks. I'm picky about what I shoot. I try to get a buck for the freezer. Maybe a doe for sausage. My wife and I both like venison."

"Use a rifle?"

"During gun season. But this is bow season."

"How'd you end up a medic? It sounds like you know how to use a gun."

"The army decided for me. Something on my aptitude test showed I'd make a good medic. I did what I was told."

"Did you carry a weapon in combat?"

"Oh, hell yes! Never went anywhere without my trusty .45. When you're working on an injured soldier, you're vulnerable for attack. Enemy doesn't give you a pass because you're nursing the wounded. Just the opposite—the enemy figures he can kill two for the price of one. And let me tell you, most of the medics I worked with were like bear sows protecting their cubs when enemy fighters tried to harm their patients. I discharged my weapon many times." He paused to see my reaction. "Does that surprise you? That I wasn't some kind of pacifist or conscientious objector?"

"Doesn't surprise me at all. I'm just trying to get all the details. I appreciate what you did for your country. Takes a hell of a lot of courage. Soldiers who take care of the wounded deserve more credit than they get."

"I appreciate that. I am working toward a nursing degree."

"You'll make a hell of a good nurse."

"Am I a suspect?"

"I don't think anyone considers you a suspect. We're just trying to figure out who left that gut pile. Honestly, I think the victim was killed elsewhere and the entrails were placed on Ibsen Ridge to confuse authorities."

"I'm glad to hear that. I've been worried that since I was there with a weapon, I might be a suspect."

"Do you ever remember seeing cars in that area when you were hunting?"

"No, it's a lonely area. Usually don't see anybody."

"Try to think back. Picture driving that road around the ridge."

"Like I say, it's remote." He squinted one eye as if to look into his memory. He was obviously a man used to taking orders. I gave him time to scroll through old memories. He suddenly made an odd facial expression and said, "You know, there was a car out there maybe a week or two earlier. Just parked along the shoulder. I slowed down to see if the driver needed help."

"Do you remember the car or driver?"

"It was woman. Probably looking at her phone or GPS. People get lost out in the bluffs, and lot of times can't pick up a satellite signal. I remember I pulled up next to her car. She waved me past, kind of frantic, like maybe she was scared of me. That seemed normal, a woman out in the boonies alone."

"Can you recall what she looked like?"

Again, he squinted one eye. "She might've had sunglasses and a ball cap. Nothing stands out."

"How about the car?"

"Big vehicle, because I had to look up to see her. Black and shiny. SUV, probably. Maybe a Cadillac." He threw up his hands. "But I'm just guessing."

"That could be very helpful."

"But I saw the woman a week or more before I found the entrails. Those guts couldn't have been there a week. Scavengers would've spread them all over the woods—or would have eaten them."

"Maybe she was scouting. That's why police work gets boring. We have to look at every possibility. Little details can be important."

"Well, whatever it takes." He finished his coffee and pushed his chair away from the table. "I better get back to work, but I'll call if I think of something."

"You got my number. And I appreciate your help. Maybe the black

SUV is connected, or maybe it's not. But I'll check into it."

Before leaving the diner, I checked vehicle registrations for Kelly Swalheim and Harley Januss. Neither owned an SUV. I decided I'd call Pat to see if he'd learned anything. Though I questioned Pat's current mental clarity, I figured it was still better to work together rather than against each other.

When I called Pat, I got his voicemail. I hoped that didn't mean he was hungover or lying in a gutter—or in jail. I was relieved when he returned my call ten minutes later.

"Shea, have you solved our murder?" He forced a cackle.

"I had that wrapped up last night. Figured I'd give you a few hours to solve it yourself so I wouldn't bruise your ego."

"My ego is beyond bruising. Seriously, did you find out anything?"

"Maybe. For one thing, I got a date Friday night with a hunter from the Kilimanjaro Society. Stealing that cell phone paid off."

"Good, but you're not thinking of meeting the guy? Not alone."

"I'm still considering that. But here's the thing. He recognized the number when I called him. Said he'd already scheduled a hunt with someone using that number. I let on I was the guy's wife and a more formidable quarry than my husband."

"Did he believe you?"

"I think his misogyny kicked in, and he drooled over the idea of hunting a woman. And"—I paused for effect—"when I gave him the location, he said he'd already been there."

"That's insane. That's got to be our guy."

"Well, except he seemed to think I killed my husband."

"What's he going to say?"

"True."

"You can't go through with it. He's an experienced big game hunter with the best weapons. Fancy rifle that'll shoot a mile."

"Nobody can shoot a mile in a thick forest."

"I'll be there too, but even the two of us won't have a chance against a guy like this. Unless you were an Army Ranger or a Navy Seal and never mentioned it."

"We got a couple days to think about it."

"Don't do something stupid, Shea. That's my department, and believe me, you don't want to end up like me."

"That doesn't sound good. You having issues?"

"You mean with the drinking? No. Two beers a night."

"Good. And I may have another lead. Zach Layman, the guy who found the gut pile, saw a vehicle in the area a week earlier. Female driver, acted suspicious."

"Kelly Swalheim maybe?"

"He didn't get a good look at her. And the car description didn't match the vehicle registered to Kelly or her husband. Or Harley Januss. But it might be something."

"You're doing a hell of a lot better than I am. I've been trying to mend fences with Lakeshore County. Januss's murder has to be connected to Swalheim's, so we're forced to work together. They don't seem thrilled about it. And they're making it clear the second murder is their case."

"Not welcoming home their prodigal son?"

"Hardly. But I'll keep at them." Pat paused, hopefully to take a swig of coffee and not something else. "Did you talk to anybody else?"

"The guy who publishes the local paper. A little weird I think, but he said he'd keep us in the loop if he hears something. He acted like a seventh grader at a middle school dance. I think he tried to flirt with me."

"Hope that works out for you."

"Thanks."

"And don't get foolish about that hunting date. I'll come up with a plan."

"God, now I am worried."


ACTUALLY, I had no idea how I was going to handle the "meeting" with the man-hunter. I wasn't equipped to face the hunter one on one. I would need warm camouflage clothes, night-vision goggles, and most importantly, a high-powered rifle with a night-vision scope. And I wasn't excited about waiting for Pat to come up with a plan. I didn't know if I wanted to let anyone else in on the absurd idea. I could talk to the sheriff, or I could try Hennie again. He's the one with hunting experience, but under the circumstances I had less faith in Hennie than I had in Pat. The first thing I needed to do was visit the ridge and get an idea of the terrain. Going out there unguided made no sense. I needed a guide to show me around. Well, I had just talked to Zach Layman. He probably knew the area as well as anyone. I could call him and offer to pay him for his time if he was willing to put a hold on his other jobs. Obviously, I couldn't tell him why I needed to learn about Ibsen Ridge, but I could pick his brain about layout of the area. Before phoning Zach, I googled the coordinates and studied the satellite images of the area. It was very remote. The western border was the Mississippi River and there appeared to be only one route to access it, Ridge View Road, where Layman saw the woman checking her phone. There was a railroad track that ran along the river with maybe a gravel maintenance road, but it looked nearly impossible to climb the sandstone bluff from the river side. To get to the peak of Ibsen Ridge, a climber would have to travel nearly a half mile through thick forest with sheer rocks and cliffs, which appeared practically vertical on the topographical map. The hiker would experience a 1,300-foot rise in elevation. That option seemed remote, but maybe Zach knew other routes to access the bluff.

ZACH agreed to take me to Ibsen Ridge the next morning but refused to accept money. He said it was his duty as a citizen to help law enforcement. From my experience, that attitude put him into a very small demographic of our population. I told him I'd at least buy his breakfast and lunch. He didn't argue with that proposition. We met at the diner, and after breakfast we took his pickup truck to the ridge.

The thirty-minute ride from town to Ibsen Ridge was a bit awkward. Zach couldn't understand why I seemed to be taking charge of the investigation if I worked for the city of Madison. I told him it was complicated, and since Kickapoo County had such a small force, the sheriff was happy to get the help. He also asked about Hennie

Duggan, whom he'd talked to the day after discovering the gut pile. I was honest and told him I didn't know where Hennie was. I said he told the sheriff he needed time to deal with a personal issue.

When we reached the base of the bluff, Ridge View Road widened a bit and there was a gravel shoulder wide enough to park five or six vehicles. Zach slowed down and pointed out the parking area and the trail leading up to the top of the ridge. He said the trail was steep but wide enough to accommodate ATVs. Then he picked up speed and drove past the parking area.

"We're not going to stop?" I asked.

"I'm going to show you a less-traveled route."

We drove a quarter mile and then turned right onto what appeared to be a logging road—barely wide enough for a pickup, unpaved and bumpy enough to jar every vertebra in my spine.

"Is this your usual route?" I asked, my voice quivering with each rut, root, and stump we hit.

"No, but I figured if you're investigating a possible murder, you probably want to know access paths that aren't so obvious. If I was going to plant a bucket of human entrails on a public hunting ground, I wouldn't want to hike up the main trail."

"Makes sense." I paused as his truck bounced what felt like three feet off the ground. "Did you ever think about being a cop? You got the brain for it—thinking about what's going on in the mind of the bad guys."

"You think maybe I am the bad guy? And that's how I know about this hidden route?"

"If you committed the crime, you wouldn't be showing me how you got there. Though I admit, this is more than secluded." For a few seconds I did wonder if maybe Zach was driving me out here to dump me in a spot nobody would ever find.

"Don't worry. I know this way because when I come out here to tramp around, I'm just trying to get away from civilization. It's normally peaceful out here. Nothing but trees, and squirrels, and birds, a few deer, maybe a flock of wild turkeys. Good place to escape."

"That makes perfect sense to me."

"Most guys are in a hurry. They race out here, unload their ATVs, and roar up the trail to the top, scaring every animal within twenty miles. Not me. I like peace and quiet. I spent many hours when I was in Afghanistan dreaming of being back here schlepping through the woods by myself. No land mines, mortar shells, or incoming rifle fire."

"I cannot imagine what guys go through over there. Nobody can unless they've been in combat."

"Lot of GIs had it harder than I did, that's for sure. I got home in one piece."

"I'm glad you did. But I bet you went through plenty of hell."

"I'll tell you this. I weighed 192 pounds when I landed at Bagram Air Base near Kabul. Two years later when I headed back to the US, I weighed 165. It's not a picnic for anyone over there."

"I appreciate what you did for the country."

"Thank you."

He slowed to a stop and shut off the engine. "Well, here we are."

"This is our destination?"

"There's a creek bed through those trees, maybe twenty yards ahead. In the spring when the snow melts, there can be forceful streams coming off that bluff. But this time of year, it's dry. Easy trail—though it's a fair jaunt to the top. I see you wore your boots and snowmobile suit. It's plenty cool, but I can tell you, you'll be sweating when you reach the top."

"I appreciate this, Zach. Since it's seldom used, there's a good chance we might find clues."

"We can hope," he said as he loaded several bottles of water, some sticks of jerky, and a couple snack bars into a well-used military backpack.

"You come prepared."

"I've made this trek before. It's a good workout."

"Let's go."

The climb presented plenty of challenges. The trail followed the dry creek bed, but the creek had numerous drop-offs, which would create beautiful waterfalls in the spring. Now, these sandstone formations produced rugged elevation changes that required us to clamber over the rocks or try to wedge our way through thick brush. I told Zach that I thought the deer could do a better job of constructing their trails. About halfway up, we paused to drink water. As I was standing there guzzling from my bottle, Zach tapped my elbow and held his finger to his lips. Without a word, he pointed to an area about thirty yards to our left. It took me a minute to recognize a herd of about a dozen pigs nestled in a small grove of hemlock trees.

"What the hell?" I whispered.

"Feral pigs. We don't want to tangle with them."

"They're dangerous?"

"Can be. Just stand still—though you may want to slowly move your hand toward your weapon, just in case."

The heat generated by the climb quickly subsided, and I felt a chill run through me. I didn't know there were feral pigs in Wisconsin.

We stood frozen for several minutes until the lead pig lost interest in us and began moving away. The rest followed. Once they were out of sight, I took a deep breath. Zach smiled, half amused at my reaction and half relieved the pigs lost interest.

"Wild boars in Wisconsin?"

"More common than you might think in these secluded bluffs and coulees. Originally, they were escapees from farms. But they've evolved over the years to adapt to the wild by growing longer hair and sprouting dangerous tusks."

"Do people hunt them?"

"Sure. Permanent open season. In fact, the DNR urges people to shoot them. They can be dangerous and cause a lot of damage."

"People eat them?"

"Supposed to taste better than regular pork, from what I've heard."

"What do they eat?"

"Everything. They're pigs. Mostly roots, and nuts, and green vegetation. But they like to raid area farms and root up fields for succulent roots and bulbs. And they'll eat meat. Whatever they can kill or find already dead."

"Sounds like a nice crew."

"Had they found that gut pile, you would not be here investigating a murder. There would have been no remains."

"Will they be back?"

"Not likely. But we better get moving if we want to have time to study the upper bluff."

"Would those pigs eat a human body if they found one?"

"Probably. But they wouldn't leave the guts—that'd be the best part."

"But if the victim was killed elsewhere in the bluffs, gutted, and left, maybe the pigs would get rid of the body without finding the guts."

"Maybe. But the sheriff's had dogs out looking. Pigs wouldn't be able to completely remove all traces. There'd be blood and bones, something to attract the dogs."

"You're probably right. Just a theory."

"If the body's out here, it's well hidden. But there are plenty of hiding places."

We started back up the bluff. I concentrated on my footing to make sure I didn't step into a pile of fresh deer droppings, and more importantly, didn't lose my footing on the loose rocks, risking not only having to re-climb the hill but also possibly suffering an injury. We hadn't spoken since our encounter with the pigs. Suddenly, to my right, I heard a rustle of leaves, and assuming the pigs were back for a deadly ambush, I drew my weapon and found myself drawing a bead on a flock of half a dozen wild turkeys.

"A bit jumpy, Detective?" Zach flashed a shy grin.

"Spooked me a little, I guess," I admitted.

"Dry oak leaves can make a couple squirrels chasing each other sound like an army. It's a good lesson, if you're planning to be a hunter. It's awfully hard to be sneaky in a forest, especially in fall."

"Why didn't we hear the pigs?"

"They were standing there watching us approach, deciding whether flight or fight was the better instinct."

When we got to the top of the bluff where Layman had found the remains, we scoured the area, even though the state crime investigators had already searched it. After an hour, we paused for water and beef jerky. As he gnawed on his jerky, Zach gave me a quizzical look.

"So, why are we here? This place has been searched several times."

"I just wanted to know what we're dealing with."

"Have you ever hunted?"

"No, not really."

"Did you think we were going to stumble onto the killer returning to the scene of the crime?"

"Do you think killers do that?" I asked.

"That's what they say."

"It probably happens. It's human nature to want to visit the sight of conquest. Or just to make sure you didn't leave evidence behind."

"You must not think I was involved, or you never would've come up here alone with me."

I was taking a drink of water when Zach spoke, and I damn near choked when I heard his words. Why had I ruled him out as a suspect? I had a sudden thought that maybe it had been Zach who I'd spoken to on the phone. He asked a couple times whether I hunted. Could he have recognized my voice from the phone call and wanted to find out how threatening I might be as an adversary? I tried to recall the voice on the phone. Could it have been Zach?

He was personable and had a commendable military record. But he obviously knew these woods. He had the medical training required for the surgical removal of entrails, and he discovered the scene. This wilderness covered hundreds of acres. Someone who knew his way around could certainly know of caves or crevices where a body could be hidden, where even trained cadaver dogs wouldn't find them. Suddenly a chill ran through my body.

# / 6 /

"MILLIE, THIS IS PAT DONEGAL. I NEED A BIG FAVOR."

"You want to talk to the sheriff?"

"I need to talk to Hennie."

"Hennie's not here. I'm not sure if he even works here anymore."

"I know he's not working, but I think you know how to contact him. I really need his help."

"Sorry, Pat, but—"

"Listen, I took this job because Hennie asked me to help him. When he disappeared, I asked Shea Sommers of the Madison Police Department to help me. She's in serious danger. Hennie owes it to us to at least talk."

"I don't know what to say."

"He doesn't respond to voicemails, but I think he'll communicate with you." I could feel my voice rise. I didn't want Millie to hang up, so I took a deep breath. "Listen, Millie, I don't want to put you in a bad spot, and I don't care why Hennie left. But he has to help me. I'm afraid Shea is going to get killed, and it'll be my fault for bringing her into the investigation. But it's also going to be his fault. I know he doesn't want something to happen to Shea, so you need to make him understand how urgent this is."

"I can't promise anything . . ." Millie sounded ready to cry.

"Let me be clear. If Hennie doesn't help us, a brutal murderer will not only go free but will kill again. And the victim will be one of my best friends." I took another deep breath to prevent saying something I might regret. "And let's just say"—I lowered my voice—"if something happens to Shea, I will track down Hennie and find him."

She hung up the phone, hopefully to try to reach Hennie. Or she might have wanted to disconnect from a lunatic.

Twenty minutes later, I had a text—from Hennie. "Where can we meet?"

I was equally terse in my response: "Ibsen R. Thurs, 1 p.m. Bring your hunting gear."

**THURSDAY** morning, I contacted Shea. She sounded pleased that Hennie and I would be at Ibsen Ridge to create a plan to trap the man-hunter. Whether or not the hunter was involved in David Swalheim's death was unclear. He'd had an appointment to meet at Ibsen Ridge about the time the remains were found, but without questioning him, it was impossible to draw a clear connection. It was crucial we capture the hunter unharmed so we could interrogate him.

When I'd talked to Shea, she told me Zach Layman, the former army medic, had offered to guide her. He knew the area as well as anyone, and she felt like she could trust him. Sheriff Grimes okayed the plan and deputized Zach to avoid liability issues. My first thought was that Layman was technically still a suspect. But if Shea and the sheriff trusted him, why should I raise any doubts? I was already on thin ice with Shea. I wanted us all on good terms when we climbed that bluff to confront the hunter. I told Shea we'd meet at one thirty because I wanted to have time to talk to Hennie before the other two arrived.

When I arrived at the parking area below Ibsen Ridge, Hennie was there, leaning on the front fender of his truck. His eyes were down. No eye contact until I was parked, out of my truck, and standing two feet in front of him.

"Pat, what's going on? Millie said it was a matter of life and death. Something about Shea."

"Swalheim was involved in a hunting club where members arranged times and locations to anonymously meet other members. Meet them to hunt. Hunt each other."

"To kill each other?" Hennie finally looked at me.

"I guess."

"How'd Shea get involved?"

"Well, I sort of found a burner phone belonging to Swalheim, and Shea used it to make a date with the hunter whose number was one of the last ones dialed on it. Now the guy is coming here tonight to hunt Shea."

"That's insane! She can't do that. This is my case—well, was my case. I got to be the one—"

"We're going try to work together to take this suspect alive. Shea will be here soon. And she's bringing Zach Layman, the medic who found the guts."

"Why him?"

"He knows the woods. Plus, Sheriff Grimes will be here at some point."

"Listen, Pat." Hennie paused, looking at his boots again. "I'm surprised you wanted me here, after—"

"Hennie, I really don't give a shit right now about what's going on in your head. I called you because you're an experienced hunter. If this works out, you can go back to wherever you've been hiding. I don't give a rat's ass. But if something happens to Shea, then you're going to have hell to pay with me."

"Fair enough. When's the meeting?"

"Friday night, midnight. But Shea and Zach will be here in a few minutes so we can plot out some kind of trap to capture the Great White Hunter and question him without anybody getting shot."

"I know the area pretty well. There are only a couple trails to the top of the ridge. An experienced hunter won't use the main trail. Too obvious. We'll need to be stationed along the other trails long before midnight. If this man is playing a game of life and death, he's not going to come stomping through the woods at eleven-thirty. Hell, he'll probably be here in the morning."

"Makes sense. Guess he could be watching us now."

"Full moon tomorrow night will make it hard to stay invisible."

"Are you sure there are only two other trails?"

"I've been coming here my whole life. One comes up from the river. Railroad tracks down there. It's a long, tough hike. But if you know what you're doing, it's possible. The other trail goes up a dry creek bed. Easier, but still a challenge. I don't know any other ways up to the top."

"The suspect is probably from out of town. How does he know his way?"

"He probably did the same thing Shea did. Hired a local guide."

The conversation ended as we saw a truck approach. Hennie opened the back of his truck and pulled out camouflage coveralls.

"It's best to look like we're hunters. That might be our guy coming to check the set up."

But when the truck got closer, I recognized Shea in the passenger seat. The driver would be Zach Layman. Hennie regained his pose, looking at his boots, embarrassed to confront Shea. I understood how he felt.

# / 7 /

I WAS DUMBFOUNDED WHEN MILLIE GAVE ME PAT'S MESSAGE. I NEVER
planned to talk to Pat or Shea again. I'd let them down. I knew I was
done in law enforcement. There was no way I could face those people again. For the past several days, I had my phone turned off, but
for some reason I got curious and decided to see who left me voicemails. When I saw several in a row from Millie, I called her. I'm not
sure why. She was new in the department. We'd talked several times
in the coffee room. It was just chitchat, nothing important. But for
some reason I felt different with Millie. I was sure there was a connection between us—something special. I never had a girlfriend, but I
liked being around Millie. It was probably a one-sided attraction, but
maybe it wasn't.

She sounded surprised when I called her. "Hennie, where are you?
Everybody's trying to find you."

"I told you. I need some time alone."

"I talked to Pat Donegal. Something bad is going on here." Her
words came slowly as if she was afraid to relay the message.

"He didn't say what happened?"

"No, but he sounded scary."

"What do you mean, scary?"

"Well, he said if something happened to Shea . . ." She paused to gather her words. "He said he'd come looking for you. I didn't like the way he said that."

"Thanks, Millie. Thanks for letting me know."

"Are you coming back?"

"I don't know."

"Why don't you come back to work? Everybody wants you back."

"I'm not sure I can do that. I got some issues I need to straighten out—one way or the other." I hung up.

I was in a small campground near the town of Chetek in northern Wisconsin. Actually, the campground was closed for the season, but it was in a remote area, so I had pitched a pup tent and built a small fire. It was a good place to get away from people for a few days. Now I had to decide if I wanted to face Pat and Shea and Sheriff Grimes. The truth is I was afraid to go back. I didn't care about Pat coming hunting for me, but I didn't want to be responsible for something happening to Shea. She was one of the nicest people I'd ever met. I had no idea what I would do next.

# / 8 /

I HAVE TO ADMIT PULLING INTO THAT PARKING AREA AND SEEING PAT AND Hennie standing there slouched against Hennie's truck waiting for us set off a flurry in my guts that felt like a swarm of wasps had just exploded. I wasn't happy to see either of them. How could I trust them? Still, what choice did I have? Though I'd had doubts about Zach Layman during our first visit to the top of the bluff, I had since decided he was probably my best bet to capture our suspect. Lately, it felt like I couldn't trust anyone. My smartest move would've been to just drive back to Madison. But then, good sense is overrated.

Our best lead was confronting a man who apparently enjoys hunting other human beings. He had admitted to me that he previously made arrangements for a hunt with David Swalheim. He also admitted he'd visited Ibsen Ridge about the time Swalheim had been killed—though the exact time of death couldn't be determined. More importantly, this man indicated on the phone that he was excited about hunting me. That meant that an experienced big game hunter would be stalking me with no other intent than to kill me, probably gut me, and I don't even want to imagine what else. And I'd be forced to capture the man alive to question him about how he was involved with the Swalheim murder. Agreeing to help Pat solve this case and then setting up this meeting with a man with no regard for human life were the two worst decisions I'd ever made. A year earlier, I would have felt comfortable with Pat and Hennie covering my ass, but their recent actions clouded my faith in their dependability. When Zach shut off the engine, I took a deep breath before facing Pat and Hennie. I decided my best bet was to stroll boldly toward them and establish myself as alpha dog—even though I really wasn't even a member of the sheriff's department.

"Pat, Hennie." I spoke matter-of-factly, avoiding eye contact. "I guess you understand why we're here. This is Zach Layman, the man who found the remains." This was followed by a silent round of nods and handshakes. "Zach knows these woods as well as anyone, and he's been helping me get to know my way around. Phil Grimes deputized both Zach and me. Phil will be joining us for the hunt tomorrow. I'll be honest, I don't know how I got into this, and I haven't a clue how it's going to turn out. I have this image in my brain of us running around tripping over each other like the Keystone Cops. I don't want that to happen. And if you don't want to get involved, I'll do it alone."

"I'm sorry you're involved, Shea." Pat spoke slowly, also avoiding eye contact. "I know you won't listen to me, but I would like you go back to Raven's and let Hennie and me handle this."

"You're right. I'm not going to listen. What we need to do is figure out a way for the five of us to intercept this maniac and take him alive before he kills any or all of us."

"I've known these woods my whole life." Hennie spoke in a low, quiet voice. "If this guy shows up, he only has a couple trails to reach the top."

"Zach showed me the trail up the dry creek bed. Do you know another route?"

"Trail up from the river. It's longer and it's dangerous to maneuver, but a determined climber can make it."

"I didn't know there was a way to scale the bluff from the west side," Zach said. "But if Hennie knows the trail, I think we should split up and cover each route. I brought two portable tree stands. We can set them up along the creek bed path and the trail from the river." Even though Zach was the outsider, I was impressed by his willingness to take charge. His military training gave him the confidence to assert leadership.

"I brought a couple tree stands too," Hennie volunteered without looking at any of us. "There are actually two paths coming from the river, but they converge at a point halfway up the bluff where there is a crisscross of boulders, trees, and tunnels that allow an experienced climber to reach the top. I'll set up in a tree where the paths meet."

"How much experience can this character have climbing this bluff—unless he's from around here?" Pat asked. "Or am I foolish in thinking this guy is coming alone?"

"Big game hunters rarely hunt without a skilled guide. Most have more money than courage. They let a guide set up the trophy for the shot, and then the hunter makes the kill. My guess is he's hired a local guide," Hennie explained, speaking more confidently than he had been.

"Who the hell around here is going to guide a hunter to shoot a human?" Zach asked.

"Probably somebody who wants the money and doesn't give a shit how he gets it," Pat responded cynically.

"Or he doesn't ask what the prey is going to be," Hennie said.

"Is it even legal to hunt at night?" I asked.

"Sure, raccoons, coyote, fox, wild pigs," Zach offered. "Here's a better question. Who gets a thrill out of shooting humans? I've been in combat. It's not a sport."

"Rich jerks get bored shooting deer and elk, so they pay to go to Africa to shoot elephants and lions. Hell, even a giraffe, which has to take about as much skill as it would to shoot a cow standing in the pasture. When that gets boring, what's left?" Pat spoke in a flat tone.

"Other hunters," Hennie mumbled.

"It's insane," I said.

"Yet here we are," said Pat.

"You guys probably read the story about the rich guy who releases captives on his island and then finds them and kills them. This is just an advanced version of the same game," I said.

"Humans are predators." Pat looked around the group as he spoke. "Some see hunting as a game. Winner take all."

"I don't know about you, but I'm not doing this for fun," I snapped.

"'Whoever fights monsters should see to it that in the process he does not become a monster,'" Pat said, as much to himself as to the group.

"Are you a philosopher now, Pat?"

"I read that in a book. I jotted it down in a notebook. Guess it hit a nerve. I had lots of time for reading while I was staying alone at Raven's house. Writer was named Nietzsche."

"I'm impressed," I said in a voice full of irony. "But I think we should get to work so we can come up with a way to capture this guy before he turns us into monsters."

"Weatherman says the sky will be clear tomorrow night. With a full moon, it won't be easy to conceal ourselves from the hunter, who will no doubt have night-vision equipment." Zach again showed it was a good decision to bring him into this operation.

"Phil says he'll have night-vision goggles for all of us," I said, trying to sound like I was in charge. "We'll be armed with high-powered rifles and our handguns. Obviously, we'll wear Kevlar vests."

"Two things I need to admit," Pat said. "One, having only one good lung and not being in the best physical condition, I will have to volunteer to station myself along the main trail. And, since I am not a crack shot with a rifle, I will take my chances with my 12-gauge shotgun. I'll be at a disadvantage if a sniper gets a clear shot at me from a distance, but judging from the density of the trees in this area, I think that will be unlikely."

"Fair enough," I said. "You can find a secure location along this main trail. Our quarry might assume we'll be covering the remote trails and leave this one unguarded. And, unless he's already here watching us, he shouldn't suspect his opponent will bring a posse."

"Can't believe he'd be here this early," Zach said. "My guess is he'll arrive just before dusk tomorrow. If he knows his trail, he'll be able to find his way with night-vision goggles. But we would be smart to set up in the morning. Why take a chance? It'll be a long boring wait, but it's our best hope of getting into position undetected."

"I like the way you think, Zach," I said.

"You know," Hennie spoke slowly, "they call this full moon the Hunter's Moon or Blood Moon. It's usually in the latter half of October, but every four years it's in early November."

Nobody responded. None of us wanted to dwell on that thought.

We went to work and spent three hours setting up blinds and discussing strategy. At dusk, we split up to gather our equipment for the morning and hopefully get a few hours' sleep. Zach reminded us the temperature tomorrow would near 50 degrees, but once the sun set it'd drop fast, especially without cloud cover. Since we had no idea how long the operation would last, he said to dress warm but in layers, and full camouflage was a necessity. Face paint was crucial. I admit, by the time we split up, I was actually excited about what we were doing. My adrenal glands were spurting hormones like a fire hose. In spite of earlier doubts about Pat and Hennie, I felt comfortable with the team. Twenty-four hours later, who could even speculate?

By 6:30 a.m. on Friday, we were in position. Sheriff Grimes had borrowed a small bus from the school district and had a rookie patrolman haul us and our equipment out to the ridge and drop us off so that we could be hidden by the time the sun rose. It was going to be a long, slow day.

With luck our antagonist would also show up early to establish his position, and we could finish the hunt without bloodshed. My position was in a tree stand three-quarters of the way up the trail along the dry creek bed. I was glad to be in a tree because I was about fifty yards from where Zach and I encountered the wild pigs. I had no desire to squabble with a hungry herd of porkers.

Zach was at the top of the same trail, where he had a view of both the trail and the eastern area of the ridgetop. Hennie was alone at the river trail. Phil Grimes was in a tree near where the intestines were found, and Pat was hidden in a rock grotto halfway up the main trail.

I've served on numerous stakeouts during my career but sitting motionless in a tree stand for eighteen hours was going to present a new challenge. Sitting still is not on my list of strong attributes. With the floor of the woods covered with leaves, mostly oak, hickory, and maple, every movement sounded ominous. Even a small creature could create commotion loud enough to ignite a major heartbeat escalation.

The hours seemed to drag on forever. We had walkie-talkies in case of emergency, but we couldn't risk using them. I spent my day snacking on peanuts, jerky, and chocolate-covered raisins. I rationed my water because I dreaded having to climb down from my tree to traipse through dry leaves to relieve myself. It was one of the rare times I experienced penis envy. I wasn't just concerned about being detected by the Great White Hunter. I was also worried about being caught with my pants down by a herd of hogs.

As darkness finally set in, I appreciated the night-vision goggles. Within the first hour, I spotted numerous rabbits, opossums, a family of raccoons, a doe and her yearling. Three hours into my vigil, I heard a frantic thrashing of leaves to my left. I scoured the area with my goggles but couldn't spot the source. Probably a rabbit running from a fox, but darkness and isolation can dramatically stimulate the imagination. My weapon was a lever-action Winchester .30-30 with an eight-round magazine. I'd shot plenty of high-powered rifles before, but Sheriff Grimes assured me I'd never touched one to measure up to this recently released model. I hoped I wouldn't have reason to test it. Yet the cop in me felt an urge to open fire just to feel the action.

As slow minutes crawled by, I tried to sort out my feelings toward Pat and Hennie. I'd worked a few cases with Hennie. He was always a bit of a mystery. He tried to act confident and cool under fire, but I sensed he was covering some secret side of his personality. He was not an easy man to trust. And Pat, well, he's a unique specimen. His reputation showed a cop who got results—clever, relentless, fearless, but always unorthodox and unpredictable. My first cases with him left me in awe. He reminded me of that all-knowing uncle who parents respect but fear their children getting to know too well. Recently, I'd seen a darker side. Maybe I set him on too high of a pedestal. Or maybe he'd changed. Maybe I'd changed.

**MY** reverie was shattered by a volley of rifle shots followed by three booming blasts from Pat's shotgun. The battle was on, and not surprisingly Pat was right in the thick of it. Pat's shots were followed by several minutes of silence. Had he shot the hunter before we had a chance to question him? Clearly, the rifle shot started the exchange, so if Pat did shoot the perp, he'd done so in self-defense. Or could the rifle shot have come from the sheriff's rifle?

The silence ended with several more rifle rounds fired in quick succession, obviously from a semiautomatic weapon. No shotgun response. Was Pat hit? Should I chase up the trail to see what was going on? What were Zach and Phil and Hennie doing? Then two blasts from the 12-gauge were followed by one rifle shot. I waited. How long would it take me to reach Pat's location? If I went back down the trail, I'd have half a mile to reach the road and then probably another half mile to reach the parking area. Then I'd have to climb halfway up the ridge without getting shot. I waited again, hoping to hear friendly voices. Nothing. I crept down from my stand and started up the trail, trying not to rustle the leaves. I was wearing the night goggles, so I could see fairly clearly.

When I was almost to the top of the hill, I heard a voice whisper, "Shea, is that you?"

Even with the goggles, I couldn't see where Zach was hiding. "Who's shooting?" I whispered back.

Zach stepped out of a cluster of shrubs, grabbed my arm, and pulled me to his hiding place. "Stay quiet. Whoever is shooting probably heard you running up the trail."

"What about the shots?" My whisper was mostly a gasp, caused partly by my running uphill but mostly by the shock of suddenly being pulled into the bushes. It flashed through my mind that I could have been wrong about Zach. What if he shot the others and then waited for me?

"We need to check on Pat. I heard a shotgun," I said.

"We need to wait. Those three guys can take care of themselves."

"Listen, this operation was my plan. I need to see what's going on," I argued.

"Then stay behind me. Try not to rustle leaves."

We started along the trail. Zach was able to move through the leaves without a sound. I tried to match his stealth, but it's not easy moving boots through dry leaves without stirring them. After twenty or thirty yards, I figured out how to walk on the outside edges of my boot soles and to lift my feet and then set them back down without disturbing the leaves. I pretended I was a cat stalking a chipmunk. Without much commotion, we reached the peak of the ridge and crept toward Sheriff Grimes's location. Zach turned around and held a cautionary finger in front of his lips. We moved at a turtle's pace as we scanned the upper ridge. No sign of Phil at the spot he'd chosen for his stand. We continued creeping slowly toward the main trail, where Pat was stationed.

Suddenly, a rifle shot pierced the silence. Zach and I dropped to the ground. The bullet whizzed over our heads, not close but a bit too nearby for my comfort. We raised our weapons. No other sound. Zach signaled for me to stay put while he climbed into a crouch, slung his rifle across his back, and started creeping quietly toward the sound of the shot. I also climbed into a crouch, shouldered my rifle, and studied the forest, ready to respond to the flash of the next gunshot.

"Drop your weapons! This is the sheriff's department. You're outnumbered by armed deputies. Put down your weapons now, and step into the clearing with your hands above your head."

After a brief pause, Zach responded in a low voice. "Sheriff, it's Zach. Shea is with me."

"Sorry. I heard shooting and didn't know who you were. I shot well above your heads. But I should've held my fire till I knew who was moving."

"Have you heard from Pat or Hennie?" I asked.

"No." There was a crackle of leaves. "I can see you. I'll come over."

"Be careful," I said.

Phil crept closer and took a position behind an oak. "I heard rustling. I guessed a deer or fox." He spoke just above a whisper. "Then I heard the shots. Too close for Hennie. Pat's the only one with a shotgun. So, he's in on it."

"Zach, why don't you come with me to check on Pat?" I said.

"I got my trauma kit."

"I'll stay here in case the guy is still around. Keep your heads down," Phil said.

Zach led the way. He was a damn sight more careful than I would've been, and it was hard not to tell him to get the lead out of his ass and find Pat. But Zach's military training convinced me to keep my eyes open and my mouth shut. We moved quietly toward the main trail.

Halfway down the path, we spotted legs sprawled out across the path. It was Pat. He wasn't moving. Zach moved quickly but without creating a target. This would be a perfect spot for an ambush.

"I'll check Pat," he whispered.

"I'm going down the trail."

"Be careful! Stay low."

Even though I was a clear target for a sniper, I hunched over and raced down the trail, my night-vision goggles illuminating my path. If someone wanted to shoot me, I was a running duck. I stayed low as I scrambled down the trail maybe thirty or forty yards. I heard a groan in the bushes. I hit the dirt and waited, trying to focus on the sound. Another snivel from the brush. I raised my rifle, ready to fire.

"Help me!" I heard a painful-sounding whimper near me.

"Drop your weapon, now!" I shouted.

A rifle flew from the brush and landed a few feet in front of me. I waited, expecting a volley of gunfire. Nothing.

"Help me. I'm shot." It sounded like a prayer.

I scanned the perimeter. Nothing.

"Where are you?" I demanded.

"Under this big pine tree."

I surveyed the area. To my right stood a white pine. I zeroed in. Movement. I aimed my rifle, ready to fire. He rolled on the ground beneath the lowest bough.

"Help me. I'm shot."

I waited, expecting a madman to bust out of the bush. Nothing.

"Step out with your hands up," I ordered.

"I can't stand up. My legs are on fire."

"Then you better crawl out because I'd rather see you bleed to death than be stupid enough to walk into an ambush."

"Seriously, I'm hurt."

"I can wait."

"Listen," he said in a weakened voice, probably an act, "I can't move. Somebody shot me. This was supposed to be a fair hunt. Kilimanjaro code. You didn't come alone." He waited, but when I didn't respond, he continued. "Are you going to finish me off?"

"I'm considering it," I snapped. "But I'm a cop investigating a murder. I'd rather take you alive so we can talk."

"I don't know about any murder. Aren't you the woman who called me to set up a hunt?"

"Yeah."

"Were you the first one or the second?"

"First or second what?"

"Another woman called a few weeks ago, said she was calling for her husband. Wanted to change the date of our meeting. I came here on the date she told me, but no one showed up."

"If I was you, I'd crawl out of that brush real slow. Because if you're hurt, you may want to get to a doctor."

I heard rustling and quickly slinked down behind a nearby tree and shouldered my rifle. Gradually, a man crawled from under the brush. He appeared unarmed.

"Lay flat on your stomach and put your hands behind your back," I shouted. He moved slowly but followed my orders. I stepped from behind the tree, focusing my rifle between his shoulder blades. I stepped behind him and straddled his back. I had a thick plastic zip tie on my belt and quickly secured his hands. "Okay, stand up," I ordered.

"I can't."

"Are you alone?" I pressed the barrel of my rifle between his shoulders.

"Yes, I'm alone. That's the rules, remember?"

"Get up," I ordered.

"I can't. My legs are full of buckshot."

"Okay, then lay there and bleed." I knelt down beside him to examine his legs. Both had suffered wounds consistent with shotgun fire. He groaned when I touched his wounds but didn't speak. I stood up and took out my walkie-talkie to contact Sheriff Grimes. He responded quickly. He had joined Zach helping Pat. He said Pat was coming around but had a nasty bump on his head. I told him our subject was in cuffs. "Suffered non-life-threatening injuries in the gunfire exchange. Was Pat shot?" I asked.

"Looks like a bullet ricocheted and a chunk of rock hit Pat squarely on the temple. Zach's treating him. I called the ambulance. I had them on call close-by. Won't take long. I've been trying to reach Hennie, but no response. Thought he'd come running when he heard the shots."

"Hopefully he's okay," I said. "He seems to have a problem responding to calls."

"I'll keep trying."

"Keep me informed," I said. "Well, Mr. Great White Hunter, I guess we wait here till our medic is finished working on the detective you shot at. If you're lucky, he'll be okay. And keep in mind, you're already looking at a murder charge."

"I didn't murder anybody. These hunting games are legal."

"We'll see about that. By the way, you're lying in animal feces. I'd hate to see those wounds develop gangrene. But, you did shoot at one of my best friends, so maybe I don't care all that much about the gangrene."

"Listen, I'm a doctor. Take off those cuffs and let me look at my wounds. I have a medical kit with me. You have the gun. I can't escape."

"Really? A doctor hunts down and shoots humans? There's a twist on the old Hippocratic oath."

"It's just a sport. We usually don't kill each other."

"Explain that to my partner who's lying unconscious on the trail back there."

"He shot at me first. I didn't know he was a cop."

"You a lawyer too?" He didn't respond. "And I distinctly heard rifle shots preceding the shotgun blasts. And three other law enforcement officers heard the same thing."

"I was defending myself."

"Well, as to me letting you loose to treat your wounds, I don't think that's going to happen. So, you better hope my friend comes around quickly, because lying there on that cold, wet, shit-infested ground is probably not doing a lot of good for your wounds. But, you're the doc, so you'd know more about infections than me."

"This was entrapment. You called under false pretenses and lured me here."

"Again, the lawyer talk?"


IT was well after midnight when we got to the hospital. Neither patient suffered life-threatening injuries—though Pat had a hell of a goose egg on the side of his head and required a couple stitches. The good doc had a dozen double-aught pellets imbedded in his legs. The emergency room staff insisted we wait till morning to question our suspect. Pat wanted to leave the hospital, but the doctor in charge refused. One night for observation. I guess concussion protocol applies to cops as well as football players. Phil and Zach stayed out at the ridge looking for Hennie. By the time I left to head out to Raven's place to sleep a few hours, there was still no word.

My phone rang before six. It was Phil Grimes. Hennie was still missing. No response on the walkie-talkie, and his phone was most likely turned off. Sheriff was sending out a search party, and he asked me to join. I agreed to meet them at the site along the river where we dropped off Hennie. Phil also said Pat was fighting the hospital staff to get released so that he could join the search. Hopefully, I thought, they'd put Pat in a straitjacket and keep him restrained for at least another day. Twenty minutes later, I was in my car headed toward Ibsen Ridge.

It was getting light enough to see when I arrived, but I waited in my car drinking coffee I'd made at Raven's. Ten minutes later, the sheriff arrived. He'd assembled eight or nine volunteers. Zach drove his own truck and brought two other searchers. The young deputy who had driven us out to the ridge in the school bus the previous day now drove a pickup towing a trailer carrying two ATVs. A tall young man wearing camouflage coveralls traveled with the deputy. I guessed he would drive one of the ATVs. A young woman and an older man climbed out of the sheriff's squad car. Once all were unpacked from the vehicles, Sheriff Grimes called the group together.

"Thanks for coming. We need to work fast to find Officer Duggan. Temperatures stayed above freezing last night, but it's still cold enough for hypothermia, especially if he's injured. There are two trails heading up the bluff. The two intersect halfway up. Deputy Meyers and Art Zander will head up first with their four-wheelers. They'll have to take a roundabout way to get up there. The route Hennie used is too steep for a vehicle. The rest will split into two groups and scour the trails more carefully. There are dangerous drop-offs and rocky ravines along these trails, so use extreme caution. I don't want anyone getting hurt." Grimes paused and nodded toward Zach. "This is Zach Layman. He knows this area. Shea and Millie, you can go up the north route with Zach. The rest of us will head down the railroad tracks about a hundred yards and head up the south trail. I don't know what we're going to find out here, so be careful, and keep your phones handy. Signals can be weak, so keep calling if you need to make contact. Zach, Deputy Meyers, and I have walkie-talkies. The ambulance crew will be here shortly."

I approached the young woman, extending my right hand. "Shea Sommers, Madison Police Department. I've worked with Hennie and Pat Donegal on several cases."

The woman shook my hand. "Millie Trainor, dispatcher. I heard about you. Hennie and I are friends at work. He says good things about you and Mr. Donegal. I'm worried. Hennie has been acting weird lately."

"We'll find him," I said, patting her shoulder.

"Shea, Millie," Zach interrupted, "I know we want to find Hennie fast, but this will be a treacherous climb, so no reckless moves. I'm familiar with the ridge, but I haven't been on this particular trail, so we'll all work together."

The first hundred yards were easy. Then the terrain changed, and we headed up a steep, rocky incline. As we reached the peak of a treacherous climb, I heard a grunt and squeal below me on my left. I quickly surveyed the rocky ravine. In the shady light, I made out the shapes of a small herd of wild pigs, probably the same ones Zach and I had seen earlier. Looking more closely, I noticed they were circled around a human form wearing camouflage coveralls—Hennie Duggan. Without a lot of thought, I pulled my weapon and emptied a nine-shell magazine from my .40 caliber Glock. The two pigs farthest from the body dropped. The rest scattered. Zach came running.

"There's a body down there, and I think the pigs were . . ." My voice trailed off.

Zach quickly unwound a rope attached to his waist. He secured one end to a tree and quickly began to rappel the rocky edge of the bluff. Millie stood in shock, unable to speak or even gasp.

"Wait here," Zach ordered as he descended. He tossed me the walkie-talkie. "Call Sheriff Grimes. Alert the EMTs." He maneuvered downward with precision and speed. Once he reached the body, he started checking vital signs. I contacted Phil. Then I put my arm around Millie's shoulder. Zach performed numerous tests, moving the body as little as possible. He dragged one of the dead hogs to the side to make more room to perform his exam.

The rest of the team, who were further down the trail, arrived quickly as Millie and I looked on in horror. Sheriff Grimes grabbed the rope and carefully rappelled down the slope. Once at the bottom, he and Zach spoke at a level I couldn't make out. There was no communication between the men attending to Hennie and the rest of the rescue crew waiting above. Before long, the EMTs arrived with a portable stretcher and additional ropes. There was little doubt that we had found Hennie too late. Now it'd be up to the medical examiner to determine if he died from the fall, or if he'd been killed and then pushed off the cliff, or whether lying injured in the rocks overnight in near-freezing temperatures or the wild pigs had caused his death. In my mind, regardless of the exact cause, the reason Hennie was dead was a direct result of the scheduled hunt with the good doctor. I gave Millie a brief wordless hug and then headed back down the trail by myself. As I walked, I asked myself, "How in the hell did I ever get mixed up in this mess?" The answer was obvious—Pat Donegal.

When I reached the bottom, without waiting for the rest of the rescue crew or even letting the sheriff know I was leaving, I climbed into my car and raced back to Lake Hope, traveling much faster than I should have on those curvy, hilly roads. I drove directly to Raven's place. I knew I should call Pat to tell him what happened. But he'd find out soon enough. Besides, I didn't want to talk to him. Had I never met Pat Donegal, I'd be leading the simple life of a detective in Madison. Instead, I was tangled up in a bizarre murder case that was getting more out of control by the minute. Hennie was dead and I was to blame. Nobody told me to arrange a hunting contest with a deranged doctor who gets his rocks off by hunting and killing people. Save people all week and then go out and shoot them on the weekends. I considered heading back to Madison right then, but I was tired and depressed. I went to my suitcase and got out a bottle of Chianti I'd brought, hoping to celebrate if we solved the case. I uncorked the bottle and poured a third of the bottle into a water glass. Wine before noon was not my style, so I poured the glass of wine into the sink and went upstairs to pack. My days as a consultant to the Kickapoo County sheriff's department were over. I knew I'd be back in a day or two to answer questions about my involvement in the case, but at that moment I simply couldn't face anyone. I didn't give a good goddamn if they solved their case or didn't. Let Pat figure it out. He was the one who screwed up the investigation.

# / 9 /

AFTER BEING RELEASED FROM THE HOSPITAL, I WALKED TO THE SHERIFF'S office to get my truck. I tried calling Shea, but her phone went to voicemail. I asked her to call me. I didn't hold my breath waiting for a response. Surprisingly, within minutes my phone rang. It was Sheriff Grimes.

"Pat, how are you doing?"

"Headache and a knob on my head. Otherwise, I'm okay. Did you find Hennie?"

"We did. I thought maybe Shea called you. She drove off without saying anything."

"How is he?"

"Listen, Pat, this is bad. Hennie didn't make it. We found him in some rocks at the bottom of a ravine. He fell at least forty feet. I can't say for sure if he fell or was pushed. We'll need the DCI to study the scene. For all we know, Dr. Grant hit him over the head and tossed him onto the rocks. It's a shitty deal."

"Goddamn it, Phil. I shouldn't have talked him into getting involved in this mess. His head wasn't in it."

"It's not your fault. He came along willingly. And goddamn it, I'm the sheriff. I approved the plan."

"And Shea?"

"She emptied her weapon into some wild pigs that were feeding on the body. Killed two of them."

"Jesus Christ, wild pigs were eating him?"

"They didn't do much damage, but enough."

"For Christ's sake. Shea has to be a mess."

"She took off after she saw he was dead. I figured she'd come and talk to you."

"Shea hasn't got a lot of love for me these days. She thinks I did something to make Hennie quit the investigation. I probably did, but I don't know what."

"You should give her a call."

"I tried but it went to voicemail. I'll run out to Raven's to see if she's there."

"Good. I'd like to talk to her too."

"I let you down on this deal, Phil. It's time to quit playing Wyatt Earp and just hang up my holsters."

"Let's stop pointing fingers at ourselves and each other and figure out what the hell we're going to do next. I'll be back in town in a half hour. Then you and me are going to grill that son of a bitch doctor till we get some answers. Even if he didn't kill Swalheim, there's a real good chance he killed Hennie, and he sure as hell tried to kill you. So that's where we start."

I picked up my truck and headed out to Raven's. I couldn't stop thinking about what I'd said to Millie. Basically, I threatened Hennie's life if he didn't help us. Now he was dead. How could I not blame myself? Not to mention what the whole incident did to Shea. I wished that doctor had been a better shot and had put a slug in my brain instead of just banging a piece of rock off my skull.

When I got to Raven's, the place was empty. I checked around for Shea's stuff but didn't find anything but a partial bottle of wine. Apparently, she'd been there and left. She got smart and headed back to Madison. I tried calling, but my call went right to voicemail again. I didn't bother leaving a message, figuring my voice would be the last thing she'd want to keep hearing.

Before heading back to town, I decided I'd take a shower. First, I had to carefully remove the gauze wrapped around my head. Glancing at myself in the mirror, I looked like the soldier on the cover of *The Red Badge of Courage*. I remember reading it, or at least attempting to read it, in high school. I decided I'd fit better on a book titled *The Red Badge of Stupidity*.

I drove back to the hospital to meet Phil. I hoped the sheriff was ready to play good cop because I sure to hell wanted to be the bad cop. He was waiting in the lobby.

"Our doctor friend says he isn't going to talk until his lawyer arrives, and he's driving from St. Louis. Probably won't get here till at least three o'clock."

"So, what if we talk to him and tell him to keep his trap shut so that he won't compromise our investigation. He may start jabbering just to spite us."

"Worth a try, but first I'm going to check in with the coroner to see if he knows what happened to Hennie."

"That's probably a better idea. Guess I'll tag along."

We walked over to the coroner's office and learned he'd finished his initial exam. Results were consistent with a person falling forty feet into a rocky ravine. Broken bones, contusions and lacerations, fractured skull, damaged vertebrae.

"I'm certain the victim died instantly. However, we can't tell why he fell at this point. Tough terrain out there. He could have slipped, or he could have been pushed. Or maybe he was hit over the head from behind." The coroner paused and looked directly at Grimes. "I hate to say it, but he could have jumped."

"Why the hell would Hennie drive all the way back from wherever he was to help us catch a possible killer and then decide to kill himself?" I almost shouted.

"I didn't say it happened. I just said it was a possibility." He spoke matter-of-factly.

"We got to consider all options, Pat," the sheriff said.

"Any chance of finding a weapon that could've been used?" I asked.

"The DCI team is still out there. But what are they going to find? A rock with blood on it? What would that tell us? Either somebody hit Hennie over the head, or he fell on the rock," Grimes said.

"I blame myself. I told Millie to get word to Hennie that if he didn't show up and if something happened to Shea, that I'd come looking for him. Stupid threat to make."

"Don't blame yourself. Hennie got you and Shea into this mess, then he walked away."

"It is a mess." I sighed. "Did the suspect say anything when he got to the hospital?"

"He said you shot first, and he was just defending himself. Me and Shea and Layman heard the rifle shots first, but that's hard to prove," Grimes said.

"Worst of it is, Hennie's dead, Shea's probably a basket case, and who knows if this guy is the one who killed Swalheim. Maybe he did. Maybe he shot Januss too. But what if he didn't?" I asked.

"Then we put him away for shooting you and maybe killing Hennie. Then we go find out who killed Swalheim. Though I'm still betting on our man-hunting doctor. He was in the hunting club, admitted he'd scheduled a hunt with Swalheim, told Shea he'd already visited the area, and he's a surgeon, skilled at removing organs from a human body."

The coroner listened politely and then announced, "I have to get back to the lab. Hopefully, we'll have more specific results in a few hours, at least by tomorrow."

"Thanks, Doc." Sheriff Grimes stood up and patted the coroner on the shoulder. "We know you'll do everything possible."

WE decided to wait to question the doctor until his attorney arrived. While Grimes went to his office to take care of paperwork, I drove out to Hennie's place to see if he'd left any clues to suggest he might

148

take his own life. As crazy as that theory sounded, I felt like I had to check it out. The door to his house was locked, but I found a window unlocked in a back pantry. Having recently become proficient at breaking and entering, I squeezed my 220 pounds through the window. The house was neat, nothing out of place. For some reason, I decided not to snoop around—it just didn't feel right. One thing I noticed was Hennie's dog was not around. Millie said Hennie had the dog with him when he left town. Maybe he'd dropped it off again with his neighbor before going out to the ridge. Since there was only one house within a mile, it wasn't hard to figure out who the dog-sitter was. I left the house the same way I entered. My head throbbed when I bent down to crawl through the window.

The neighbor's place was a dilapidated-looking farm in a valley at the crossroads that led to Hennie's. There were a few beef cattle strewn across the grassy pasture, but no sign of any corn or soybean fields. Much of this area is too hilly and rocky to be worth trying to cultivate. Those who still farmed in that area typically raised thirty or forty head of Angus or Herefords as well as maybe a few chickens and hogs. There was a hard-driven Ford pickup sitting in front of the house, so I parked in the driveway and walked across the yard to the front door.

I knocked on the door but got no response. I tried again and then walked around the porch trying to look in the windows. The house was dark. I knocked again. This time there was a response.

"Whatever you're peddling, I don't need any."

"I work with the sheriff's department. I want to talk about Hennie Duggan," I said.

"Ain't seen him. Go away!"

"There's been an accident. I need to talk to you." There was no response.

Finally, I heard a dead bolt snap open and the door opened a few inches. "Never seen you before. Where's your badge and uniform?"

I reached in my jacket pocket and took out my badge. I held it up so he could see it through the slit in the open door. "I'm a new detective. I work with Hennie."

The door opened further, and I saw the occupant set down a shotgun and lean it against the wall. "You say Hennie's been hurt?"

"Can I come in and talk?"

"Wife died a couple years ago. I don't keep the place in condition to have visitors."

"I'm a bachelor. I'm not interested in your housekeeping habits. We need to talk about Hennie."

The door opened the rest of the way, and the elderly man waved me into the house. It was dark and smelled of rotting food and human sweat. My host moved slowly from the door and switched on a lamp standing beside an old recliner covered with clothing and blankets. He waved me into the kitchen and pointed toward a chair next to a table covered with food scraps and dirty dishes. He flipped on a light switch and a bare bulb in the center of the ceiling illuminated the mess. He extended his calloused hand. "Marlin Noble. I've known Hennie since he was a baby. What happened?"

He again pointed to the chair, and I moved a stack of papers from the seat and sat down. Noble continued to stand. He was a big man dressed in bib overalls over a flannel shirt, both needing mending and a good wash.

"My name is Pat Donegal. I've worked several cases with Hennie. He's a good man. We've been working on a homicide case that happened out on Ibsen Ridge."

"Heard about it. So, what happened with Hennie?"

"I'm sorry to have to tell you this, but Hennie had a bad fall last night when we were trying to apprehend a suspect."

"Gonna be all right, is he?"

"Hennie died in the fall. We're not sure if it was an accident or whether he might've been pushed. Hennie's been out of touch the last couple weeks, and we're just trying to piece together what's been going on."

"Goddamn it," he muttered. "I can't believe he's dead."

"It's a real shock." I watched as Noble lowered himself into the chair facing me. "Have you talked to Hennie lately?"

"Week or two ago he stopped by in the evening. Said he just wanted to let me know he'd be out of town for a while. He didn't say where to, and I didn't ask. He just wanted to let me know he'd be gone so I wouldn't wonder about not seeing him drive by. I asked if I needed to watch his dog while he was gone. I did that when he left town. But he said no, he'd take the dog."

"Was that the last time you talked?"

"No, I was gonna tell you. Thursday night he stopped by about suppertime. I offered him some eggs, but he said he'd already ate. Acted kind of funny. Then he asked if I'd be interested in taking his dog permanently. Said he was going away and wouldn't be able to take the dog. Damn nice spaniel, good bird huntin' dog." He pushed aside a couple plates on the table, sat down in the other chair, and folded his big paws in front of him. "I questioned him about where he was going, but he just said 'away.' Hell, I said, I can barely take care of myself, and I'm damn near eighty-five years old. I can't take in a good young hunting dog like that."

"What did he say then?" I asked.

"Asked if maybe I knew somebody who'd want a good dog. I thought about it and said, sure, my grandson lives down on Sand Creek Road. He hunts all kinds of birds and rabbits and squirrels. I said, I bet Jake would be glad to get a good dog like Presley, that was the dog's name."

"So, Jake took the dog?"

"Sure as hell. Glad to get him. Hennie drove over that night. Craziest damn thing. I mean, that Hennie was going someplace where he couldn't have a dog. Not like Hennie to do that. Course, maybe he found a woman, and maybe she said, 'You can move in but your dog goes elsewhere.'"

We talked another twenty minutes, but Noble couldn't tell me anything to explain Hennie's recent behavior. I thanked the old farmer for his help and gave him my card in case he thought of something else. He took the card but confessed he hadn't paid his phone bill in six months, so he knew he wouldn't be calling.

I headed back to town hoping our suspect's lawyer had arrived so we could get into the interrogation. Unfortunately, the lawyer was running late and planned to arrive around nine. I decided to call Shea. My guess was she still wouldn't answer, but I wanted to let her know that nothing that happened was her fault. It was Hennie and me who'd screwed things up. And now that he was dead, I was willing to shoulder the blame myself. Not surprisingly, Shea's voicemail still picked up immediately. I left a message apologizing for all that had happened and asking her to call me when she felt up to a talk.

Since I still had a couple hours to kill before our chance to question the suspect and his lawyer, I decided to drive out to Raven's, where I could kick back, have a snack, and do a little web searching to find out about Grant. About all I found in the refrigerator was some cheddar cheese and beer. There was no way I wanted to walk into this interrogation reeking of hoppy IPA, so I found some saltines in the cupboard and ate cheese and crackers—the exciting life of a detective. I made a pot of coffee and popped a couple of pain pills the doc had given me to fend off the headaches that result from owning a large goose egg on one's noggin from a ricocheting rock.

Doing a web search, I found plenty of articles about our suspect, Dr. Simon Grant. He was indeed a renowned cardiac surgeon, with degrees from Stanford and Johns Hopkins. Recently published a study on cutting-edge innovations in mitral valve reconstruction—whatever the hell that means. In addition to practicing surgery at multiple hospitals, Dr. Grant also lectured for a while at Harvard and at Washington University. There was no mention of his skills in hunting and gutting other men. I was skimming through the various articles when I stumbled onto a recent posting about a seminar he presented at in Italy. The part that caught my attention was the date, October 16–20 of this year. Those dates would have been very close to the time Swalheim's entrails were deposited on Ibsen Ridge. If Dr. Grant spent even a few days in Europe after the seminar, then he would have an alibi. I was glad to know this before the evening's interrogation.

# / 10 /

IT WAS AFTER NINE O'CLOCK WHEN DR. SIMON GRANT'S ATTORNEY STEPPED out from a meeting with his client to announce they were ready to talk to us. "Us" referring to myself, Sheriff Grimes, and County Prosecutor Elizabeth Magnuson, who had been grilling the sheriff and me about what hard evidence we had to hold Dr. Grant. I didn't mention the alibi issue I had discovered.

Once we were all seated at a long rectangular table, and once all introductions were exchanged, Grant's lead attorney, Milo Benning, assumed the alpha dog position and quickly proclaimed that not only was his client not guilty of any crimes but that he and his associate Jenna Haley were planning to file a lawsuit on Dr. Grant's behalf that would ask for punitive damages for the sheriff department's illegal entrapment of their client and also compensation for his injuries and for lost time from his medical practice. Before he could conclude his remarks, Prosecutor Magnuson stood up and dramatically cleared her throat.

"Excuse me, Mr. Benning, this proceeding has not even begun yet, so please hold your theatrics until you have at least heard if there are charges against your client." She paused to allow everyone in the room to come to order. "To begin with, this meeting tonight is our first chance to actually talk to Dr. Grant about what transpired on Ibsen Ridge last evening. He has for the most part refused to speak with Sheriff Grimes or Detective Donegal—which is within his rights, but which also means my office has had no opportunity to determine exactly what happened last night. We have patiently waited for your arrival so that we could proceed with our investigation. So, before you start puffing up your chest and threatening us, let's all try to figure out what happened that resulted in the death of our county's chief deputy, Hennie Duggan, and in the serious injury to Detective Donegal."

"Let's not forget, Dr. Grant suffered severe gunshot wounds as a result of being ambushed and shot by one of your police officers. Let me remind everyone that Dr. Grant committed no crimes last night. It is perfectly legal to hunt at night in Wisconsin." Benning took a deep breath to let his words soak in.

"Dr. Grant was armed with an AR-15 assault rifle," I said. "To be specific, a Winchester .308 caliber semiautomatic weapon with a twenty-round capacity. A weapon with that power is not designed for hunting rabbits and raccoons. It is designed to kill people—a lot of people. Not to mention, he also carried two additional cartridge magazines. That is sixty bullets."

"Excuse me, Detective? Am I correct, that is your title with the sheriff's department?"

"Yes, that's my position," I responded.

"The weapon you described for us, Detective, is that weapon legal in this state?"

"Yes, it is legal, but it's hard to believe a skilled hunter would bring a weapon that powerful on a simple hunting trip." I tried to remain composed.

"Do you have wild pigs in this area?"

"We do," Sheriff Grimes said.

"Is it legal to hunt wild pigs with a high-powered rifle, Sheriff?" Benning asked.

"It is legal. Yes."

"I believe your state Department of Natural Resources even encourages citizens to shoot these dangerous animals. Is that true?"

"There is no closed season or bag limits on wild pigs, so, yes, I guess what you said is reasonable." Grimes spoke frankly.

"We are not in court, Mr. Benning, and you are not addressing a jury, so why don't we just focus on the inquiry we came for?" Prosecutor Magnuson held her professional demeaner.

"So, I take it you are not prepared at this time to file any charges against my client. Is that correct?"

"We haven't had a chance to even speak to Dr. Grant, so how would we be prepared to file charges? We are here to try to find out exactly what happened last night." Magnuson's voice remained calm. "Our chief deputy is dead, and Detective Donegal sustained a serious head wound. Your client is at least responsible for the detective's wound, and he may be responsible for Hennie Duggan's death. Not to mention he is the primary person of interest in a murder that took place in this county recently. So is Dr. Grant ready to answer our questions?"

"If you are not charging my client with a crime tonight, then the answer is no. Dr. Grant is not ready to answer your questions. My client is a highly esteemed surgeon whose skills and talents have saved thousands of lives. He has a busy schedule, and many people are counting on him to perform life-saving surgeries. Not to mention, he has suffered serious injuries to his legs and wants very much to get home to a medical facility with—how do I say this?—a more competent medical staff. If in the future, your department actually finds evidence to support an arrest warrant, then you can contact my office." Benning looked down, closing a file folder on the table. Then he looked up again, directing his gaze directly at me.

"Detective Donegal, would you mind telling me how long you have been an officer with this department?"

"I've worked as a detective for over thirty years," I responded, understanding exactly where Benning was headed.

"Thirty years in this county?"

"No, thirty years total," I said.

"Yes, I was able to research your work history during our trip here today. Quite an interesting career you've had, but I couldn't find any mention of your being a detective for Kickapoo County. That must be very recent."

"Detective Donegal is in fact an employee in our department. In addition, he has served as a consultant in our department for several years prior to being hired as a detective. All the official paperwork is in my office if you'd care to stop over when we're finished here." Sheriff Grimes again managed to maintain a professional manner even when his county was obviously coming under attack.

"No, we'll be heading back to St. Louis tonight. We have our car waiting outside. We brought an extra driver to take Dr. Grant's truck home—that is unless you have a warrant to impound his vehicle."

"You may take his truck." Elizabeth Magnuson appeared to be seething under her words. Clearly, she planned to have that vehicle carefully searched for evidence linking Dr. Grant to the Swalheim murder, but she realized none of us were prepared to challenge Grant's attorney. The evening was a complete bust. I now knew how Shea felt when she simply drove away this morning. I felt like doing exactly the same thing.

After a brief post-meeting conference with the sheriff and the county prosecutor, which was basically a session of licking our wounds and scratching our heads as to where the investigation needed to go next, I admitted what I had discovered about Simon Grant's trip to Italy. Sheriff Grimes shook his head, realizing an alibi would likely end the investigation.

"Why didn't you mention this before we met with Grant and his attorney?" Grimes asked.

"Guess I didn't think it was an issue to bring up. I'm not a hundred percent certain the dates conflict." I looked down as I spoke.

"If you knew he was out of the country, you should have told us," Grimes said sternly.

"We may never get a chance to question him now. Plus, it would be an ace up his sleeve if we did charge him." Magnuson sounded tired.

"I really messed this up, didn't I?" I gently massaged my head wound as I spoke. "So, do we call in the State DCI?"

"For now, let's keep this whole business as quiet as possible," Grimes said. "I need a little time to digest this."

The sullen group broke up and headed out into the darkness.


I decided to return to Raven's house to try to figure out if there was any way for a small, undermanned police force to deal with this situation that had spiraled out of control. What started with the discovery of a pile of human intestines in a heavily wooded area of one of the most remote places in the state had now become three related deaths with no real evidence to solve any of them. I considered how simple life would have been if the hunter discovering the entrails would have assumed they were from a deer or pig and simply left the pile for the pigs and crows to feast on.

I was out of my league on this investigation. And now that I'd be working primarily by myself, I couldn't see any way forward that had a happy ending. As I drove the county roads toward Raven's place, I realized the smartest solution was probably to rule the Swalheim murder a cold case, let the Lakeshore County sheriff's department worry about Harley Januss, and have the coroner rule Hennie's death an accident. That would allow me to drift off into the sunset, where washed-up old lawmen go to die. I had convinced myself to throw in the towel until I turned into Raven's driveway and saw Shea's car parked near the front door.

# / 11 /

**WHEN I HEADED BACK TO MADISON EARLIER AFTER EMPTYING MY WEAPON** into the herd of wild pigs that were eating Hennie's remains at the bottom of a rocky ravine, the last thing I ever planned to do was return to Kickapoo County. Everything about this investigation was wrong. Hennie walked away from the case and then apparently walked off a cliff at Ibsen Ridge. Pat was breaking every law and code of ethics he could think of, and I had just arranged a disastrous and deadly scheme to try to trap a suspect who probably had nothing to do with the crime. So, after pulling into a wayside and crying my soul out—something I've had very little experience doing—I foolishly turned my car around and headed west, back to Kickapoo County.

I knew I should call my friend Jill Connor to fill her in on what was going on, but that relationship was rather rocky at the moment. Plus, I didn't want to hear one of Jill's lectures about how every time I worked with Pat it turned into a near cataclysm. Jill abhorred the way Pat put me into perilous predicaments. I told her it was a two-way street. He'd bailed me out many times. But she had blinders on when it came to Pat. And if she had any clue what was going on with this case, I would hear a blistering I-told-you-so sermon. I sometimes think she's a little jealous of Pat. Anyway, that kettle of crawfish had to wait. Maybe it was all a moot point. There was a chance I would never see her again.

My first stop was Ibsen Ridge, where I watched from a distance as DCI agents looked for clues to determine how Hennie ended up at the bottom of the ravine. I could have joined the search since I was officially deputized by the sheriff. But I didn't want to talk to anyone. Hennie's body was gone, being studied no doubt in the coroner's lab at the hospital, but a flock—I guess the proper, and in this case more appropriate, term is a murder—of crows fought with several turkey vultures to feast on the carcasses of the pigs I'd shot. It occurred to me that this was the real meaning of life—an endless chain of one creature feeding on the misfortunes of another. Isn't that the real history of this planet? I have to admit I fleetingly considered joining Hennie at the bottom of that abyss.

Worse than sitting on the ridge watching investigators figure out how a friend of mine had died hours earlier—died because I had a wild-hair-up-my-ass idea about solving a murder by entrapment and ended up catching some assault-rifle-toting doctor who felt he had the right to balance the good karma he earned in the operating room by going out on weekends and shooting other idiots who thought killing human beings for sport was a clever idea. For some reason, as I sat there on that desolate bluff, I remembered a paper I'd written in a literature class in college about some French writer who said something like, *Man is a useless passion. It is meaningless that we live and it is meaningless that we die.* If only I'd known then what I knew today.

It was dark by the time I ended my existential sojourn on the bluff top. I headed back to Lake Hope, which in my bleak state of mind seemed to be the most ironic name imaginable for this town. I wasn't sure where to go next. I drove around town for a while, passing Zach Layman's house and the courthouse. I knew I should join Pat and Sheriff Grimes in their interrogation of the Great White Hunter Doctor. But I couldn't face any of them, so I drove out of Lake Hope, a town with no lake and no apparent hope, and headed to Raven's house. The downside of that decision was knowing Pat would probably end up there when he finished questioning our suspect. I didn't want to see Pat. I certainly didn't want to talk to him, but I told myself that I'd dug myself into this quandary, and I was going to have to find a way out. While sitting on the bluff, I decided to call my boss in Madison and tell him straight out that I'd gotten into a situation that I needed to see through till the end. I had plenty of vacation time coming, so I told him I needed two weeks. If I couldn't solve the case in two weeks, I'd throw in the towel and come back to work. If I solved it earlier, I'd find a hole in the wall somewhere and simply crawl in and allow my brain to decompress. At first, he told me to walk away from whatever I was entangled in. But when I said I couldn't do that, even though that's what I wanted to do, he told me to take care of myself and to let him know if there was any way he could help. I warned him to be careful what he offered.

I finished a couple glasses of Chianti and was jotting down ideas in a notebook about any positive leads we had in any of the cases. It was a short list. When I saw headlights in the driveway, I knew I was going to have to talk to Pat. I took a deep swig of wine and gritted my teeth.

He walked in cautiously, obviously not knowing what to expect. When he saw me sitting on a chair next to the dining table, he made a nervous attempt to smile. "I didn't expect to see you," he said slowly. "But I'm glad you're here. I've been trying to call you."

"Here's the thing, Pat. The only reason I came back is because I decided I owed it to the county to try to figure a way out of this mess. I don't want to talk about what happened. I just want to resolve it. So, I know you got things you want to say, but I don't want to listen. It makes sense that we both stay here, not to mention work together, but for now, let's not talk."

"Fine, but let me say just one thing. Then I'll keep my mouth shut till you ask me a question."

"One thing."

"I know you're beating yourself up over what happened to Hennie—"

"No, don't try to tell me it's not my fault."

"It's not. It's mine. I basically threatened Hennie's life if he didn't show up. I told Millie, who was probably his only friend in town, that she needed to get word to him. And, yes, my threat was perfectly clear, and he knew it."

"But it was my harebrained scheme. Had I taken time to consider the consequences, none of this would have happened. So, no more talk. Put some ice on that knob on your head and go to bed. I put my stuff upstairs. I hope that works for you."

Pat nodded sheepishly and headed toward Raven's bedroom. I poured the last of the wine and headed upstairs. I knew this was going to be a grueling two weeks.

After a night of relentlessly wrestling my pillow and always losing, I fell asleep around four thirty. When I woke up, the clock on the stand next to the bed read seven thirty-eight, later than I ever slept. I pushed myself off the bed, threw on an old sweatshirt over the Packers T-shirt I'd slept in, and trudged toward the door. I was not ready to face Pat. I knew we needed to work together, but I dreaded the idea of actually talking to him. As I dragged myself down the stairs, I caught the welcome aroma of fresh coffee. Maybe I would survive this day.

As I reached the bottom of the stairs, I looked around and didn't see Pat. Could he have overslept too? But he must've made the coffee, so he had to be up. I found a mug in a cupboard and poured the steamy brew. It smelled good and strong. I went to the kitchen table, blowing over the rim of the cup, anxious to get a mouthful of caffeine. As I pulled out a chair, I noticed a box of Cheerios and one of Raisin Bran. I headed back to the cupboard and grabbed a bowl and spoon. I took the carton of milk from the fridge, smelled it for freshness, and decided it would do fine for cereal. As I sat down to eat, I noticed a handwritten note scribbled on a scrap of paper on the table: "Shea, something urgent in Lakeshore County. Need to talk to sheriff. Pat."

This mess was spiraling faster and faster toward a total shitstorm. On the bright side, I didn't have to talk to Pat today. I finished breakfast, headed upstairs, and got dressed without bothering to shower. Having BO and looking like Medusa were going to be the least of my problems today.

I went directly to Sheriff Grimes's office without calling first. When I got there the office was empty. No receptionist and no Phil Grimes in his office. I called out, "Anybody here?" No response. I decided to sit down and call Grimes to let him know I was back on the case—if he even wanted me. After seven rings, his voicemail picked up. "Sheriff Grimes, this is Shea. I'm back in town if you want me to continue on the case. Give me a call."

As I was putting my phone back in my coat pocket, Zach Layman walked in and did a double take, shocked to see me standing there. He said, "Shea, I'm glad you're here. Are you okay?"

"Not exactly, but I'll survive. Where is everybody?"

"I talked to the sheriff. The county prosecutor let the doctor go back to St. Louis. Apparently, he had an alibi for the week before I found Swalheim's guts, and they had no evidence to hold him."

"Are you shitting me? Christ, did I screw up. Hennie's dead for helping me with my crazy scheme, and now we find out it was the wrong guy. I should go back to Madison."

"It's not your fault. We all went along with the plan. Who knows what happened with Hennie?"

"What's your plan, Zach?" I asked.

"I don't know. I'm a deputy now, at least till this mess is settled. I'll wait and see what Sheriff Grimes wants me to do. We can wait together till he calls."

"Since we're both here, I'll grab my notebook and we can figure out if we got any leads worth pursuing. Maybe it's the wife. We can start there."

# / 12 /

SIX FIFTEEN IN THE MORNING, I GOT A CALL FROM DETECTIVE CHASE
Norman, Lakeshore County sheriff's department. He must have been
hired after I left the department. Probably my replacement. Hell, I
was still asleep when he called. He told me he's leading the Januss
investigation now and needs to see me right now. I said I was in Lake
Hope to interview a suspect. He informed me that my plans are going
to have wait. He needed to talk to me about Harley Januss. "This is
not a good development," he said. "It's gotta happen right now."

"Take me damn near three hours to drive there. What's so
important?"

"Just get in your car and start driving. And don't bother with
speed limits!"

"I'll be there as soon as I can," I muttered and clicked off the
phone. A break in that case would be wonderful, but based on the
tone of the call, I knew I wasn't going to like the discovery.

At ten o'clock I was sitting in Detective Norman's office. Norman
looked young and physically fit. He had a military haircut and a
pissed-off-at-the-world look on his face. He had a two-inch scar along
his left cheek. Yeah, this was probably the guy they hired to replace
me. "You had coffee yet?" he asked.

"One cup as I was heading out the door, but I could use another."

Norman left without comment and returned a couple minutes later with a mug of coffee and a glazed donut. "All cops like donuts," he said sarcastically without looking at me. "Least that's what the public believes."

"Thanks. So, what's so important to drag me away from my investigation?"

He spread notes across his desk, avoiding eye contact. Finally, he took a long, slow breath and then spoke.

"Nasty lump on your head there. I won't even conjecture where that came from."

"I'm sure you couldn't guess," I snapped, thinking about how close I was to being in a coffin instead of an interrogation room—on the wrong side of the table.

"We don't know each other Donegal, but I heard a lot about you."

"Don't believe everything you hear." I smirked.

"Some was good, some bad, but that's water under the bridge. I have been put in charge of the Januss investigation. Not a hell of a lot to go on. But there are some things I need to clear up with you. We know you were out in the area of the crime scene about the time it happened."

"I went through that with the sheriff. I drove by the place just to see where it was and what kind of property it was. We were sure there was evidence there pertaining to a murder in Kickapoo County."

"That's all here in his notes."

"Does it also say Januss was killed with a high-powered rifle and that I don't even own a rifle?"

"That's what you told the sheriff the morning after we found the body—found it after getting an anonymous tip. That doesn't necessarily prove you didn't have access to a rifle the night Januss was killed."

"I've never used a rifle because I'm a horseshit shot. I'm right-handed so I use my right eye to line up the sights. But my right eye is slightly crossed, sort of like what they call a lazy eye, so my bullet doesn't always go where I'm aiming."

"Really? You were a cop all your life and you can't shoot a gun?"

"Not good with a rifle. I can hold my own with a handgun or shotgun. It was a drill sergeant in the army explained it to me. Probably why they made me an MP in New Mexico rather than an infantryman."

"Judging that theory is way above my pay grade."

"I didn't kill Januss, and I didn't borrow a rifle. If you find a weapon with my prints or DNA on it, then you call me in here. Otherwise, I got a murder to solve." I started to rise from my chair.

"Sit down. I got a murder to solve too. And it seems to me like you're right in the middle of it. How hard would it be for a guy who knows police work as well as you do to dispose of a weapon so it was never seen again?"

"I didn't have a rifle, and I didn't kill Januss." It was my turn to take a slow deep breath. Detective Norman shuffled through his notes.

"Do you use a notebook when you work on a case?" This time he looked directly at me.

"Of course I do."

"Maybe a little notebook, cheap little 3×5 type?"

"I got a bunch of them. Got a fresh one in my pocket right now." I reached into the front shirt pocket and pulled out a small notebook. "Like this one?"

"That's what I'm talking about." He reached into his desk drawer and pulled out a baggie with some writing on it. He held it front of me.

"Does this look like your notebook, Pat?" He paused for my reply.

"Looks like one of mine. Why?"

"Did you ever use a pen from a Motel 6?"

"I stayed at a Motel 6 for a few nights, so, yes, I might have used their pen."

"Okay, here's the thing, Pat. One of our officers was looking for evidence not far from the crime scene. Actually, right where the DCI team said the shooter probably stood when he killed Januss. He didn't find any shell casings, but he did find this notebook and pen. Kind of wedged in some rocks where the shooter probably sat waiting for his victim."

"And you think I left that notebook out there when I killed Harley Januss?" I felt a chill run through me.

"Actually, the notebook and pen have your fingerprints on them. And inside the notebook, there were notes about the Swalheim case. Included in these notes was the name Harley Januss, along with a description of his vehicle, a license number, and his address."

"I took those notes. Januss was a person of interest. Part of my job when I first arrived here was to do surveillance on Swalheim's wife. See where she went and who she met. I followed Kelly Swalheim to Januss's apartment one morning. After a couple hours, they came out of the apartment together, argued, and drove their separate ways. That led me to believe Januss was a person we needed to keep an eye on."

"So you followed him out to the hunting lodge where he was killed?"

"No, I followed him to a restaurant where, I later found out, he worked and was part owner. That's the last time I saw Januss."

"So how did your notebook and pen get there?"

"I don't know. But I do know I never carried that pen outside of my motel room." I again reached into my pocket and produced a Parker T-Ball Jotter. "Only kind of pen I ever carry with me. Got one for Christmas from my dad when I was in high school. Since then it's the only pen that feels right in my hand. If you analyze the ink in the notebook, I bet it doesn't match the pen from the motel."

"Maybe true, but why were your notebook and a pen from your hotel room found at the scene of a crime, where you were caught on camera driving to and from, at about the time the crime occurred? That's a lot of coincidences."

"There usually are no coincidences on a murder case, Detective. Most likely somebody planted that notebook there. Either took it from my hotel room or from my truck."

"Who would do that, Mr. Donegal?"

"Whoever shot Harley Januss and wanted to make it look like I did."

"Another interesting theory, but right now, I got to put your name on top of my list of possible suspects. I hate to do that to another cop, but we both know you're not exactly a typical cop."

"What is a typical cop, Detective Norman? Are you a typical cop?"

"A typical cop goes by the book, follows the law, works with his fellow officers. And, yes, I'd say I'm a typical cop. I gave you coffee and a donut, didn't I?" He forced a slight chuckle at his attempt at humor.

"Are you going to arrest me?"

"Not yet. Maybe you can figure out how to convince me, and who knows, maybe further down the line, convince a jury that all this evidence was planted by the real assailant. I'm going to let you go, but if you leave the area, say to go back to Kickapoo County to work on your case, I want you to give me a call and tell me where I can contact you."

"That I will do, Detective Norman." As I spoke these words, I slowly stood up, pushed back my chair, and headed toward the door. Last night I thought things couldn't get worse. I was so wrong.

Before I reached the door, I turned to ask Detective Norman a question. "Can you tell me when your officer found my notebook?"

"Yesterday. We often go back to a scene a few days after the initial search, just in case we missed something."

"So almost a week after your officers and the investigators from the DCI scoured that area, suddenly your deputy finds a key piece of evidence. How likely does that sound to you?"

"Like I said, it was wedged between some rocks. It could easily have been missed."

"Your officers don't look between rocks when they do an evidence search? I bet the state crime lab people do."

"Shit happens. The notebook and pen got missed on the earlier searches."

"Has it rained since the night of the crime?"

"Yeah, rained a few nights ago."

"Was the notebook wet when your guy found it? It would surely show effects of being soaked if it sat outside in the rain."

Norman paused to consider the question. He rubbed his hand through his butch haircut. Finally, he spoke. "Like I said, it was between some rocks. Maybe the rain didn't get between the rocks."

"That's bullshit and you know it. Somebody planted that evidence well after the time of the crime. I'd suggest you try to figure out who planted it. Then you might find the killer."

"I don't need investigative lessons from you, Donegal. Your reputation around here is less than stellar. I know what I'm doing."

"You know, Norman, this department has had a hard-on for me since I solved a string of the worst crimes ever committed around here. Solved them without help from anyone. Maybe they didn't like my methods, but without my work, your stack of cold cases would be a hell of a lot thicker than it is. I got things done. And I made sure the right people came to justice."

"From what I heard, you enforced your own methods of justice. You didn't always give the courts a chance to do their job."

"Well, I didn't have to plant evidence in order to frame a suspect."

"You think the department's out to frame you?"

"Look at the evidence you just showed me. If you were me, what would you think?"

"You think this frame job goes all the way to the sheriff? Just because the whole department is jealous of your great police work ten or twenty years ago? That's bullshit."

"I don't know who's behind it, but I know I didn't leave that notebook and pen out in those rocks. So, I hope you will find out who killed Januss and then tried to blame it on me."

"You're still our prime suspect, so let me know if you leave the county."

"Consider yourself informed. After stopping back at the motel and trying to figure out who might have had access to my room, I'm heading back to Lake Hope to do some real police work."

"Well, don't get too comfortable back there. The county DA is putting together a file on you. Next time I might have an arrest warrant."

"Yeah, I'm sure you're working on a way to transfer my prints onto a rifle that you can plant where it'll look like I hid it."

"Get the hell out of here!"

I have to admit I don't scare very easily, but I was scared now. Somebody was out to pin a murder on me, and they were doing a damn fine job. I thought about hiring a lawyer before Detective Norman showed up with an arrest warrant. But who? I had made a career of alienating defense attorneys. Might be tough finding a good one to back me up. Clyda McCabe crossed my mind. She was successful, and we'd been on friendly terms—too friendly, unfortunately. But Clyda represented a key suspect in my murder investigation. Chances are there would be a whole snake's nest of conflicts of interest.

As I drove, I tried to piece together any conjectures about who planted my notebook and pen at the crime scene. The bigger question was how they got my notebook and pen. Shea visited my room briefly when she first came to town, but there was no way she would do it. Not that she was enamored with me right now, but there was no reason to frame me for shooting Januss. Then there was Hennie Duggan. He visited my room before his mysterious disappearance. In order to figure out why he might want to frame me, I first had to figure out why the hell he went AWOL from his job. Perhaps that was where I needed to start my search.

Of course, one other person also visited my motel room—Clyda McCabe. This was an incident I'd like to strike from my past. If it turned out Kelly Swalheim was charged with the murder of her husband, how was the court going to deal with the issue of the defendant's attorney and the detective in charge of the investigation having been together in a hotel room? My hope was that Clyda would be at least as protective of that secret tryst as I planned to be. It was clear to me from the time I sobered up the morning after the event that Clyda was intentionally getting me drunk at the Wagon Wheel Bar. Not, I'm sure, because she wanted to take advantage of my good looks and sexual prowess but because she wanted to find out how strong our case was against her client. Lifting my notebook and a pen from the table beside the bed would make perfect sense. A free insight into the investigation. But why plant the notebook at the scene of Januss's murder? Simple—to protect her client.

If Kelly did kill her husband, it is possible that her lover found out. Maybe she told him during their pillow talk, and he tried to use the information to extort money? If she was willing to kill one man, why not two? And if she told her lawyer, her primary confidant, maybe Clyda decided the best defense was a good offense. Attack the cops in charge of the investigation. Maybe that's why Hennie jumped ship. Maybe they had something on him. But Hennie, really? Hennie seemed squeaky clean—well, except for the investigation of the murdered priest eighteen years ago. Could Clyda McCabe have learned something about *that* case that involved Hennie? Unlikely, but he did quit his job at the sheriff's department without solving the Father Johnny case. Life was turning into a labyrinth that, like the universe, just seemed to keep expanding by the second. How could I solve the Swalheim murder case without also figuring out who killed Harley Januss and then framed me? Where could I start?

What about Hennie? What did he find out that would cause him to run away from the case? Hennie was a hunter. Could he have been involved with the Kilimanjaro Society? To me the odds of that were a billion to one. Unless Hennie was the one who hunted and killed Swalheim. He did know the ridge area as well as anyone. Kill someone in your jurisdiction and then take charge of the investigation. Sounds pretty much like what his former boss did eighteen years earlier when he helped Father Johnny's murderer. But Hennie knew the ex-sheriff didn't get away with it. Maybe Hennie wasn't so clean in that old murder case. Maybe he shot the former sheriff to keep him quiet. I took a deep breath, realizing my theories were sounding like a poorly written paperback mystery. I decided I needed to find out more about Hennie's life.

And how about Clyda? She had the best opportunity to steal my notebook and the motel pen. Plus, she had a motive—to protect her client. She might have taken the notebook just to see what information I'd already gathered against her client. The idea of planting the notebook to frame me might have conveniently occurred to her well after Januss was killed. And since her client owned the land where the crime took place, Clyda would have easy access to the crime scene. If Kelly Swalheim killed Januss, then planting evidence against the cop in charge would provide a perfect case of reasonable doubt. Clyda McCabe had to be a strong possibility.

I tried to remember exactly what was written in that notebook. As I'd told Chase Norman, I used several little notebooks during an investigation. The only way to be sure what was scribbled in that notebook was to get a look at it and see what Clyda might have learned. I could call Norman to see if he would let me look through the notebook just to see what information could've leaked out. Chances are he'd say no, but considering the information was crucial in the Swalheim murder, I had a good argument for seeing the notebook, especially if I was willing to let his department keep it for evidence. Too many loose ends. Where should I start looking? I decided I'd first call Norman. After that, I'd head back to Lake Hope to try to figure out what Hennie's role was in this botched investigation.

I was surprised when Detective Norman answered his phone on the second ring.

"Detective, this is Pat Donegal. I know our meeting today didn't end on the best terms, but I want you to consider doing me a favor."

"Donegal, why the hell didn't you tell me about your partner Hennie Duggan? I just got a call from my sheriff telling me what happened. He said you damn near got your brains blown out. I didn't know that, or I would have gone a little easier on you. I got a murder to solve too, but I should've cut you some slack."

"We are trying to keep that quiet for now—to protect the investigation. And don't apologize for being a hard-ass. I've been one all my life. In this job you got to forget your manners sometimes. Don't worry about it. What I'm wondering is, can I peek into that notebook just to see how much information I let slip out to whoever stole it? You can keep it after I read through it."

"Not a problem. And I wish I would've known. Losing a partner on the job is as tough as it gets. I wish I would've known."

"Thanks. Hennie and I worked together on several cases, plus he's on the short list of people I'd call a friend. In this line of work and with my personality, you don't make many. And I honestly don't know what the hell happened to Januss."

"Stop at my office and I'll show you the notebook, but I'll have to hold on to it for evidence."

"That's fair. Be there in an hour."

On my way back from Norman's office, I decided I'd pop into the Wagon Wheel Bar around five just in case I could run into Clyda McCabe. She was the most likely person to steal my notebook. Which also meant she was probably the one trying to frame me for Januss's murder. I needed to talk to her. She was not a person I wanted for an enemy. After that, I'd slip back to Lake Hope.

# / 13 /

I OPENED MY NOTEBOOK AND ASKED ZACH TO HELP ME LIST CLUES THAT
might lead us in the right direction.

"Start with the gut pile," Zach suggested. "If the doctor wasn't the
killer, then someone else had to have experience cutting up bodies.
What are the chances of another medical person being involved?
Maybe an undertaker." He paused, looked embarrassed, and said,
"And, yes, I guess we have to reconsider the army medic who discovered the remains. Though I'm certainly not a surgeon, and I can
assure you I didn't do it."

"I believe that, Zach, but like you say, we better write it down."

"If we knew where the body was, our job would be easier. Could it
still be on the ridge somewhere?" he asked.

"You know that area better than I do, but it has been searched by
state investigators and cadaver-sniffing dogs. Dogs are normally hard
to fool. But there are places on that bluff where even highly trained
dogs couldn't find a body. I'll write it down as an area we need to
look at."

"How did the doctor find his way up the ridge without knowing the area? Hennie and I know that area as well as anyone, and we
thought we had all the trails covered. He had a way in we didn't know

about. His truck was parked on a side road by a cedar swamp. I don't see how he walked through that."

"He must have hired a guide. Someone who knows a route you're not aware of. Let's get feelers out about possible guides."

"If he showed the doctor the way up there, he might have shown the killer too," Zach suggested.

"I'll note that." I looked at our short list of leads. "How about the woman you saw parked along the road?"

"I just wish I could remember more."

"You said she was wearing a baseball cap, which means she didn't want to be recognized if she was from this area, or she didn't want to be remembered if she was from out of town."

"I think she drove a black SUV."

"I jotted down possibly a Cadillac Escalade in my notes."

"It's a guess. Could've been a Suburban or Yukon."

"What else?"

"I hate to bring it up"—Zach spoke slowly, considering each word—"but how does Hennie fit in? First, he leads the investigation, then he quits the case, then he ends up dead at the bottom of the ravine."

"We need to find out what he discovered. Did he know too much? Was he pushed to his death? Why leave the case if he had relevant information?"

"Million-dollar question." Zach scratched his head. "What next?"

"We can cover more ground if we split up. You head back out to the ridge and take a fresh look. Something might pop out that everybody missed during earlier searches. Try to find another path up the bluff. Maybe you can snoop around and find some names of hunters who know every tree and rock on the bluff. And who might be willing to use that info to make a few bucks."

"I can do that." He got up and headed toward the door.

"I'll leave a message telling Phil what we're up to. Then I'm going to look into suspects who might have experience with human dissection. Pathologist maybe? And I'll hunt motor vehicle records for big black SUVs in this area. Long shot, but we got to keep searching."

Zach and I went our separate ways. I left him a message in the afternoon and suggested we meet at the diner the next morning to compare notes.

When I got there, Zach was already drinking coffee and going over his notes. I went to the counter and ordered black coffee and wheat toast and pointed toward the booth where Zach was sitting.

"You're up early," I said. "You must be getting into this police work."

"I couldn't sleep. Things keep swirling through my brain when my head hits the pillow."

"Spoken like a career cop," I said. "The job gets into your head, and if you're not careful you'll end up a cranky old gumshoe like Pat Donegal. And that is a scary thought."

"You don't like Pat?" Zach asked.

"We've worked some tough cases together the last couple years. Our results have turned out well, but some of Pat's methods are hard to deal with."

"Why do you work together?"

"Good question. Most of the time I really like the guy. Love being with him. He knows how to close cases. But sometimes he just goes way over the line." I took a deep breath, not wanting to say more. "But let's get to our investigation. What did you find?"

"Nothing new when I went back to the crime scene, but I might have a lead on a guide."

"Good work."

"There's a little grocery store with a gas pump and a five-stool bar about two miles from the ridge. Very rustic. I go there once in a while when I'm hunting. They sell great summer sausage, so I stop by and grab a loaf of bread or crackers and half a pound of sausage for my lunch. Maybe a beer to wash it down. I stopped yesterday. I was wearing camouflage coveralls, so I fit right in. Three old-timers were playing ship, captain, and crew at the bar, so I slid in beside them and ordered a Pabst tallboy, a half-pound of summer sausage, and a box of saltines. I pretended to be minding my own business, eating and drinking, till the bartender walks by and I say, 'That ridge is one goddamn maze to try to navigate. I'd be willing to pay a hundred bucks if I could find somebody could show me how the hell to get around up there.' The bartender gives me a noncommittal nod and smile and walks away." Zach paused to be sure Shea was following the story.

"Sounds like a good idea," Shea said.

"So, I drank my beer and ate," Zach continued. "Few minutes later, one of the dice shakers speaks up. 'If you're willing to spring for a round of tallboys, I might be able to help you out. You're not from around here?' I told him I lived in Lake Hope, recently back from Afghanistan, working as a handyman, finishing a nursing degree, and looking for a good place to hunt in my free time. 'Where do you find free time?' he asked. I told him I didn't have much, that's why I wanted to learn the lay of the land. 'May take more'n a hundred,' he says. I told him I might be able to go higher. I ordered four cans of Pabst from the bartender, who seemed a little wary of the conversation. The other two dice shakers seemed bored, sipped their new tallboys, and started shaking without their buddy. 'I'm listening,' I said, snapping the tab on my fresh tallboy.

"The guy continued. 'There was an Indian grew up down along the river just south of here. He knew this area better than anybody. But he moved up around La Crosse. He must be sixty or seventy now. Rumor has it he comes back once in a while to do a little guiding.' I asked if the guy had a name. 'Not sure.' He moved to the empty stool between us and spoke softly. 'But maybe for a couple sixers of tall-boys my memory would improve.' I nodded and signaled for the bartender, who was also running the grocery counter."

"A real helpful citizen there." Shea smiled.

"I ordered two six-packs to go, and while the bartender was filling my order, I took a healthy swig of beer and wrapped up my meat and crackers. I paid my tab and started toward my truck. The dice shaker waited a couple minutes then followed me out. As I was climbing into my truck, he stepped up and said, 'The guy's name is Clancy Lone Owl. But you didn't hear that from me.' He took the beer and headed toward an old Ford Taurus parked next to the front door."

"Damn, Zach, first week on the job and you're looking like a pro. You know Sheriff Grimes is never going to let you quit after we solve this case."

"I got plenty of irons in my fire already. My wife thinks I'm crazy doing this police work. Especially now that I'm working with a strange female detective from Madison."

"I'm not all that strange. Well, some people might not agree with that."

"I didn't mean it that way. Just that in a little town like Lake Hope, Madison sounds exotic."

"Tell your wife not to worry. I'm damned boring."

"I'll tell her that." Zach smiled, suddenly looking shy and embarrassed.

I then reported that my search for black Escalades turned up four vehicles in the county. Almost twenty Suburbans and Yukons. I'd printed a list and planned to run them past the sheriff, though I was certain it'd be a dead end.

"Why don't you take a few hours to catch up on your homework and spend some time with your family. I'll see if I have any luck tracking down Clancy Lone Owl."

I ran Lone Owl's name through the state database. No criminal record. Actually, no record at all until he was in his twenties and had a couple minor violations. Then he worked as a part-time game warden for the state for seventeen years. He was a licensed fishing guide. His current address was listed as a rural route outside a little town on the Mississippi River just north of La Crosse. Thanks to Zach we might have a real lead.

I stopped to talk to Sheriff Grimes to find out if he'd heard anything from Pat. I was surprised I hadn't heard a word since he left.

"I wish I had better news, but Pat's in another predicament. Lakeshore County found one of his notebooks and a hotel pen at the Harley Januss crime scene. Apparently, they still consider Pat a suspect." Grimes looked grim.

"Any chance Pat shot Januss?" I asked.

"God, I hope not or we'll never solve our murder. You know Pat better than me. You think he could do this?"

"I thought I knew him, but how well does anyone really know another person? We worked several cases together, and to be honest, most of the time I felt more comfortable with him than any cop I'd worked with. But he sure knows how to get into trouble."

"How's Hennie fit in? He and Pat seemed like a good team on earlier cases, but shit, this one has me baffled. Could those two have gotten themselves into some kind of mess they couldn't climb out of?" Grimes shook his head and exhaled heavily.

"Beats me," I said. "I was ready to say screw it to the whole operation, but I hate to start something and not see it to the end. I don't know who to trust anymore."

"I'll contact Pat tonight, see what's going on. I'll let you know if I hear anything."

"Thanks."

I explained what Zach had found out, and he told me to find this Lone Owl character. When I left the office, I was still unsure whether I was afoot or on horseback. Nothing in this case made sense. I thought about calling Pat to see if he'd like to go with me to visit Lone Owl, but I decided I really didn't want to spend three hours alone in a car talking to Pat. Sometimes flying solo has its benefits.


USING my phone for navigation, it took less than two hours to find Lone Owl's cabin, which was located on a slough on the Mississippi about twenty-five miles north of La Crosse. To get there required weaving through a maze of narrow, barely paved township roads with names like Bull Head Trail, Beaver Path, Pickerel Lane, and Hoof Print Lake Road. My primary concern winding through this labyrinth was getting to the address and discovering the cabin abandoned, or more likely simply finding no one at home. To my relief, when I arrived at the designated fire post number, I spotted an elderly man bent over the engine of a restored Ford pickup truck. He looked up with a quizzical expression when he heard my car and realized I was pulling into his driveway. I tapped my Glock, realizing I was a long way from civilization, a type of location where many people do not want to be found.

I was dressed in my usual attire of jeans, boots, sweater, and black ski parka. I'd decided on the way that I wouldn't identify myself as a police officer. Rather, I'd pretend to be in search of a guide. I planned to say I'd gotten his name from an acquaintance in Lake Hope. If pressed, I figured I'd use Zach Layman as my source.

Remembering the Tony Hillerman novels I'd read, I decided to follow the Navajo custom of greeting Lone Owl from my car and waiting for him to invite me to visit. It was unlikely Lone Owl was Navajo, being in Wisconsin, but I thought there was a chance the custom was common among Native Americans. I rolled down my window and waited. Apparently, it was a good idea, because after studying me for a couple minutes, Lone Owl approached.

"Lost?" he asked, pulling down the brim of his baseball cap to shade his eyes from the sunlight reflecting off my windshield.

"I wonder if I could talk to you a minute?" I said, still sitting in my car.

"Not many people drive all this way to talk. You must be looking for something." He stepped closer and bent down to get a better look at me.

"All right if I get out and talk?"

"Suit yourself."

I eased open the door and climbed out. "Nice setting you have here," I said, looking over the expanse of trees running along the water.

"If you're a realtor, I'm not selling."

"No, I'm not a realtor. But I heard from a friend that you sometimes guide hunters in the bluff areas in Kickapoo County."

"Are you a hunter?"

"Not exactly." I tried to think quickly. "I'm a writer working on a mystery. In my story, a convict escapes prison and is reportedly seen hiding out in the area near Ibsen Ridge."

"How the hell did you ever come up with Ibsen Ridge for a place to hide out?"

"I closed my eyes and put my finger on a map. That's where it landed."

"That seems like a strange way to write a book."

"Well, I didn't say I was a good writer, but I try."

"So, who was it gave you my name? I haven't lived in that area since I left high school and joined the army."

"A young guy named Zach Layman. He lives in Lake Hope and does a lot of hunting."

"I never heard of him." He paused, probably trying to figure out why the hell I was really there. "If he's a hunter, why doesn't he show you around? There are people who live around there that know the ridge as well as me."

"Zach says he knows the two main trails up to the ridge, but if I want to write a decent story, I should find somebody who really knows the area. He said one of his drinking buddies at a little tavern up near the ridge told him stories about you knowing every inch of that remote river country."

"I grew up there, but like I said, I haven't lived there in many years. Places change."

"My publisher would cover guiding fees if you'd show me around for a day or two. I can't describe an area unless I've been there. Readers know when you're making stuff up."

"Nobody at that little tavern knows where I live. How the hell did you find me?"

"I got your name and started digging around on the internet. Found a Clancy Lone Owl who used to work as a game warden. Figured that was you."

"I helped out the DNR from time to time. But I never worked full time."

"You worked enough to get on their retired employee list. Once I had a name, it wasn't hard to track down an address."

"Nothing private in this goddamn world anymore. A guy wants to mind his own business and fish and trap along the river, and the whole damn world has to know right where he is."

"Listen, I won't blame you if you tell me to get the hell off your property. I just thought it was worth a try." I turned and edged slowly toward my car.

"Well, you came all this way, might as well come up and set on the porch. I'll make a pot of coffee."

"I'd appreciate that, Mr. Lone Owl. I would like to stretch my legs a bit."

"No indoor plumbing, so if you need a toilet, you're welcome to use the outhouse. It's clean."

"Thank you, but I stopped for gas in La Crosse and used their facilities. Coffee sounds great if it's not too much trouble."

"No trouble." He turned as he spoke and headed toward the cabin. I followed. The cabin was one story, probably no more than one or two bedrooms, with a rustic pine log exterior. It looked comfortable. Half a dozen coil spring animal traps hung along the side wall—looked the right size for muskrats or beaver. A fish cleaning table stood under a tall white pine tree thirty feet from the cabin. A canoe and Lund fishing boat were tied to a pier along the river. Clancy Lone Owl's place was designed for convenience. For a man who enjoyed nature, this place appeared ideal.

On the porch, Lone Owl had three cane-back chairs that looked handmade from some kind of willow wood. I took the one farthest from the door and sat down. A flock of cranes flew overhead, raising a harsh chorus of discordant bugle calls. I stepped off the porch to watch them pass over. Must have been about two dozen flying in a loosely developed V-formation. Their loud cackles and cries sounded like they were just a few feet away.

"Amazing creatures," Lone Owl said, surprising me as he opened the door and stepped out.

"Did you ever wonder why one side of the vee is longer than the other?"

"I never thought about it," I answered.

"Because one side has more cranes." He suppressed an embarrassed chuckle.

"You learn something every day. This trip was worth the drive already. Maybe I'll put that in my book."

"You should see them in spring when they do their mating dances. Cranes mate for life, you know. More than can be said for most people. No disrespect if you've been married more than once. I'm just talking."

"No harm. I have never experienced matrimonial bliss."

"Twice for me, and I wouldn't say there was much bliss involved." I went back to my chair and sat down. Lone Owl followed and sat in the chair closest to the door, leaving the middle chair as a buffer zone.

"Coffee will be ready in a few minutes."

"Thank you."

"I'm still trying to figure out how the hell you found me out here. Lone Owl is not exactly my God-given name. Renamed myself after I came back from Vietnam. Officially, I am still Clancy Big John on my Social Security card. Ho Chunk name. My people once controlled most of the land in the southwest corner of Wisconsin. Government called us Winnebagos back then. When I came back from service, I got involved in some political organizations. Maybe you heard about the Catholic novitiate we took over north of Shawano. Plus, I was involved in protests out on Pine Ridge Reservation in South Dakota. I didn't really want to drag my family into my politics, so I chose my own name. I've used it ever since. Lot of native cultures routinely have young adults chose their own name."

"I appreciate your service in Vietnam. From everything I heard, it was hell over there."

"I didn't have it as bad as most. I was picked to be the assistant to a colonel stationed in Saigon. More like a personal servant. A bit humiliating, but it kept me out of the jungle. I worked in an office all day and drank most of the night. But, like you say, nobody comes home from war without scars. Not always physical."

"Having never been in the military, I can't even imagine."

"Funny. I don't usually talk this much. I don't talk at all most days. I used to have a dog. Named Chief. Talked to him a lot. But he got old and died. Good old mutt. Now I just talk to myself if I got something to say."

"Why not get a new dog?"

"Hell, the dog would outlive me. Then what?"

"Dog would find a new place to live. Dogs are smart."

"You're a good talker. Bet you're a good writer too." He paused, maybe thinking he'd said too much. Then he stood up. "Coffee should be ready. Milk or sugar?"

"Black, please."

Clancy returned with two mismatched mugs and handed one to me inscribed with a drawing of a duck flying above a patch of cattails. I took a slow sip. It tasted good.

"I still don't quite understand you coming all this way to hire me, but if you want a guide, I'll help you out. No cell phone or computer, so we'll have to make a plan today."

"That'd be great. I'm free the next several days."

"I can meet you at that little tavern you talked about next Tuesday, 8 a.m. Three hundred a day. May take a day and a half to really get the lay of the land. So figure $450 cash. No reason to get the IRS involved. They got plenty to do already."

"That sounds fair, Mr. Lone Owl."

"Just Clancy," he said. "And if you don't mind, I'd just as soon nobody else knows about this deal. Like I said, I grew up there and we'll just leave it at that. Some folks weren't always too welcoming to the noble savages. Now we're Native Americans, but I heard a lot of less flattering names growing up."

"Then we'll keep it between us. Cash will work fine."

"I've done all the talking here. You never gave me your name."

I quickly thought about throwing out an alias. But I figured I'd lied enough, and besides, if he didn't have a computer or a cell phone, it was unlikely he'd be doing a background search. So, I simply extended my hand and said, "Shea Sommers, a pleasure talking to you."

"Do you have any books published?"

"Not yet, but I'm working to change that."

I finished my coffee, and we talked a little while longer about life along the river. The way Clancy explained it, it didn't sound half bad.

On the drive home, I realized I hadn't even tried to find out who else he'd shown around Ibsen Ridge. He made it sound like he hadn't been in Kickapoo County in many years, but if Zach's source was right, Clancy Lone Owl had offered his guiding service fairly recently. Now I had to decide my next step. I told Clancy I'd keep our plan quiet. I wanted to keep that promise, but did that make any sense? How much trust did I put in a man who spent much of his life keeping to himself? Did I owe it to Sheriff Grimes to let him in on my plan? How about Pat? Or would he find a way to screw it up? I was sure I could trust Zach, but was there any reason to drag him into another of my goose chases? I had a few days to plot my next move, so I decided to just keep my cards close to my vest. After my debacle that got Hennie killed and almost got Pat's head blown off, maybe it'd be best to try this plan alone.

Maybe Clancy Lone Owl killed David Swalheim. Clancy was a hunter, trapper, and fisherman. Maybe he got bored shooting animals and developed a taste for hunting men. Maybe he wanted revenge for the racism he'd faced growing up. Maybe he was on the ridge the night Hennie died. Clancy could've led Dr. Grant up the bluff and then slipped down the back trail, saw Hennie, and pushed him into the ravine. Hell, a man who spent his life hunting and trapping had to be damn skilled at skinning and gutting. He probably realized the minute I stepped out of the car that I was a cop. Lot of people can spot a cop a mile away. Instead of killing me on his turf, he decided to secretly head back to Kickapoo County and do it in a place where he'd had no apparent connections for fifty years. He asked me to keep our plan a secret. Did he think I'd be stupid enough to meet him without backup? Why wouldn't he believe that? It was exactly what I was planning to do. Whatever happened to normal cases?

# / 14 /

MY STOLEN NOTEBOOK HAD VERY LITTLE INFORMATION OF VALUE. OTHER than my observations about Kelly Swalheim's rendezvous with Januss and the details about his address, car and license plate number, and place of work, it was mostly just chicken-scratch observations I made during my surveillance of the victim's wife. This was a major relief. I was also pleased that Clyda McCabe didn't show up at the Wagon Wheel. I knew at some point I was going to have to confront that whole situation, but as things were going now, I was satisfied to keep that one on the back burner as long as possible.

About eight o'clock I stopped by my hotel, grabbed a few items, and headed for Lake Hope. It was almost midnight when I got to town, so rather than waking up Shea if she was sleeping at Raven's, I pulled into what I called the Bates Motel, got a room, and actually slept soundly for the first time in days.

Next morning, I looked through the items I'd collected from my motel room. Among the stuff were two thumb drives. It took me a minute to remember I'd taken them from the filing cabinet the night I'd broken into Swalheim's hunting lodge. In all the commotion of finding Januss's dead body, being accused of his murder, and then the fiasco on Ibsen Ridge the night Hennie died and I nearly had my brains surgically removed by Doctor Psycho's rifle, I'd forgotten about the flash drives. I booted my laptop and decided to check the data on the files. The first thumb drive was simply labeled "JS." The second was "HD." I loaded the JS drive and waited. To my surprise, there were no facts and figures on the flash drive. Rather, there was a very raunchy video of Kelly Swalheim in bed with one of the Sangiovese brothers—I recognized Johnny, who was a couple years older than my friend Sammy. The brothers looked a lot alike. This was a no-holds-barred porno flick, complete with sound effects, mostly groans, screams, and heavy breathing. When the performance reached its climax, David Swalheim popped into the room. He did not act surprised or upset. In fact, as Sangiovese rolled off the bed and scrambled into his clothes, David explained that if Johnny wanted this little orgy to remain discreet, he would deliver two thousand dollars in cash on the first day of each month. Otherwise, Johnny's wife and kids would receive a copy of the video of his performance. Johnny, now in shock by what had happened, simply grabbed his jacket, and as he moved to the door, angrily spit out, "Miserable cocksucker! People end up in the bottom of Lake Michigan for pullin' shit like this."

David Swalheim shouted back, "Yeah, well, first of the month is next Tuesday. I'll take my chances!" Then he turned to Kelly and said, "Great performance, babe."

"Eat shit!" she snarled as she walked toward the bathroom.

David chuckled and the video ended.

This sex video provided more motivation for Kelly to kill her husband. But it also provided motive for Johnny Sangiovese. The file could prove helpful—except for the fact that I'd obtained it illegally the same night I was accused of killing a man. How could I explain being in possession of the file? I couldn't.

I removed the first thumb drive and loaded the second. What I found this time shocked me even more. HD stood for Hennie Duggan. My first thought was to eject the drive and bust it into a hundred pieces. Unfortunately, the cop in me said I had to see what was there. It was painful to watch. Hennie seemed to have no idea what was coming. He was asking Mrs. Swalheim questions about where she was during the days preceding the discovery of her husband's remains. Before he finished his questions, she skillfully dropped off the robe she was wearing and stood there in sheer panties and bra. Hennie backed away, stammering something about coming back later.

Kelly spoke in a low, seductive voice: "Okay, Detective, I'll give you what you asked for. Just follow me into my bedroom."

"That's not what I said," Hennie mumbled. "And I'd feel more comfortable if you were dressed."

"Come on, Detective. This is what you demanded. You said you'd drop the investigation if I *cooperated*." Kelly suddenly appeared as awkward as Hennie, like she was reading a script in a seventh-grade play. She turned and stepped closer to him. She undid her bra and moved to within inches. "I'm ready to *cooperate*."

Hennie stepped back. Kelly Swalheim was a beautiful woman, but this video was nothing like the first one I watched. "Don't you like what you see, Detective?" Again, the words sounded forced.

Hennie turned to leave, but before he escaped, he looked back, confused, like he was ready to cry.

"If you still feel like you have to consider me a suspect, you may want to know the past five minutes have been recorded on video. Once edited, it'll look like this was all your idea." The words were flat, contrived, like she'd been ordered to recite them.

Hennie never spoke. Instead, he simply beat a beeline for the front door. Now I knew why he left the job. He was afraid his sex video would be made public. I had so many answers and no way to disclose them. I wondered about trying to sneak back into the lodge to replant the thumb drive. Then when I got a warrant, I'd be able to find them legally. But did I really want Hennie's performance made public? I also wondered if there was any way Hennie could have been at the hunting lodge the night Januss was killed. Could Hennie have come looking for the thumb drive, found Januss there, shot him, and then left before he had a chance to enter the house to find what he had come for? Maybe I scared him away. It was a crazy theory, but everything about this case was insane. I stashed the drives in my duffel bag and headed down to the motel office for a free cup of coffee.

I wondered who was on the thumb drives I hadn't stolen. There were just too many loose ends.

I knew my best next move would be to call Shea to see if she had come up with new leads. But there was a barrier between us that I didn't feel like batting my head against. Since I wasn't ready to disclose the information I'd found, not even to Shea, I decided to move on without calling her. Since my phone had not been ringing the past couple days, I figured she was doing the exact same thing.

I elected to stop by the sheriff's office to check in with Phil. When he asked what was new, I simply responded that I was working on something and would let him know if anything worked out. Chickenshit answer, but it bought time. I also got permission to go through Hennie's house and everything in it, something we should have done right after his fall. But this case had nothing to do with doing things the way they should be done.

On the way out, it started snowing—just like the first time I went to see him at his place. That was when I was stirring up a reinvestigation of the fifteen-year-old murder of Father Johnny. During my first drive out to Hennie's, I was considering Hennie a possible suspect for that murder. As it turned out, he later saved my bacon in a shootout and helped me solve the cold case. After that we teamed up three or four more times. We worked well together and always got the results we wanted. It suddenly hit me while I was driving those crooked backcountry roads, watching big flakes of wet snow dance in front of the windshield, that I hadn't grieved at all for Hennie. Things were so frenzied I hadn't felt the impact of what happened. Hennie Duggan was dead. I didn't know how or why, but the fact remained he was dead. I suddenly felt a rush of sorrow. I pictured him walking out of Kelly Swalheim's house on the video—lost, confused, broken, hating himself. That's why he'd vanished. Then I remembered how I spoke to him that morning at Ibsen Ridge as we prepared for that disastrous night of hunting. I'd done nothing but berate and threaten him. Why didn't I try harder to find out what was wrong? Why couldn't I ever put myself in someone else's shoes? In my self-pitying reverie, I damn near slid off the road and into the ditch. Once I regained control of my truck, I stopped on the edge of the road and slammed my fist down on the steering wheel several times, setting the horn blaring every time I beat the wheel. I guess it was a Neanderthal's way of grieving for a friend.

Before I started back down the road, it occurred to me that this had been my lifelong pattern of dealing with loss—anger and denial. Instead of a five-step grief process, I'd abbreviated it to two. Hadn't I done the same thing when my parents died? When my wife left me for my oncologist, and when my sons moved to places unknown? Hell, yes. Get pissed off and then pretend nothing happened. Shea Sommers would be next. When this case ended, she'd head back to Madison, and we'd probably never speak again. I'd crawl into a hole somewhere and wait for my next situation to screw up.

I had a key for Hennie's house now, so I went in through the back door. This time I actually looked at the house. Last time I came through, I was in a daze. The first room was the kitchen. It was small and neat, with an electric stove, refrigerator, small sink, and a few white painted cupboards. In one corner was an old wooden table big enough for two ladder-back chairs. Nothing was out of place. I looked around the house. Everything seemed to be tidy and efficient. Furniture looked old but well kept. Probably the same furniture used in the house when Hennie was growing up. Hennie inherited the house and everything in it, and he took good care of what he owned. He probably lived in the same house his whole life, same bedroom, same bathroom, same kitchen. And now he was dead before having any chance to see the world.

It seemed like a comfortable life in some ways, but at the same time it was sort of pathetic. I didn't snoop through closets or drawers. What was point? Before leaving, however, I did page through a small stack of papers on the kitchen table. A couple manuals for appliances. A list of directions for starting the furnace. A plat map of the forty acres accompanying the house. And, finally, a will, signed the night before he died. Without reading through the document, I placed it in an envelope next to it that was labeled Final Requests and tucked it into my jacket pocket. I figured I should give this material to Phil

Grimes. Since the will had been recently written, it might serve as an indication that Hennie took his own life. Had I been able to explain what I'd seen on the thumb drive, this would make more sense to the sheriff. But no one else was seeing that video unless it was completely necessary.

Phil acted surprised to see the will. When a young guy dies suddenly, more often than not he hasn't even considered who he'd leave stuff to. Unless he knew he was going to die and he gave a shit what happened to his possessions. Phil read the brief statement out loud. Surprisingly, Hennie left his house to Millie Trainor, the department dispatcher. Millie was new to the job, and Phil had no idea there was a strong connection between them. I had suspected they were friends when I used Millie as a conduit to order Hennie to have his ass at Ibsen Ridge for the hunting disaster. Apparently, Hennie had no family. Along with the house, he'd left Millie three acres of land. The remaining thirty-seven acres were donated to the county to serve as a wildlife conservancy. Hennie had put thought into the document. His clothes and any household supplies not wanted by Millie were to be given to the local Catholic church to be distributed to the needy. His books went to the public library. His truck was left to the old farmer who had arranged for the adoption of Hennie's dog. Finally, the antique Browning shotgun that had been passed down to Hennie from his grandfather was willed to Pat Donegal. I was shocked, considering the will was written after I'd essentially threatened his life regarding the Battle of Ibsen Ridge. I quickly realized that other than Millie and the old farmer, I must've been Hennie's closest friend. Though not accustomed to emotions, I damn near started crying right there in the office. Regrets are powerful forces, especially if those regrets are self-imposed. Golfers get mulligans, but there are no do-overs in real life. I had majorly screwed the pooch. Hennie was a simple, honest man caught in a mess he could see no way out of, and I was literally one of the forces that pushed him over a cliff.

I'm quite sure Phil Grimes spoke some appropriate healing words, but I didn't hear a thing he said. My mind was back in the warehouse behind the local utility company in Lake Hope, where Hennie

Duggan and Phil Grimes, neither knowing jack-shit about me at the time, risked their lives to back me up. Now Hennie was dead, and at least a healthy portion of the blame fell directly on me. Without a word, I left the sheriff's office, got in my truck, and started driving to who knows where.

# / 15 /

I REACHED RAVEN'S HOUSE JUST AFTER DARK. NO SIGN OF PAT. I ASSUMED he was still working in Lakeshore County. I considered calling him to compare notes. We were working the same case and theoretically working as a team. In previous cases, I couldn't wait to meet with Pat to bounce ideas off each other. But things were different now. I'd lost confidence in Pat, and I'm sure he lost it in me as well. Hopefully, he was making headway getting Kelly Swalheim to cooperate. Obviously, it's a stereotype to blame the spouse, but statistics backed that theory. And Kelly had done nothing to help solve the murder. It occurred to me that I should check car rental dealers in the Milwaukee area to see if maybe Kelly Swalheim rented a black SUV around the time of her husband's disappearance. I don't know why I hadn't thought of that before.

Raven's house was dark and felt cold when I walked in. I was hungry and couldn't remember what I'd left in the refrigerator. When I opened the fridge, the first thing I saw was the remains of the Driftless IPA I'd bought when I arrived, knowing it was beer Pat would like and we could share together. Instead, I grabbed one for myself and snapped the cap with the opener I'd left on the counter. The beer went down easy. I took out a pack of hot dogs and grabbed a can of baked beans from the shelf. In the middle of nowhere with beer, hot dogs, and pork 'n' beans, it almost felt like I was on vacation. In a sense I was—burning my vacation days from my job in Madison. What the hell did that say about my life? At what point in life did I lose my mind?

After devouring the hot dogs and beans, and having a second beer, I curled up on the couch with an afghan and my notebook to try to decide what I'd do in the morning.

I'd just dozed off to sleep when my phone rang. It was in my jacket pocket about eight feet from the couch. I seriously considered letting it go to voicemail but gave in and hustled over to answer.

"Sommers here," I answered.

"Hello, Shea. It's Pat. Thought I'd check in." His voice was flat, none of his old smartass vigor.

"Pat." I tried to force a little enthusiasm. "I was just wondering how you were doing. Where are you?"

"Actually, I'm in Lake Hope. Got here last night. Was late. I didn't want to bother you, so I got my old room at the motel. It hasn't changed much. I doubt they've changed the sheets."

"You coming out to Raven's? I just had hot dogs and beer. Got some left."

"Thanks. I had pizza at Murphy's. I'm on my way back to face Norman Bates."

"Why don't you stay out here? We should talk."

"I do have something to tell you, but I don't want . . ."

"Drive out, Pat. If we're going to work together, we're going to have to talk to each other."

"Are you sure you're up for company?" Still no emotion in his voice.

"It's more your house than mine. Yeah, come on out. We'll compare notes."

"Twenty minutes."

"See you then."

Pat looked five years older when he walked in. His shoulders stooped, his face sagged, and his eyes looked dead. The knob on his head had deflated but was still discolored. I was scared when I saw him.

"I don't need a hot dog, but I could use a beer," he said as he set his duffel bag down beside the door. "I bought a couple more six-packs of Driftless—we might have some tough days ahead."

"There are cold ones in the fridge. Help yourself."

Pat opened a beer and plopped down on a kitchen chair. He took a long swig from the bottle. He stood up and put the new beer in the refrigerator.

"Got stuff to tell you, Shea, but I'm not sure where to start."

"Beginning, middle, or end. Take your pick."

"Maybe I'll start at the end." He took another swig of beer. "Went out to Hennie's place today. The house looked all right. But on his table, I found a will. Dated Thursday night before the Ibsen Ridge adventure. Must've done it after our meeting that afternoon."

"Hennie wrote a will? That's strange."

"He had it witnessed by the old guy who lives down the road. Written the day before he died. Do you think Hennie was psychic?"

"Either that or . . ."

"Right, or he knew it because he planned it."

"You think Hennie . . ."

"What else can you think?"

"Maybe he realized how stupid my plan was to capture Dr. Grant. Probably knew there was a chance we'd all be killed."

"That could be it." Pat spoke with little conviction. "Anyway, it gets sadder than that. The guy must not have any family or friends. He left his house to Millie, the department dispatcher. I talked to her this afternoon. She had no idea they were that close. He left most of his land for a conservancy, other stuff to charity." Pat paused, and I could see his eyes mist up. His voice cracked slightly. "And, Christ, this is the real kicker. He left me an old shotgun handed down from his grandfather." He paused again and sniffed his nose. "After the way I chewed his ass that morning, he leaves me his shotgun. Makes me feel like more of an asshole than I usually do."

"He had a lot of respect for you, Pat. He probably agreed with every word you said that morning."

"Yeah, I respect you so much I'm going to jump off a cliff."

"Sounds like he had this all planned before he came back to town."

"He must have."

"Any ideas why?"

"Unfortunately, yes. Remember when I broke into the hunting lodge?"

"The night Januss was killed."

"Right. I took two throwaway phones. You used one to trace Dr. Grant. The other was blank."

"Okay."

"Well, I'm not sure I told you this, but I also took two thumb drives. I forgot all about them till yesterday when I was going through stuff in my duffle bag. So, I opened the thumb drives. They were videos. First one was a mob guy I knew when I worked in Lakeshore County. One of the Sangioveses. On the video this guy is getting it on with Kelly Swalheim. I mean moves I never imagined."

"So Kelly played around. And recorded it."

"Her husband recorded it. He steps in after they're through humping and tells Sangiovese the price for screwing his wife. Two grand a month. Or the video goes public."

"So it's a team event. How many drives were there?"

"Couple dozen probably. So that's where all the money came from. Kelly screwed powerful people, recorded them, and David blackmailed her costars."

"And Hennie found this out?"

"The hard way, unfortunately."

"Are you going to tell me more?"

"The second drive featured Hennie and Kelly. She must've lured him over to her place. Probably said she was ready to talk. Anyway, she drops her robe and is in her underwear. Poor Hennie looked like a fish out of water. Who knows if he was ever with a woman? Nothing happened, but she made it look like the whole thing was his idea. It was depressing."

"And once it's over, she tells him it's been recorded."

"Yup. Poor guy never had a chance. That's why he ran away. And why he jumped into the ravine."

"So, it wasn't you or me."

"You're clear, but I sure didn't help any. If I would have watched the video, I could've destroyed it. Told him he was clear. But I didn't see it in time."

"That's not on you, Pat. He couldn't live with the possibility of being accused of demanding sex from a suspect."

"But I might have stopped him from jumping if I'd taken the time to figure out what was bothering him."

"You're not Superman."

"Not even close." He looked at the floor as he spoke.

"Now what?"

"I go back and find a way to nail this murder on Kelly Swalheim. She killed her husband because she was tired of splitting the proceeds of their sex scheme."

"What if it was *his* scheme? Maybe he forced her to screw around with these guys."

"Husband was dead when Kelly recorded Hennie. Nobody made her do that."

"Have you got a plan?"

"I need to get the rest of those thumb-drive files. I can't use the two I have because of how I got them. Chances are Lakeshore County already confiscated everything in that lodge for evidence. I need the rest to use against Kelly. My guess is the Swalheims kept separate thumb drives to make it easy to extort money. Each performance was saved on a drive."

"Will Lakeshore County cooperate?"

"Good question. They still think I look good for the Januss murder."

"What if I approach them? Leave you out. Me and Zach can go over tomorrow and make an official Kickapoo County request. How can they not cooperate?"

"Might work."

"Once we get the videos, we got motive. Too bad we can't slip that phone back into evidence."

"Be nice, but it'd have the record of your call to Doc Grant. Open a new can of worms."

"Good point," I said.

Pat rose from the table, walking with a bit more bounce in his step, as if he saw some light in the tunnel. "Beer?" he asked. "I can use another."

"Sure. I'll call Zach in the morning. He has put his online classes and his life on hold until we solve this."

"You like Zach? Think he's a good guy?" Pat asked.

"I do. I trust him. But, there's always a chance he did the killing and made fools of us all."

"I doubt it. Not with all the seedy bastards involved."

"We still need to check black SUV rentals. It would be nice if we could put Kelly Swalheim at the base of Ibsen Ridge a couple days before the guts turn up."

"Long shot, but worth a try."

Pat came back with the beers. We clinked bottles and gave a silent toast, both careful not to step over the line we had been avoiding for several days.

"Hennie always seemed comfortable with us," I said after a couple meditative swallows of beer. "I'm surprised he didn't have friends or family."

"Lived ten miles from town on a tangle of back roads on top a hill. Had one neighbor. An old farmer. And Hennie gave him his pickup truck in the will. It was an isolated life. The way he liked it."

"How about Millie. She okay?"

"Nice woman. Artistic, I think. She was taking care of her aunt or grandmother till she died. Then had to find a job and a place to live. Now she's got both."

"So, were they dating?"

"According to her, they had coffee together at the station once in a while. I think she said he offered her his house while he was out of town. I don't remember the whole story."

"I'm tired, Pat. I'm going to bed."

"I may have another beer. Then I'm turning in."

"Hot dogs and coffee for breakfast."

"Works for me." He took a couple drinks of beer. "And, Shea, I'm sorry for dragging you into this. I think this'll be my last go-round. I cause more trouble than any good I do."

"It'll all look better when we wrap this up."

"Thanks, but I doubt it."

When I'd cleaned up and climbed into bed, I could still hear Pat pacing around downstairs.

**WE** met Zach at the diner for a quick breakfast. The plan was for me to ride in Zach's pickup to Lakeshore County, where we'd hopefully get access to the Swalheims' collection of home movies, which, for the record, we didn't know existed. We had, however, previously requested access to materials in a missing filing cabinet. A request Kelly and her lawyer refused to grant. Now with a second murder, this one located in Lakeshore County, we felt we had a better chance of gaining access to that material. Meanwhile, Pat planned to head to the Milwaukee area to try to make connections between the two murders, plus figure out the Kilimanjaro Society's role in the whole thing. He'd also check local car rental agencies to see if Kelly Swalheim rented a large black SUV in the time period her husband was killed. We were assembling a collection of loose straws, which was better than no straws at all.

As we waited to pay our tabs, a familiar-looking man approached me. "Detective Sommers, we meet again." He shyly extended his hand, ignoring the surprised glances from Pat and Zach. "Joe Flaherty."

"Right, the newspaper publisher. How are you doing?"

"Could be better. It would be nice if the sheriff's department would release details about the mysterious events out at Ibsen Ridge. I need a story."

"Unfortunately, we don't have many details. But I'll keep you in mind if something develops."

"You said that Halloween night when we had a beer at Murphy's. But you never called."

"Sorry, I had no information to release. But we're hoping."

"Maybe I can help. I'm a reporter. I've been digging around."

Flaherty fidgeted as he spoke. I wasn't sure if he was nervous talking to me or if that was just his personality. Pat and Zach paid the tabs and sauntered toward the door.

"And?"

"Maybe we can meet for that beer you owe me." He glanced up at Pat and Zach. "Looks like your friends want you to leave."

"We're heading to Milwaukee to try to expand the investigation. But when we get back, I'll stop by your office. Maybe we can help each other."

"I like that idea, Detective." He nodded and walked back to the table in the corner where he had been drinking coffee alone.

Outside, I got a roll of eyes from Pat, and even Zach flashed a curious smile.

"I'm not saying a word." Pat smirked.

"Yeah, well, unless we want to get into your recent starry-eyed meetings in bars, you better drop it. He's a possible source." With that I walked over to Zach's truck and climbed in.


MEETING with Detective Chase Norman of the Lakeshore County sheriff's department was even more dreadful than I expected. Admitting that I was working with Pat Donegal was going to be a black mark from the start, but the fact I was *volunteering* to work with him painted an even brighter target on my back. Pat was probably the best cop the department ever employed, yet he was held in low regard by his former colleagues.

Most police officers resent outside cops entering their domain. Competition far exceeds cooperation. Like a new dog moving into a neighborhood. First thing he does is piss on a fire hydrant. Every hound on the block feels like its rank in the pecking order is threatened. I expected this to happen when Zach and I walked into Norman's office. What I hadn't counted on was being treated like the new girl in middle school. I'd been a detective long enough to forget about the creeps always looking to impress the new "little lady." Detective Norman quickly reminded me.

After explaining why I was there and what we were looking for, Norman leaned back in his chair, smiled, made an awkward wink, and spoke in a low tone. "Well, Shea—I should say, Detective Sommers—maybe we can work something out here." He completely ignored the fact that Zach was sitting beside me. "What I'm thinking is maybe we could set up a joint task force and try to work together on both murders. Obviously, they're connected."

"Good idea," I said. "We're willing to share our information in exchange for any leads and evidence you may have that will help us."

"Great." He smiled as he spoke. "But there's no way Donegal can be a part of the task force because he's still a person of interest in our investigation. Not that I'd be excited about working with him anyway, though I feel bad about his losing his partner. But I think you and I could work well together. Pool our notes. I could find you a space here in my office, and in a few days, we'd probably have both cases wrapped up."

"Well"—I hesitated, trying to decide what would be best for the investigation—"there's also Deputy Layman here who's been assigned to work with me."

"I see." He spoke slowly, running his fingers through his brush cut hair. "What I'm thinking is, now that Donegal's partner has been tragically lost from the investigation, maybe it'd be best if Deputy Layman teamed up with Pat."

"Makes sense." I gritted my teeth as I forced out the words. "I'll run it past our sheriff, and if he agrees, I'll be back this afternoon to start working."

"I'll get you a chair and make a space for you to work. I assume you'll have your own laptop, otherwise, I can get a computer."

"Not necessary. So, like I said when I came in, the first thing we'd like is access to a filing cabinet that was moved from Swalheim's house in town."

"You sure such a cabinet exists?"

"It only makes sense. It had been recently moved from the house because we could see the tracks in the carpeting. The lodge seems like the likely location it was moved to."

"We'll look into that when you get back. I'll buy lunch if you're back before one thirty."

"No, I'll grab something."

"Then, Detective Sommers, I will look forward to working with you."

"Appreciate your willingness to cooperate, Detective Norman."

"Call me Chase. Now that we're a team, we can cut the formalities."

I think there was steam shooting out of my ears as Zach and I walked out of the municipal building. I suddenly felt grimy, like I just crawled through a barnyard. Zach tried to keep up as we walked to his truck. He didn't speak till we were driving out of the parking lot.

"Now what? You gonna call Sheriff Grimes?"

"No. You're going to drive to the nearest car rental lot, and I'm going to rent a cheap piece-of-shit car for a couple days. I refuse to be left working with that man without having a quick means of escape."

"Use my truck. I can tag along with Pat."

"Thanks, Zach, but you haven't worked with Pat. You may need a handy escape route of your own. I'll rent a car. All I want right now is the contents of that cabinet. Once I get that, I'll make an excuse to head back to Lake Hope. Once I get a car, you'll need to head to the Motel 6 where Pat stays. I'll also get a room there. They'll have plenty of vacancies, trust me. Just tell them to put it on Kickapoo County's tab."

"How many nights you think we'll be here?" he asked.

"One. I'm leaving tomorrow, evidence or no evidence.

# / 16 /

I USED TO WALK AROUND FEELING LIKE I HAD AT LEAST A MODEST AMOUNT of control over what direction my life took. But over the past few months I've realized that was a pipe dream. All the bizarre twists life had taken since Raven moved out of her own house to pursue a life totally devoid of my presence should have been fair warning that I should never expect anything to make sense again. I think philosophers have a word for this, but I don't remember it. I should have learned long ago that there was no logic in our lives. But I'm a slow learner—an old dog content to fetch tennis balls and bury rubber bones in the yard. I'm not too skillful when it comes to adapting to new ways. So, this case and everyone involved in it had totally screwed with my brains. Nothing was rational anymore.

After I left Shea and Zach, I called Clyda McCabe. Yes, I'd had a rather strange relationship with Clyda. She was a wealthy, successful lawyer, the type who would do anything to protect a client with deep pockets. And yes, Clyda and I had spent a night of unprofessional behavior in my motel room. And, yes, she'd offered me a job working for her firm. But now I knew it was time to put pressure on Kelly Swalheim. I knew she and her husband had teamed up to extort money from wealthy, powerful men. Kelly screwed these dumb bastards one way, and her husband screwed them another. Now, apparently Kelly had decided she didn't need her husband anymore. Why finance his gambling and big game hunting when she was doing all the dirty work? So, she killed him. Now the money was all hers; after all, she earned it. And, worst of all, Kelly had also used her sexual magic to destroy Hennie Duggan, a good man and one my few friends in this world.

It was time to confront Kelly and Clyda with what I knew about this lucrative scheme. Unfortunately, I couldn't let on I knew about the sex operation because I'd discovered the evidence by breaking into the Swalheims' hunting lodge—at the same time someone murdered Kelly's boyfriend, Harley Januss. My naïve ego told me I could confront Clyda and by some clever device I hadn't figured out yet could trick her into disclosing some deeply protected secret that would allow me to unravel the twisted web of this case and miraculously uncover needed evidence and even better, a full confession. As I mentioned before, my connection with reality was rapidly fading.

So, five minutes after arranging a meeting with Clyda, I get a frantic call from Shea, all distressed because Chase Norman was a pervert, and she was going to have to work with him in order to get the evidence we needed, and that Zach would be working with me the next couple of days. Zach seemed like a good guy, but he didn't exactly fit into my plans. But I begrudgingly agreed to take Zach under my wing while she worked the joint task force with Chase Norman. What could I say? She was sacrificing a lot to get evidence I needed. Evidence I asked her to get. So, I agreed to meet at the Motel 6.

"Jesus, Shea, I didn't mean to put you into this kind of pickle," I said when I saw her face to face.

"We need that evidence. And if I do my job right, I should have it by tomorrow. Then Zach and I are heading back to Lake Hope, and hopefully you'll be able to put together enough to get an arrest warrant for Kelly Swalheim. If we don't wrap this up in the next week, then you'll do it without me. Another week, and I'm done."

"I don't blame you. I feel bad about dragging you here, and I appreciate everything you're doing to resolve this mess. If we can't solve it in the next couple days, it's not going to happen. We know who did it, why she did, now we just have to figure out how she did it."

"Tell you what," Zach said. "I don't know what the hell I'm doing here. I'm not a cop. I'm just in the way. I'll head home tonight, and, Shea, you can call me when you get back if you want help out at the ridge."

"No," I said. "I want you here tonight when I meet with Clyda. I want an extra set of eyes. Plus, I need a witness to verify everything I say happened. I can't say as I trust this lawyer very much."

"If you think I can help," he said.

"Yup, this is your official undercover training. I want you to go ahead of me to the Wagon Wheel Bar. Try to get a stool at the end of the bar, close to the door. I'll find a booth within easy view. Just nurse a few beers and watch. When I leave, follow me."

"Listen, Zach," Shea said, "I've worked with him many times. His plans don't seem to make much sense, but they usually work. So, do what he says."

"I can sip beer at a bar with the best of them. And I get a free night in a fleabag motel. This cop work is great. I may give up nursing."

"All right." Shea jiggled the keys to her rental car. "Then I'll go spend a romantic afternoon with Prince Charming. And I'll pick up a twelve-pack, and you guys can join me when you get back. We'll drink beer and compare notes."

"I may become a cop even if I don't get paid. This sounds like fun." Zach shook his head as he spoke.

"Don't get your hopes up," Shea said. "We may be drowning our sorrows by the end of the night."

I spent the afternoon filling Zach in on the investigation. He listened, asked questions, and seemed excited about the chance to help us solve a case. I had to admit he seemed like a straight shooter, but people probably said the same thing about Jeffrey Dahmer and Charles Manson.

Earlier I had called Clyda. She agreed to meet me at the Wagon Wheel. I went through fifty plans in my head, trying to figure out a way to get Clyda to slip up and reveal some opening into Kelly's secret world. I hate to admit one scenario had me luring Clyda back to my hotel room for a replay of our romp in the sheets. From the little I can remember, the night we spent together was pleasant. But after all my screw-ups on this case, and knowing Shea was at the end of her rope with me, I knew I had to secure real evidence to help us close this case against Kelly Swalheim. As usual, since I couldn't come up with a plan, I decided to just wing it and trust my instincts. Some might say the definition of a fool is someone who refuses to learn from previous mistakes. That definition fits me to a tee.

Zach and I drove separately to the bar. He entered first, ordered a beer, and claimed a stool at the bar. I arrived ten minutes later and took a booth across the room. I was halfway through my first beer when Clyda walked in. She looked good, wearing tight-fitting black pants, black boots, and a silver blouse and black blazer. If I was having a problem figuring out a strategy to entice Clyda into my trap, she was way ahead of me. She was a tiger on the prowl, and I was the prey. I told myself to sip beer. Don't even think about a gin cocktail or I'd end up in the motel unraveling the pathetic details and evidence we'd collected so far. I was glad Zach was sitting at the bar serving as my guardian angel, pushing me through the maze between right and wrong. Scruples have never been the strength of my character.

"Clyda." I tried to sound suave. "Glad you could join me."

I stood up and ushered her into the booth.

"I'm happy you called. I thought I'd be sitting home eating a frozen pizza and watching Stephen Colbert."

"I already got a beer. What can I get you?"

"Vodka gimlet. And get yourself a gin and tonic—as I recall, light on the tonic and heavy on the gin."

"I'd love to, but I better stick with beer. I may be heading home tomorrow with my tail between my legs, so I better be on my best behavior. I'm afraid the sheriff of Kickapoo County is ready to pull the plug on this investigation. Label it a cold case. Why should the county spend money on a bodiless victim that isn't even a resident? Makes sense to drop the case, I guess."

"Don't try to fool me, Pat. We both know the famous Detective Donegal will never give up until the perpetrator is either in prison or in the ground." She flashed a sinister smile.

"Ooh, that is a low blow." I forced a dejected frown.

"Sorry. I didn't mean that the way it came out." She reached across the table and put her hand on my wrist and winked. "I thought you were going to buy me a drink."

I signaled the waitress. When she came to our booth, I ordered a vodka gimlet, light on the Rose's lime juice, and another IPA for myself. I drained the rest of my beer and excused myself to visit the lad's room. I had noticed Zach trying to get my attention, and I hoped he'd follow me to the restroom so I could explain to him the first rule of undercover surveillance—don't look like you're doing undercover surveillance! He played it cool and waited to follow me in.

No one else was in the bathroom, so I confronted Zach as soon as he came in. "Relax, man. It's obvious you're watching us. Just act cool. Talk to the bartender or the people around you. Act like you're having fun."

"I need to tell you something," he interrupted. "I've seen that woman before—at Ibsen Ridge."

"What the hell are you talking about?" I made a careful canvas of the toilet stalls to make sure no one was in the room.

"The first time I talked to Shea," he said in a low tone just above a whisper, "she told me to close my eyes and try to picture anyone I might have seen when I was hunting at the ridge. I thought she was crazy. But I did what she said, and out of nowhere, I remember seeing a woman parked there one day, maybe a week before I found the guts. She was wearing a ball cap and driving a big black SUV. I asked if she needed help, but she said something about her phone and waved me off. So I left. I didn't think anything of it till Shea cast her voodoo spell on me."

"And you think Clyda was the woman in the SUV?"

"Almost positive. I noticed something when she came in. I remember when I saw her at the ridge, her mouth seemed curled in a permanent frown, but when she told me she was fine, she forced the edges of her lips into a smile. She just did the same thing when she greeted you at your booth. Something flashed in my brain."

"Are you sure?"

"Well, not a hundred percent, but something clicked. I can picture that woman in a baseball cap sitting in a tall black SUV."

"Thanks for the heads-up. I better get back. Stay in here awhile before you come out. Then move to a table where she can't see you. Play a video game or something. If you recognized her, there's a good chance she'll recognize you too. Better yet, just go out and wait in your truck. Follow me when I leave. I may need you."

"Okay. I hope this helps."

I didn't respond. My guess was he was letting his imagination get the best of him. First undercover assignments can play tricks with the brain. I just hoped he hadn't blown the operation.

Back at my booth, I tried to act cool—something that was not inherent in my genetic makeup. Our drinks arrived, and Clyda clinked her glass against my beer mug. "To better times, when your investigation ends!"

"Cheers," I said. "That may be sooner than we both think—but probably not in a positive way."

"You still think my client is involved in her husband's death? You know, Pat, I'm pretty good at my job, and when I take a case two hundred miles from my office, I make sure to build connections in the area of the investigation. Well, my connection tells me something weird took place on Ibsen Ridge the other night. And you were in the middle of it. Apparently, Kelly Swalheim is not your primary suspect. Think about it, Pat, whatever just happened on Ibsen Ridge would raise so much reasonable doubt with a jury, you couldn't convict Ted Bundy. Besides, Kelly didn't do it."

"You might be right. Without a body or a witness, we don't have much to go on. I think my policing days are over."

"How's your head, by the way?"

"It's all right. Takes a lot more than a flying rock to make a dent in this old coconut."

Clyda forced a smile. I easily pictured what Zach was talking about. Then her expression turned somber. "My source told me about Deputy Duggan. Very sad. Was it an accident? Or was he pushed?"

"He probably just fell," I said. "The sheriff is investigating. I'd rather not talk about Hennie. I feel responsible. Another reason I think this might be my last case."

"Did you forget my offer? Set your own hours. I'll pay twice what you are making now. And best of all, you'll have me for a boss."

"Tempting offer, but I think it's time for me to throw away my phone, find a remote cabin in the woods, and fade into oblivion."

"Whoa, you are drowning in self-defeat."

"Or self-pity?"

"Well, I wasn't going to say that. No, Pat, you got a lot of good years of investigating left. You just need to work on the good side for a while."

"You mean finding ways to save criminals from going to jail?"

"Is that all you think I do? Did you ever hear of protecting the rights of the accused? Isn't that what our justice system is based on?"

"Not my justice system," I snapped. "My goal is to prosecute those who break the law."

"There are two sides to every story, Pat. But let's not talk it till this case is over." She paused and took a long drink of her gimlet. "So, why did you ask me to meet you? Certainly not to berate my occupation and begrudgingly congratulate me for convincing you my client is innocent."

"Maybe that's what I was planning. Or maybe I hoped you'd walk in here and tell me your client is willing to admit she killed her husband and is planning to fill in all the missing details of the case and top it off by showing us where to find the body."

"Are you sure you've only had one beer?"

"Maybe I just wanted to see you again before I threw in the towel, tucked my tail between my legs, and slinked off into the sunset."

"Man, that is some pickup line."

"I guess I'm just a bad loser."

"Come on." She stood up as she spoke. "Let's go for a ride. We'll take my car. I'll drive you out to my place. Show you a different side of town. Who knows? A look at the brighter side of life might improve your perspective."

"I got my truck here. I can follow you."

"We can get your truck later. Who knows? Maybe in the morning."

"Okay, I could use a fresh perspective."

I waited by the front door while Clyda used the restroom. I hadn't seen Zach since our summit over the urinal. I assumed he was discreetly waiting in his truck ready to follow us to Clyda's house.

ONE of my primary reasons for accepting Clyda's invitation was to see her car. If she drove a Cadillac Escalade, then I'd have to concede Zach was probably right. Could Clyda be the killer? Not likely, but it was possible she was involved in a cover-up. But if Zach had seen Clyda a week before he'd found the guts, then she had to have been involved in the planning and implementation of the crime. Or could Zach Layman be dragging another clever red herring across our path? Logically, he should still have been a person of interest. But he had so thoroughly won over Sheriff Grimes and Shea Sommers that he had now become part of the investigation. Could two good cops be completely taken in by a killer? Sure, he acted like a good guy, but I wasn't quite ready to rule him out as a suspect. On the other hand, could I be walking into a trap set by Clyda? If she was involved, why wouldn't she want to get me out of the picture? If I was off the case, or dead, Sheriff Grimes would end the investigation. A stranger's pile of intestines found in remote woods was not worth the lives of two officers. The case would remain open and cold for decades.

When Clyda returned from the restroom, she greeted me with that unusual expression Zach had just described, a frown suddenly curled on the edges to form an embarrassed, coy smile. How could he have made that up if he hadn't seen her before?

Clyda said her car was in a public lot about a block away. As we walked, she took my arm and curled her elbow around mine. We didn't speak. When we reached the parking lot, she clicked her key fob, and I was disappointed to see lights flash on a sporty silver Audi coupe—a far cry from a large black SUV. Maybe Clyda was right. I probably should forget this investigation and accept her offer. What had all my years of trying to catch bad guys gotten me? A lot of scars and broken bones, a couple bullet wounds, and a bad reputation? What did I owe to law enforcement—to anyone for that matter? Why not just enjoy the remaining years? Why not enjoy my night at Clyda's house?

"You're rather sullen, Pat." Clyda broke the silence as I climbed into the surprisingly roomy cockpit. "You didn't say if you liked my car."

"It's great," I mumbled. "I wouldn't have guessed I'd fit in here, but there's plenty of room."

"If you're a good boy, maybe I'll let you drive later. Six speed, zero to sixty in five seconds." Again that twisted smile.

"How do you define a good boy?"

"We can talk about that when we get to my house."

As she spoke, Clyda eased out onto the street, slipped into second gear, and laid twenty feet of rubber. "Whoops." She smiled. "Foot slipped off the clutch."

Why be a hero? Why not enjoy life a little?

# / **17** /

I WAS CRUISING TOWARD THE MOTEL 6 IN MY CUTE LITTLE KIA RENTAL,
celebrating my good fortune of getting my hands on the sex videos
we needed. Even though working with Detective Norman made me
feel clammy, like I'd been lying in a tub full of night crawlers, I had to
admit Norman had given us evidence that was probably our last good
chance of closing the case. I was feeling a little guilty about turning
down his high-pressured invitation for dinner.

I was almost back to the motel when my phone rang. It was Zach.

"Zach, where are you?" I asked.

"Lost."

"What happened?"

"I was supposed to wait in the parking lot to follow Pat and the
lawyer when they left the bar. They came out, jumped into her sports
car, and tore out onto the street like she thought she was Danica
Patrick. I tried to follow them, but there was no way I could weave
through traffic and keep up with her. After eight or nine blocks, they
were gone."

"Damn him. That's it. I'm busting my ass working with some jerk
who thinks I want to spend the night in his apartment, and Pat's out
trying to get laid by the attorney for the suspect. Son of a bitch"

"Sorry. I tried."

"It's not your fault. It's him. He's had a screw loose since Raven Quinn dumped him. Amend that. He always did have a screw loose, but now he's worthless to work with."

"I should've stayed with them."

"Why? So you could sit out on the street all night while Pat gets his rocks off? Not your fault."

"I guess I'm not much of a cop."

"Can you find your way back to our motel? I'm almost there. Meet at my room. We'll figure out what to do next."

"I'll meet you there. And there's something I need to tell you about the attorney."

"Oh great, more good news. I'll see you in a few minutes." I don't know why I was so short with Zach. He hadn't done anything wrong. But that goddamned Pat—I was done putting up with his crap.

When I got to the motel, Zach was waiting. He seemed nervous or embarrassed, not making eye contact and fidgeting with his keys. Probably because he lost Pat when he was supposed to be following him and perhaps because he was going into a motel room with the "strange" woman. We went to my room, and I immediately opened my cooler and grabbed two bottles of beer. I definitely needed one, and I figured Zach could use one too. Zach waved off the offer but took my bottle and snapped off the cap on the opener on the side of the cooler.

"So, what happened? You just watched him and Clyda, like he told you to?"

"Yeah, at first, but then I realized something and tried to get his attention without her noticing. He went into the toilet and I followed him. I told him I'd seen Clyda before—out at the ridge."

"What?"

"When we talked the first time, you told me to close my eyes and try to remember seeing anybody in the area when I was hunting. I told you about the woman in the black SUV."

"That was McCabe?"

"As soon as she walked into the bar, I noticed a facial gesture that reminded me of the woman at the ridge. I'd wager money it was the same woman."

"What'd Pat say?"

"Told me to go outside and wait. In case she might recognize me. Then he said I should follow him when he left."

"What the hell's he up to now?"

"I just did what he said. Except I couldn't keep up with her. That woman drives like a maniac."

"Maybe she knew you were tailing them, or more likely she was showing off for Pat. She apparently really has a thing for him. Either that or she's just crossing the line and playing him to keep her client out of jail."

Zach waited for me to tell him what to do next. The problem was I didn't know what to do. If Pat actually had some logical strategy, then he was on his own. I could try calling him, but he was with Clyda. What could he say? I considered another beer but thought better of it.

"How did they act when they left?"

Zach hesitated before answering. "Well, they walked arm and arm to her car."

"Oh, shit, now what do we do?"

"Maybe he'll call us."

"Not likely. Any idea where they'd go?"

"How would I know?" He shrugged his shoulders.

"Well, we better find out where she lives and head there."

I grabbed my laptop and started searching. Not a common name, so I doubted there'd be more than one in the Milwaukee area. It didn't take long to find two addresses for Clyda McCabe. One was an apartment building in Brookfield. The other was listed on Lake Liwaksha Road in Waukesha County. From what'd I'd heard about Clyda, the lake home seemed fitting.

"We'll take your truck, Zach. You drive, I'll navigate."

"My driving performance hasn't been too good so far."

"You just need me telling you where to go."

Using the GPS on my phone, we found directions by the time we were out of the parking lot and heading away from Milwaukee. According to our robotic guide, our arrival time was twenty-two minutes. Traffic was fairly heavy, but Zach maneuvered the crowded streets like a veteran cop. We arrived at the address in less than twenty minutes. The house was located in a wealthy neighborhood of three-story mansions on half-acre lots with perfectly manicured yards and gardens. I told Zach to drive past the house listed for Clyda so that we could develop a plan. Her house was situated on the side of the road away from the lake, which meant we could not gain access via water, but it also meant there was no escape by boat.

That was assuming Clyda had a reason to try to escape. Her only connection to the murder thus far was that she represented Kelly Swalheim, our primary suspect. But if Zach was right about having seen her at the ridge prior to the discovery of the gut pile, then it was probable her involvement was more than secondhand. Could she have been an accomplice in the murder? Or could Zach be imagining seeing her at Ibsen Ridge? And finally, and I hated to have to consider this, but could Zach be telling us this to mislead us? I liked Zach a lot, but technically he was still a suspect. He had messed up his assignment from Pat. On purpose, maybe? Plus, he found the pile of intestines.

"See that house with the lights off?" I asked. "Pull up there till we decide what to do."

"Lots of lights on in Clyda's house, so they're probably in there," he said.

"No car in the driveway, but she would have parked in the garage if she planned to stay for the night."

Zach gave me a curious look but didn't say anything.

"I warned you Pat does things his own way."

Zach shook his head and smiled. No comment necessary.

"There are windows on the side of the garage, but the neighborhood is lit up like a damn shopping mall."

"In my bag in the back, I got camouflage clothing and face paint that will blend with the snow." He paused and flashed an embarrassed grin. "Hey, I'm a hunter."

"So, you're thinking about sneaking up to the house and looking in the windows?"

"The house next to Clyda's is dark. We drive to somewhere remote so I can change. Then you drive back, and I'll slip out of the truck and do some reconnaissance from the backyard. Trust me, I've been trained. Plus, I practice in the woods. Nobody will spot me."

"Are you armed?"

"I got my .45 from Afghanistan."

"You're an official deputy now. I'm sure Sheriff Grimes registered your weapon with the department."

"He did."

Zach drove to a nearby boat landing with an empty parking lot. He went behind the truck and changed into his hunting gear. I moved over to the driver's seat. As I waited in the cab, I asked myself what the hell I had gotten into. Eighty miles from my jurisdiction, working with one untrained rookie deputy, who was also a person of interest in the case, and one crotchety retired detective, who I sometimes considered a possible menace to society. I decided I had to start making better life decisions.

I parked again at the same dark house. We waited till we were sure no one was outside walking their dog or catching a late-night smoke. Then Zach quietly slid out the door and moved quickly across the dark lawn. I worked on my story in case someone called the police. Fortunately, Zach's truck had an insignia on the door for his handyman business. So the vehicle wouldn't seem totally out of place in a neighborhood where residents were constantly remodeling and updating. I leaned my head back against the seat and hoped for the best.

Ten minutes later I had a text. It was Zach. "They're inside. Drinking."

I responded, "Be careful."

I envied Zach's cleverness for coming equipped to jump into action. I wondered if maybe I was wrong about Pat. Maybe he was playing Clyda the same way she thought she was playing him. I cynically thought to myself that they deserved each other. Probably a perfect match.

I decided to text Pat, telling him we had the sex files. If he was applying pressure to push our case forward, it would be helpful to be able to tell her we knew about the sex-and-extortion scheme. That was motive. They had obviously tried to hide the evidence when they dragged the filing cabinet out of the house and stored it at the lodge.

A new text from Zach: "P checked phone, now seem to be arguing."

My guess was he just hit her with the news about the sex recordings. Now what? He has no car. Will she drive him back?

From Zach: "P grabbed coat. C yelling." I watched the front door, nothing. "C talking, pointing finger, P listening."

"Get back to the truck," I wrote, "in case he makes quick exit."

I started the engine. The front door opened and Pat came out followed by Clyda, who was still talking, slightly animated, but apparently quite serious. Pat walked to the curb and looked up and down the street. Naturally, he assumed Zach had followed them. He spotted the truck and marched toward it, not fast but clearly determined. I leaned over to throw open the passenger door. Zach had switched the dome light off in the truck, so the cab was dark when Pat climbed in.

"Shea?" His voice sounded high-pitched, surprised. "What the hell?"

"Don't ask. Gotta wait for Zach." As I spoke there was a sudden thump and the truck rocked. I looked through the rear window and saw Zach on the truck bed waving for me to leave. I popped the clutch and tore off down Liwaksha Road.

# / 18 /

"THANKS FOR THE TEXT, AND FOR GETTING THE THUMB DRIVES. THAT really stirred things up in there," I said.

"Tell me when we get back to the highway." Shea was intent on driving.

"She won't follow us. But I know she had something to do with Swalheim's death."

"More than just covering for her client?"

"There is a black Lincoln Navigator in the garage. Looks just like an Escalade."

"So, Zach was right?"

"I'd say yes," I responded. "Hey, shouldn't we ask if he wants to ride up in the cab? It's his truck."

"Think three of us will fit in here?"

"If we squeeze."

"I don't feel like squeezing. Besides, he's dressed for battle, and he's tough."

The rest of the ride back to the hotel was quiet. I asked a few questions and Shea threw back one-word answers. I decided I was better off sitting back and enjoying the scenery.

When we got to the parking lot, Zach hopped down from the truck bed. He didn't speak, but his face clearly showed he was thinking, *What the hell? I got to ride the back end of my own truck?*

Shea didn't speak. She tossed him the keys and headed toward her hotel room. Zach followed her, so I followed Zach. When she entered the room, she didn't ask us in, but she also didn't slam the door in our faces. Zach walked in and I followed.

"I'm gonna have a beer. Help yourself." Shea spoke without looking at either of us.

"I could use some whiskey to warm up," Zach mumbled. "But I'll sit by the radiator and have a beer."

"Me too, if you got one to spare," I said cautiously.

Shea opened the cooler and pulled out three beers. Zach reclaimed his job as opener. Once we had a few swigs, I spoke first. "Good work with the videos. How'd you convince—"

Shea cut me off halfway through my sentence. "I acted cute and flirted with a disgusting detective aptly named Chase. I don't like to act cute, and I certainly don't like flirting with disgusting men. But I got your evidence."

"I appreciate that. I won't ask you for anything else. You've done more than your share."

"That's good. Because tomorrow Zach and I are heading back to Lake Hope. I'll tell the sheriff what I found out. Then I'm heading to Madison. Zach can decide for himself what he does next."

"Fair enough. I feel like I have things going in the right direction. Clyda might be ready to cooperate. When I mentioned the witness seeing her near Ibsen Ridge a week before it was a crime scene, she got nervous. Then when I hit her with the sex-and-blackmail evidence, she got downright belligerent. I'm sure she's talking to her client right now." I paused for a drink. "It's easy to defend a killer but being accused of being party to the crime is a whole new game. I don't think she liked that."

The room was quiet for a couple minutes. Zach had warmed up enough to take off his fur-lined hat and unzip his camouflage snowsuit. Shea grabbed another beer for herself and left the cooler lid open, which I assumed meant she was offering us a refill. This time she opened her own bottle. Zach didn't respond to the offer, so I flipped the lid closed.

"I'll take Shea back tomorrow and stop and see my family for a while, but then I'll head back here. I was in this business from the start, so I'd just as soon see how it ends."

"I appreciate that, Zach, but don't feel pressured to come back. You've done good work already." I changed my mind, opened the cooler, and helped myself to another beer. I held one up toward Zach and he nodded acceptance. "Besides, I may be heading back to Lake Hope tomorrow or the next day, depending on how things work out with Clyda and her client."

"Give me a call when you want me to come back. Otherwise, I'll wait at home till you return."

"We got a plan." I paused to see if Shea wanted to join the conversation, then continued. "There is one thing that confuses me. How the hell did you follow Clyda through all that traffic and end up with Shea sitting in the driver's seat? She was damn near an hour away."

"Military secret." Zach smiled. "Classified."

By this time, Shea was totally bored with the talk and had started searching for something on her phone. Without looking up, she said, "I told Clancy Lone Owl I'd meet him at the ridge on Tuesday. No phone or email. I got to figure out a way to cancel my date."

"Think he showed Clyda around the ridge?"

"First, I assumed he guided the doctor who cracked your noggin, but then I thought maybe it was Kelly Swalheim he showed around. Maybe it was Clyda."

"What if the victim's wife killed her husband and then got her lawyer to find a remote place to dump the intestines?" I was surprised that Zach had entered the speculation. Maybe he would make a good cop.

"Good theory," I said. "But why Ibsen Ridge? And why plant evidence in a place so remote nobody'd ever find them?"

"But I did find them."

"You had medical training. Ninety-nine percent of hunters

would've walked right by that gut pile and left them for the wild pigs."

"Maybe she planted them for the doctor to find," Zach said.

Shea looked up at me from her phone. "Remember, Simon Grant told me another woman called him before I did? Maybe Grant had nothing to do with the murder."

"But that'd mean Kelly knew about the Kilimanjaro hunting club and about the throwaway phones," I said.

"Or Clyda did." Shea set down her phone and leaned forward. "Maybe Clyda or Kelly set up the doctor to take the fall. That's why the victim was perfectly dissected. But then the doc didn't show up for the hunt because he was giving a speech in Sweden or something."

"How could they know he was a doctor?" I asked. "It was all done by code names."

"Who knows?" Shea yawned, finished her beer, and stood up. "You boys can continue this meeting, but you're going to have to find a different room. I'm beat. I'm going to sleep."

Zach and I stood in unison and finished our beers. Then like tin soldiers we turned and headed toward the door. Shea ignored us and headed toward the bathroom.

Before I exited, I turned back to Shea. "How early you plan to leave? Maybe we could get coffee and eggs. My treat. I expect Clyda to call early, hopefully, to discuss some kind of deal."

"If you're ready at six thirty, I'll do breakfast. That work for you, Zach? You're the driver."

"Sure, that works. I'd like to be on the road by seven thirty. We're supposed to get five or six inches of snow starting midmorning. I'd just as soon beat that."

"Great. I'll get to drive from Lake Hope to Madison in a blizzard."

"You can always spend the night at the Bates Motel if the roads get bad. I'm sure they'll welcome you back." I wasn't sure shady hotel humor would impress Shea, but I tried.

"Rather get stranded in a ditch."

"Sleep on our couch. My wife said she'd like to meet you."

"I may take you up on that."

"No one's at Raven's. Sleep there."

"Or I might do that. But I hope I can drive home."

"Let's meet in the parking lot and walk to the diner," I said.

Zach said he was ready to crash too, unless I wanted to work more on the case. I told him a night's sleep would do us all some good— though I had no intention of sleeping when I got back to my room. A lot had happened during the previous few hours. I needed time alone to try to unravel the tangled clump of fishing line that was our investigation.

I knew Shea was at the end of her wits with the case and with me. I didn't want to get her more involved, so I decided not to tell her any details about my conversation with Clyda. This was something I'd gotten snarled up in, and it was going to be something I needed to find a way out of. Based on what I had recently learned, I was sure Clyda was ass-deep in this mess. She was at least involved with the cover-up, but she may well have been abetting Kelly Swalheim from the get-go.

Before I left Clyda's house, she'd basically challenged me to a hunting contest. This started earlier at the bar when she asked if I was a hunter. I told her I never got into it. My old man didn't hunt and neither did my friends. Hunting is usually something you start as a kid or you never start at all. The conversation started innocently enough. But she kept pushing it.

"You hunt humans, don't you?"

"That's my job. It's not a sport," I replied.

"But cops must get a rush of adrenaline when they're chasing some vicious killer or kidnapper." She paused and flashed that strained smile. "I've read a lot about you. You've survived some harrowing cases. Hunting down a man who's armed with a rifle has to be more dangerous than stalking a lion or bear. I bet you've put a few trophies on your mantel."

"Like I said, I never did it for sport. No trophies."

"I don't believe you. You're too humble. Once you've put your life on the line in quest of prey, then you've known total exhilaration. Better than sex, some people say."

"Talking from experience?"

"Plenty of experience, Pat. More than you'd want to hear about."

"I'm hard to shock. Tell me about your adventures, Clyda."

"That will take a while. Maybe we should go to my place." That's when she talked me into leaving with her.

When we got to her house and pulled into her garage, I saw the black SUV Zach had mentioned. Now I knew I was up for a challenging evening. Her first move was to mix me a stiff gin and tonic. Her plan was to get me drunk and get me into the sack. This event would likely be recorded in Technicolor and high definition. I'd be set up exactly the way Hennie had. Of course, Clyda didn't know Hennie's video would never be entered in evidence. I'd taken care of that. I sipped cautiously at my drink. Who knew what drug it was laced with? I had to find an escape plan. Was Zach outside waiting for me?

Clyda grew more talkative as she drank her gimlet. She didn't seem to mind that I was nursing my drink. Maybe she forgot to notice. I think the hunting talk had gotten her juices flowing. She was ready to talk. Maybe she thought I was never leaving her house—for one reason or another. Maybe she could seduce me into staying for the pleasure of her company. If that didn't work, maybe she foresaw me as a new trophy above her fireplace. After our first drink, I took over the task of tending bar. Maybe she didn't care if she got me drunk. I actually think she was more consumed with her own hedonism than with loading me with gin. Whatever the reason, it worked for me.

"Would you believe, Pat, that I was born on a hog farm in Iowa?"

"If you tell me you were, I'll believe you."

"A hog farm. Me, a woman of intellect, grace, and culture. Who would believe it?"

"What's so bad about a hog farm?"

"The constant smell of pig shit and pig blood. That's what wrong. And living with an old man who is cruder than the hogs." She took a slow drink. "Yes, my old man!"

"We don't have to talk about this. You were going to tell me about your hunting adventures."

"We'll get to that," she said, holding up her glass and wiggling it back and forth. No doubt what that meant. I watered down this drink. I was afraid she'd pass out before she told me what I needed to know. When I returned with her drink and sat down across from her, sipping my straight tonic, she continued to speak, but now with an obvious slur in her enunciation.

"My dad wanted sons to carry on the business. But he got stuck with two daughters. Blamed my mother and blamed my sister and me. I was fifteen when my mother died. My sister was seventeen. I have no doubt the ol' bastard murdered her, though the official cause of death was accidental electrocution caused by a radio falling into the bathtub while the victim was bathing. Who knows? Maybe it was suicide. Who could blame her? My sister and I weren't home. A rare occasion when he actually let us go to a school dance. Coincidence, huh?"

"Why are you telling me this? You were in a good mood when we were at the Wagon Wheel."

"Because you want to know why I like to hunt. It's because every time I shoot an animal, I'm really shooting my *father*—what a joke he was. He was no father. He was a tyrant. Made my sister and me clean stalls, ankle-deep in hog shit. Made us help him butcher. And if we wasted even a morsel of meat, we'd be forced to sit on a pile of shit for an hour. We learned to carve very carefully. I hated him. Then he started on my sister. Goddamn pervert! I knew what he was doing, but she wouldn't say anything. She wanted to protect me. Son of a bitch died accidently right before my sister turned eighteen. There was no real investigation because everybody in the county detested the bastard. Sheriff figured good riddance."

"I won't ask about his accident." I spoke cautiously, not wanting to break her talkative mood.

"He passed out in a silo. Died from the nitrogen dioxide fumes. It happens on farms."

"Then it was an accident."

"On paper." She tested her gimlet. "Little light on the Grey Goose, Pat."

"Sorry, I can add a little."

"That would be sweet of you," she cooed as she handed me the glass.

It was while I was adding vodka that I got the text from Shea. Clyda never noticed me reading it, but I didn't take the chance of responding. Now we legally had the evidence we needed to confront Kelly Swalheim with a motive for killing her husband. She killed him because she was tired of being pimped out to powerful, wealthy men so that he could finance his expensive hobbies and affairs. Was this the right time to throw this at Clyda? She was drunk and angry about her mistreatment by her old man. Maybe this was the perfect storm.

"Did I tell you about the break in our murder investigation?" I asked.

"I thought that case was over. You said you were running home with your dick between your legs."

"That may have not been completely accurate. We do have new leads."

"Why are you saying that now? We're talking about hunting."

"Sorry.

"Sorry, shit. You've been trying to dupe me. Get the little lady drunk and let her talk. Is that your plan, Pat? Cause that's shit, man. You've got crap for a case."

"Sorry, let's change the subject." I took a long, slow drink of my phony cocktail. "Let me catch up to you. Then we'll get back to having fun."

"Fuck you, Pat. I'm not some dumb bitch you can con into spewing secrets just because I had a few drinks. I'm one of the best-paid attorneys in Milwaukee. I made over a million dollars last year. Who do you think you're talking to?"

"Hey, I said too much. I shouldn't be talking about a case after so many drinks. Maybe I should just leave."

"Are you gonna walk back to the city? Cause I'm sure to hell not taking you to your motel."

"I'll call a cab."

"Not too many taxis out here in the burbs." She drained her gimlet. "And don't even think about sleeping here."

"I'll call somebody. I'll start walking to sober up a little in the cool air."

"Good riddance. I was trying to treat you right, and you pull this shit. Tell me you got this great new evidence, then say you're gonna walk home. That's crap."

"I said I was sorry." I stood up, put my glass in the sink, and picked up my coat.

"Oh, no, not till you tell me about this new evidence."

"Let's talk tomorrow when we've had a chance to sleep it off."

Clyda stood and pointed her finger in my face. "No fucking deal, Pat. I want to hear what you came to tell me. I knew you didn't call just because you wanted to play bury the bologna. Tell me. Then you can walk wherever the hell you want. Walk into Lake Michigan for all I care. But tell me now."

"Sex videos," I blurted out. "And blackmail."

"Bullshit."

"Couple dozen flash drives, featuring Kelly and a cast of thousands. Maybe you didn't know."

She came closer. I thought she was going to hit me. Then she pointed to the door. "Get out of my house. And don't think those recordings are going to ever get into court."

I put on my coat and headed toward the door. Clyda followed.

I allowed a pregnant pause before hitting Clyda with the real bombshell. "Oh, and one more thing. We got a witness says he saw you out at Ibsen Ridge a couple days before the guts were discovered."

"That is shit, Pat, and you know it."

"Source seems reliable."

Clyda stood there fuming, trying to digest what I'd just told her. I opened the door and stepped out. She followed.

"Here's my idea." She sounded almost sober all of a sudden. "You and me settle this case out of court. I like to hunt, and you like to catch bad guys. Let's meet up at Ibsen Ridge, and you and me have a little contest. Winner take all. I win, you drop the investigation. You win, I spill my guts—provide full confessions of all involved."

"Not sure how that'd work."

"We discuss the rules tomorrow when we've both had time to get our heads on straight."

"We'll talk about it. But now, I'm leaving."

"You really gonna walk home?"

"I don't have to. I had a deputy follow us here. He's waiting outside."

"Bullshit."

As I walked through the door, I hoped like hell that Zach really did follow us and was waiting for me. Then I saw the pickup truck.

NEXT morning at breakfast, Shea was still quiet. Zach made conversation about the upcoming Packers game against the Bears, just trying to get through the meal. I decided not to tell anybody about this hypothetical contest proposed by Clyda. Chances are she'd have forgotten the whole conversation by the next time we talked. However, during the long hours of fighting my pillow and struggling to sleep while rehashing the scene with Clyda, I settled on the conclusion that Clyda was serious. She was proposing a mano-a-mano showdown. And she wasn't thinking about hand-to-hand combat. She was a hunter and she'd be armed to the gills. Meeting her would be insane, but, hell, when had that ever bothered me? At that point, I'm not sure I cared if I lost.

After forty-five minutes of awkward conversation and dry scrambled eggs, Shea looked at Zach and said, "Are you ready to hit the road?"

"Whenever you are," he responded, finishing the dregs of his third cup of coffee.

I decided to keep this farewell simple—no handshakes, no clever parting words, and certainly no attempts at hugs. Shea was ready to end our work as an investigative team, and I didn't blame her. She was young and had a good career in Madison. She didn't need a has-been old fool complicating her life. And I knew once this case ended—however that should work out—that this would be my last rodeo. So, when Shea and Zach stood to leave, I remained seated. I thanked Shea again for all the help and told Zach to stay in Lake Hope till he heard from me. I think everyone was pleased with the lack of ceremony. They drove off for Lake Hope, and I wandered back to my hotel.

I was going through notes when my phone signaled an incoming text. I figured it'd be Clyda, but I was wrong. Sheriff Phil Grimes wrote: "Need to talk about the case and what to do about Hennie. Call me."

Instead of calling Grimes, I texted: "Be in Lake Hope this p.m. Will give update." I preferred to discuss my possible developments face-to-face rather than over the phone.

BY the time I reached Lake Hope, the roads were covered with snow. I wondered about Shea. Would she head for Madison through a blizzard? She mentioned staying at Zach's, but I offered her Raven's house without thinking I might be staying there. I didn't want to put Shea in the uncomfortable position of spending a night in a house with me. Our situation was too strained for that. Best if she stayed with Zach and his family.

My first stop was the sheriff's department. Phil Grimes was doing paperwork at his desk when I got there. He saw me enter and quickly ushered me into his office.

"Goddamn hornet's nest you got yourself into here, Pat. We may be smart to just dump the case in Lakeshore County's lap. It seems like most of the players come from there. Or we can just call it a cold case and let the state worry about it."

"There are fresh leads we uncovered. I'm sure Swalheim's wife is in the center of it. And it appears that her lawyer is involved—at least in trying to cover things up."

"The Januss killing's connected?"

"Makes sense. He was having a fling with Kelly Swalheim, and he was killed on her property. But that one is Lakeshore County's problem to solve."

"Have you got evidence to back your theories?"

"We got some, and I'm waiting on a call from Clyda McCabe that may open the door for more details. That could happen any minute."

"Shea and Zach still helping?"

"Hell, yes. They've done a lot—though I think Shea's had enough. I don't blame her. She's got a full-time job to worry about."

"I know she's been frustrated. She blames herself for Hennie."

"I tried to convince her that isn't true. But I think it's time she goes home. Me and Zach'll keep plugging away."

"Let me know when you need me. I'd do damn near anything to get away from this desk and telephone for a day or two."

"You can count on a call as soon as I hear anything."

"Are you holding up all right, Pat? It's been a tough grind, especially losing Hennie like we did. Not to mention that head injury."

"I'm good. How you going to handle Hennie's death?"

"Officially, he died in the line of duty while trying to help apprehend a murder suspect. We're calling it an accident. No other way to say it."

"Good. That's as it should be. Hennie deserves the benefit of the doubt."

"He'll get full hero's honors. I'd like to do a ceremony as soon as we close this thing down. I want you and Shea to be part of it."

"I'll be there, and if I know Shea, she will too. We both thought a lot of Hennie."

"I'm glad you feel that way. Now, what's next?"

"Like I said, I'm expecting a call any minute. If things work the way I hope they will, I got a feeling closure won't be far off."

"Good." Phil's voice was firm. "Oh, one other thing, and I don't think this will make your day any more pleasant. Our county prosecutor has decided not to charge Simon Grant with anything. His lawyer claims our department entrapped Grant and caused serious physical and mental injury without any evidence that he was involved in a crime. Lawyer claims Grant was out of the country when Swalheim was killed. I still lobbied for a charge for assaulting an officer—namely you, but their argument is that Dr. Grant was acting in self-defense. He did not know you were a police officer. Well, bottom line, the county was afraid of a lawsuit, so both sides agreed to say no harm no foul."

"Tell my head there was no foul."

"It's a shit deal, but it's done."

"To be honest, we did royally screw up that mission. Good idea, but it backfired."

"We're all just doing the best we can, Pat."

"Yup."

"Keep me in the loop." Grimes spoke as I turned to leave. "And, Pat, thanks for sticking with us. Our department isn't big enough to handle a case like this—especially without Hennie. It means a lot to have you working with us."

"I'm not too sure I don't cause more problems than I solve, but thanks for the vote of confidence. May be the last one I'll ever get."

"I know it's been tough on all of you, but hang in there."

"Got to hang somewhere, I guess," I mumbled as I left his office. The snow was tapering off as I walked to my truck.

Next, I drove out to Raven's house. Figured if Shea's car wasn't there, I'd stop, make something to eat, and clean up a little. I hadn't showered in two days and was feeling gamy—probably smelled it too.

I was disappointed to see Shea's car in Raven's driveway. It wasn't long ago that sight would have been a real bonus, but things change. So I didn't even slow down. Headed to the next farm up the road, turned around in the driveway, and headed back to town. I decided I would be nesting at the Bates Motel for at least one night.

I ate a turkey sandwich and bowl of soup at the diner. Doodled in my notebook trying to diagram some kind of strategy to deal with Clyda. I considered driving out to Hennie's just to see the place again, but with the new snow I wasn't too eager to attack those back roads. Instead, I broke down and headed to the motel to rent a room. As usual, I was the only customer. I carried my gear inside, turned on the television, and immediately fell asleep.

I must've slept a couple hours when I heard my phone signal an incoming text. I jumped up and grabbed the phone. It was from Clyda: "Noon Tuesday, bluff where guts found, come alone!" That was it. So, I was being called out for an old-fashion duel at high noon. It made me feel like Gary Cooper. It would've been funny if I had someone to laugh with, but I was alone and there was a good chance I was going to die alone at noon on Tuesday. I had less than twenty-four hours to come up with a plan. It was probably a good idea to rent the room one night at a time.

My first problem was figuring out how I was going to get to the top of Ibsen Ridge. With my health limitations, not to mention the snow, climbing to the top of the ridge was out of the question. When we went to the top before, I used an ATV provided by the sheriff's department. Now that there was four inches of snow, I wasn't too sure how well that vehicle would climb those steep, narrow trails. Besides, in order to get the ATV, I'd have to go through the sheriff's office. That would mean involving other officers, which I didn't want to do. This was a solo gig. Clyda said to come alone, and I planned to do just that—not because I wanted to make Clyda happy but because this was my mess and I didn't want anyone else getting hurt or killed. The last time I told somebody to go on a goose chase on Ibsen Ridge, it caused a good man to end his life. I didn't want the same happening to Shea or Zach or Phil. I would leave a note in my motel room letting people know who I was meeting and why I was doing it. In case I didn't make it off the bluff, the sheriff would know who to look for.

It was a stupid idea to meet Clyda alone, but what's new? Once I found a way to climb the bluff, I was going to have to gather the clothing and equipment I'd need to survive. I had good boots and camouflage coveralls. I'd take my 12-gauge shotgun and a couple of handguns, which work well in a close-range shootout. But if Clyda managed to get me in a sniper battle, my weapons would be essentially useless. Fortunately, the thick cover, especially the evergreen trees, would limit the efficiency of a long-range showdown. Maybe I was misreading the situation. Maybe Clyda just wanted to talk. No, that was a crazy theory. No one drives three or four hours and climbs a thousand feet up a treacherous snowy bluff just to talk. No, this was war I was preparing for, and somehow I needed to come up with a plan where I could survive without involving anyone else. As I said, I've had bad ideas before and somehow managed live through them. Maybe I could do it again. Or else, tomorrow would be recorded in history as Donegal's Last Stand.

# / 19 /

I SLEPT MOST OF THE WAY FROM MILWAUKEE TO LAKE HOPE—GOOD WAY TO
avoid conversation. I felt like a coward running back to Madison in
the middle of a case, but I was sick of the whole business. I'd lost confidence in Pat, and I'd lost confidence in myself. That is not a good
formula for success when stalking a killer.

I thought about asking Zach to drop me off in Madison on our way
past, but that would leave me without a car, since mine was parked at
the sheriff's office in Lake Hope. By the time we got back to town, the
roads were dicey, so I decided to stay the night. Zach again offered me
a bed at his place, but his family's life had been thrown enough cur-
veballs since he started working as a deputy. They didn't need a tired,
grouchy stranger moving in for the night. I should have stayed at the
local motel, but the place was dreadful, so I opted for Raven's house.
I knew there was a chance Pat would show up to sleep there too, but
I decided we could coexist for one more night even if we were not
on good terms. I understood I was probably being unfair blaming
Pat for everything that happened. It was my idea to lure the doctor
to the ridge. And even though it appeared that Hennie chose to end
his life, the fact remained that he would not have been on Ibsen Ridge
that night if it hadn't been for my goofy scheme. And now it was clear
Simon Grant had nothing to do with killing Swalheim.

Midafternoon, I got a phone call from Grimes. He told me Pat was in town. They had talked earlier in Phil's office. He wasn't sure what Pat had planned, but he called a while later saying he needed to borrow the county's ATV tomorrow. He said he just wanted to get away from things for a few hours. He needed to blow off some steam.

"Do you know what he's up to, Shea?"

"We have not been communicating too well lately."

"It's been stressful on all of us."

"But I can assure you Pat is not taking a joyride tomorrow. He has something planned."

"Any clue?"

"None," I said.

"My guess is Ibsen Ridge."

"I don't know why, but where else would he need an ATV?" I asked.

"He told me he was waiting for word from Kelly Swalheim's lawyer."

"Clyda McCabe. I don't know what the hell's going on between those two."

"Whatever it is, I think Pat wants to do it alone," Grimes said.

"I don't blame him. I mucked up our last trip to Ibsen Ridge."

"That's not it. He just doesn't want to see anyone else hurt. He's stubborn."

"He was a lone wolf most of his life from what I heard. It seemed to work." My voice trailed off as I spoke.

"Are you heading to Madison when the roads clear up?"

"That's the plan. I'm just running in circles here."

"We appreciate all you've done for us. And remember you were on the clock here, so you'll be getting a check in the mail."

"Not sure I did anything to earn it."

"You did plenty. Thanks."

"I feel bad leaving you before the job's done, but . . ."

"Don't worry about it. Like you said, Pat may work better alone. And we got Zach. I will probably call him and the two of us will try to keep an eye on Pat without getting in his way."

"Probably smart. But don't let him see you."

"Oh, I know how to lay low."

"Zach is good. He did nice work when we staked out the lawyer's place. He has good instincts, and all that military training."

"I'd like to keep him on the team."

"One more thing, Phil. I made arrangements to meet a guy named Clancy Lone Owl."

"I've heard of him."

"He does some guiding for hunters. I figured he might have guided whoever was out there to meet the murder victim. So, I told him I was a writer and wanted to learn about Ibsen Ridge for a novel I was working on."

"Interesting idea."

"The thing is, I'm supposed to meet him at a tavern out by the bluff in the morning. And he doesn't use a phone or email, so I can't get hold of him to cancel."

"Zach and I can meet him. He might have some info that'll help."

"I promised him 450 bucks. You can deduct that from my pay."

"It will be worth it to the county if he has anything to tell or show us. I'll take care of it."

"Thanks, and good luck."

"You too. And take a day to recoup before getting back in the harness."

"I will do that."

So now I was clear to get back to my life. Catching drug dealers and car thieves should be a picnic after the crap that was going on here. Still, I felt guilty walking away from an unfinished job. Pat could be a pain in the ass, but I hated thinking about what could happen to him up on that ridge alone. He was a piss-poor shot with a rifle, and he was missing a lung. Not exactly a winning combination for a shootout on a rugged bluff top. But Pat did what he did without asking for advice, so I guess he had to sleep in his own bed—whatever the hell that means.

The weather forecast predicted a lull in the snowstorm for late afternoon and evening, then a new wave of snow and wind during the night. There should be a couple good driving hours early in the evening. Good time to make my escape.

I rummaged through Raven's pantry and found packets of some ready-to-eat Indian lentil meal that could be heated in the microwave in the envelope it came in. Not my usual cuisine, but with enough oyster crackers it filled the void in my gut. There were still a couple bottles of Driftless IPA in the fridge, so I chased down my lentils with beer. Not bad.

I gathered my stuff, checked email messages, packed the car, and prepared to say adios to Kickapoo County. I rationalized my guilt about leaving by reminding myself that Pat lived by some outdated Hemingway code of behavior that suited him but bugged the shit out of people who had to work with him. Plus, I told myself, he had Phil and Zach to back him up if he needed them. I told myself to just push aside those ugly guilt feelings I used to experience when I was a little girl waiting to enter the confessional on Saturday morning. Slap a Kenny Chesney CD in the car stereo and let it blast. Au revoir, Lake Hopeless!

# / 20 /

HAULING AN ATV ON A BORROWED TRAILER ALONG WINDING HILLY ROADS
covered with several inches of snow and drifts up to a foot deep was
no waltz around the ballroom, but I made it to the base of Ibsen
Ridge in just over an hour. Now the challenge was to figure out how
to maneuver a vehicle, which I had little experience driving, up a half
mile of steep narrow trails no wider than a deer path. Then if I made
it to the top, I had to find a way to avoid getting shot and gutted by
a psychopathic trophy hunter. The reality was, if I did make it to the
top, I'd probably find myself on another wild goose chase. What were
the odds Clyda McCabe would really travel three or four hours over
snow-covered roads to confront a part-time cop with minimal evidence to even get an arrest warrant? Still, I couldn't resist the chance
to close this case—which in all likelihood would be my last one.
What other chance did I have?

The ATV was equipped with tire chains, which made easy work of
the steep, snow-covered terrain. Once I got to the top, I drove around
the bluff both looking for tracks that would indicate my adversary
had arrived while at the same time trying to create enough tracks to
make my own location difficult to follow. There had been plenty of
wildlife activity since the snowstorm hit, but I saw no sign of human

traffic. Clyda had set our meeting time at noon, but I was hidden in a thick grove of hemlocks by 9 a.m. Now I waited.

Temperature was near freezing, so staying warm in my insulated coveralls wouldn't be a problem. I had plenty of water plus a two-quart thermos of coffee. I also had a stash of beef jerky and peanuts. I was set for the long haul.

Once settled in, I heard nothing but light stirrings of leaves still clinging to a couple old bur oak trees. Two deer burst into the clearing, stood alertly sniffing the air for a few seconds, then bounded into the woods. My instinct said they'd been spooked by someone climbing the bluff. I cradled my twelve-gauge and waited. Nothing. I stood motionless. Would Clyda come out guns blazing? Doubtful. She wanted to negotiate. Otherwise, why bother setting up this meeting. What was her plan? A bribe? A video of our night in the hotel? Who would care? What would she offer me to abandon the case? She already tried luring me with a job. I'd kept my word about coming alone. Would she?

Well over an hour passed. A clump of snow slid off a white pine bough and smacked the fender of the ATV, which was parked forty yards from my hiding place. Would the metallic clank start the action? A flock of crows swept into the oaks and erupted in a raucous argument. Another signal of human intruders?

"Pat, I know you're here. Let's talk." It was Clyda. "Are you alone?"

If I responded, I'd reveal my location. She sounded to be within fifty or sixty yards.

"Pat, we came all this way to talk. Meet me at the head of the path you drove up. There's a big oak tree there. It still has its leaves. We need to talk."

If I stayed in the pine trees, my shotgun was more effective than her rifle, but if I stepped out into the clearing, I wouldn't have a chance. Still, if I didn't answer her, what did I gain? I had to hear her offer. If her only plan was to kill me, she could've done that anywhere. Why travel all this way?

"I'm in a grove of pines thirty yards east of your oak tree. You come here."

"I'm not stupid. You probably got a whole posse waiting in there."

"I'm alone."

"Come out. We'll talk. I don't want this to end badly any more than you do. We can resolve it. My client wants to end it. She knows she won't be found guilty."

A branch snapped close by. I huddled behind a tree trunk and raised my shotgun. With the snow muffling footsteps, it was hard to detect Clyda's approach. How close was she? Would her high-caliber rifle penetrate my cover? Probably. Another twig snapped, but this time behind me. Deer? Or could Clyda have brought reinforcements?

"Come out, Pat." Her voice low, hypnotic. "I'm sorry about the other night. I drank too much. I counted on you staying and lost my temper when you said you were leaving. We need to talk."

"Talk from there. What's your offer?"

"No offer. My client's innocent."

"Then we have nothing to talk about. I gave the evidence to the sheriff. He knows about the sex videos and the hunting club. You admitted you're a skilled butcher. You said you never wasted an ounce when you butchered pigs. You could easily disembowel a man. You helped Kelly kill her husband. At least you covered up evidence."

"Evidence, shit. Where's the body? What about the doctor you hunted down up here? There's our reasonable doubt. You got jack-shit, Pat."

Suddenly, behind me came a quick rush of branches. "Drop your gun, Donegal!" A woman's voice was close behind me.

I froze, avoiding the natural instinct to turn to face the voice.

"Drop it now!"

I let my shotgun fall into the snow at my feet. "Now step out into the clearing."

I followed instructions and made my way through the boughs of hemlock and spruce. I saw Clyda standing in the open, her rifle trained on my chest. She was about to speak but suddenly pivoted left and discharged two shots. I heard a groan in the distance.

"You said you were alone, Pat. Now you caused another cop to die. Hennie wasn't enough?"

I gasped, unable to respond. Who followed me? Shea? Zach? Phil?

"What the hell are you doing?" I finally shouted. "I did come alone. You just shot an innocent bystander." I had trouble breathing. First Hennie, now another victim of my stupidity. Shoot me, you psychopath, I thought. But before I could say the words out loud, I heard another shot. This time Clyda tumbled backward. I turned to look behind me and saw Kelly Swalheim in shock, staring stupidly. Her rifle hung limply in her arms. I leaped and smothered her with my bulk. She wrestled to get free, but I pinned her arms and wrapped my legs around hers. She was half my weight and in spite of her struggles to get free, she finally succumbed. I heard someone running toward us. I looked up. Shea was standing above me. She pushed me off Kelly and skillfully cuffed her wrists and ankles with zip ties. Kelly squirmed violently in the snow.

I stood up, stunned, unable to grasp what was happening. Shea moved slowly toward Clyda's quivering body. She applied her fingers to Clyda's throat.

"Pulse. I feel a pulse," Shea shouted.

I got to my feet, not knowing what to do next. It was too fast. Did Shea shoot Clyda? Or did Kelly shoot her? I stumbled in a trance.

"She's semiconscious. The wound is right below her sternum. Quick, apply steady pressure. Stop the bleeding." Like a zombie, I fell to my knees to follow Shea's orders. I opened Clyda's snowmobile suit and saw strong gushes of blood pulsing from her upper abdomen. I grabbed my stocking cap, wadded it up, and pressed it against the wound. Blood still streamed through my fingers. I applied pressure with the open palm of my hand. The gushing slowed. I saw Shea running back into the woods. I didn't know what was happening. It was like a dream. I continued to apply pressure. Kelly squirmed around on the ground, swearing incoherently. Where was Shea going?

Clyda tried to speak. Terror filled her eyes. "Don't talk. Help is coming." I tried to sound calm.

Minutes later I heard someone breathing heavily behind me. Shea? No, it was Zach bending beside me to examine Clyda and grabbing equipment from his emergency kit. I watched, stunned.

"Pat, I need your help. Keep pressure on the wound while I make an assessment." He started at her nose and mouth and checked breathing. "Breathing okay. Pulse steady. We need to roll her on her side and draw her knee forward." I awkwardly followed orders.

Zach drew a syringe from his bag and quickly administered a shot. "Sedative. I don't want her resisting or going into shock." After the injection, he withdrew another syringe. "Antibiotics," he said. "The bullet should have missed her bowels but there's still a chance of infection. He grabbed a packet of something called QuikClot. "Okay, Pat, gently remove your pressure on the wound." I did as told. Blood was still pouring from the wound. Zach took the gauze material from the packet and began carefully stuffing it into the wound. Clyda jerked from the pain. Once the wound was stuffed, he put a thick pad of gauze over the wound and told me to apply steady pressure. "Keep your hands still," he said. As I did this, Zach riffled through his emergency case and drew out long, pointed tweezers. "Just hold for a few more minutes."

"What happened in the woods?" I asked.

"Sheriff Grimes. Bullet in upper thigh. I got his wound clotted. Shea's with him. She called an ambulance. He'll be okay. But I'm not so sure about this one. Abdominal wounds are hard to treat in the field. May make it, may not." He spoke quietly to me even though the sedative had already kicked in and Clyda looked asleep. Zach was the epitome of grace under pressure.

"Did you say Clyda might die?" I'd forgotten about Kelly lying cuffed in the snow.

"I can't say one way or the other. We have to get the bullet out. Then we need to get her to surgery—fast." Zach spoke as he worked.

Clyda's breath was steady. Zach rechecked her pulse. "Not bad," he mumbled. He held an instrument in his right hand. "Now I need to get that bullet out. Slowly remove the gauze." As I released the pressure, I was surprised to see no bleeding. "Now my problem is I'm going to have to remove the QuikClot so I can find the bullet. I'm sure it hit bone, so maybe it didn't go deep." As he spoke, he carefully pulled the clotting gauze from the cavity. A slow ooze of blood appeared. He dug around inside Clyda.

"Think I feel something. Hopefully not a bone fragment." He continued to dig. The blood trickle increased to a slow flow. After another minute, he shouted, "Got it." He brought out the tweezers holding the intact lead from a bullet. "Now we got to repack the wound. Then we need to keep her warm till we transport."

Zach carefully stuffed the gauze from a fresh packet of QuikClot into the wound.

I removed my coveralls and draped them around Clyda. Zach did the same. "Just stay here with her, Pat, while I check on the sheriff. Yell if something changes. Keep light, steady pressure on the wound."

"Will do."

Kelly rolled in the snow. "Take these goddamn cuffs off."

"I don't have a knife."

"Then find one."

"I'm busy saving your murder accomplice's life."

"I didn't kill nobody."

"Then why were you creeping around with a rifle?"

"Clyda's idea."

Shea came running toward me. She leaned down to look at Clyda. "Zach says she won't last till EMTs arrive. We need to move her."

"How?"

"Clancy ran to get a sled he uses for his ice-fishing stuff. He knows a quick way up and down the bluff."

"Who's Clancy?"

"A guide who brought me here. He also showed Clyda the route a few weeks ago. We just followed her tracks today."

"What about her?" I pointed at Kelly.

"She'll keep till the other squad car arrives."

"How's Phil?"

"Good. Zach's amazing. Sheriff will be fine till help arrives, but we gotta get Clyda to a clearing where we're meeting Med Flight from La Crosse."

"Nice shot, by the way. She would have killed Phil and Zach, and probably me."

"It wasn't me." She stood up. "I'll keep an eye on Phil and let Zach come over to prep her for the trip down the bluff. Are you okay to help Zach and Clancy?"

"I'm fine."

"I'm glad." She almost smiled. "It's nice to see you wore your vest. Too bad she didn't."

"Can't you please take off these cuffs?" Kelly pleaded.

"Shut up!" Shea barked as she stood to leave.

"Shea, I didn't want you to have to be here for this, but I guess I can't accomplish much without you." I paused. "This is my last hurrah. I'm done."

"Yeah, I will believe that when I see it."

# / 21 /

**THE AIRLIFT FOR CLYDA MCCABE SUCCEEDED. THE CHOPPER HAD TO HOVER** above the trees and lower a stretcher. After emergency surgery on her spleen and patching things back together, she was listed in stable condition. Since Clyda was under arrest, Pat was lifted up to the helicopter also and rode along to stand guard outside her room. Phil Grimes went to the local hospital for his thigh wound. They kept him for observation. After the required paperwork, Zach went home to his family, and I returned to Raven's for beer, frozen pizza, and a chance to crash alone. The sheriff scheduled a debriefing meeting at nine in the morning. I planned to be flying down the highway by ten. I didn't plan to see Kickapoo County for a long, long time.

**THE** meeting was in Phil's hospital room. Zach was there when I arrived, and Pat was on his way back from La Crosse. Millie from the office stood beside a stack of papers on a table by the wall. Phil was in good spirits, happy no deputies were injured. He credited Zach for work well above the call of duty.

"I'd like to have you full-time," he said. "I talked to the county supervisor, who told me with Hennie gone, our budget could allow for a decent salary—patrolman, EMT, registered nurse. Three jobs in one. County will cover your school costs till graduation. Good offer if you're interested."

"I'll talk to my wife. Our boy will be ready for school in a couple years. It would be nice not to have to move and look for a job."

"It's here if you want it."

"The county would be lucky to get you," I added.

"Did you talk to Lone Owl about stopping in, Shea?"

"He said he'd be here."

"We need him to make a formal statement. Plus, I'd like to work out some compensation for stopping McCabe before she killed us all."

"I already owe him $450 for guiding service. But he deserves more," I said.

"There will be some papers for him to sign, but there shouldn't be any question about the shooting."

"Did they bring back the body from the cave?" I asked.

"Not yet. DCI crew's out there now. Not much question who it is," Phil said.

"A gutted male corpse," I said. "Lot of damage from animals and time. But plenty left to test for DNA." I stopped speaking when I heard steps behind me. Pat and Clancy Lone Owl walked in together. "I see you two have met."

"In the lobby," Pat said. "I got a few details from the patrolman who relieved me at the hospital, but for the most part I'm in the dark about whatever the hell happened yesterday."

"We'll catch you up," Phil said.

"I'll start." I spoke like a cop reading a report. "I headed back to Madison yesterday morning. Then got a guilt flash and turned around. I'd talked to Phil about meeting Clancy for our tour of the ridge. But I called and said I'd meet them at the tavern. Damn glad Clancy was here. Followed Clyda's tracks up the secret route." I paused and turned to face Pat. "Pat, I don't know if you heard, but we found a body in a cave. It's Swalheim, no doubt."

"I heard something about that from the deputy who relieved me."

"We also learned from Clancy that Clyda hired him a few weeks ago. He led her up a trail not many people know. It involves tight-roping along a narrow natural land bridge through a cedar swamp. Then through a cave. Once you get that far, it's an easy climb to the top. And, you might not know, but it was Clancy who shot Clyda."

"How about Simon Grant, did you guide him too?" Pat asked.

"Nope." Clancy spoke slowly. "Somebody else must know that route—or a different one."

"Clancy saved your life," I said.

"He probably saved everybody in this room." Zach grinned as he spoke.

"Including me," said Clancy. "When I saw Shea draw her handgun at that distance, I realized the person with the rifle better take charge." He tried to hide an embarrassed grin. "I've been hunting since I was seven. It was an easy shot." He paused before adding, "But I'm glad she's going to make it. Good thing I didn't have my deer rifle."

"She'll have plenty of time to recover behind bars," Phil said. "I hope she talked once she regained consciousness."

"She talked and I recorded," Pat said.

# / 22 /

WHEN THE MED FLIGHT ARRIVED AT THE HOSPITAL, A SURGICAL TEAM WAS waiting in the triage center. Clyda remained heavily sedated during the flight, but she knew I was there and talked mostly incoherently, going in and out of focus. She talked about her father and Swalheim as if they were the same person. She sometimes referred to Kelly as her older sister. She obviously confused two phases of her life. "Shot the son of a bitch to save my sister," she said. She frequently mentioned rape and sex slave. I wasn't sure who she was referencing, but I guessed she considered both her sister and Kelly victims.

Clyda was in surgery for two hours, so I spent most of that time in the cafeteria, studying my notes and trying to tie details together. Kelly was in custody in Lake Hope. As she lay cuffed on the ground, she vehemently swore she was not involved in her husband's death. Was she lying? Did Clyda mastermind the entire plot? Maybe?

After surgery, her doctor said she'd be heavily sedated for a few hours. If I needed to interview her, I'd have to wait till he approved. One of the hospital staff showed me to a bunk area where staff members slip off for a couple hours' sleep when working extended shifts in the ER. I accepted the offer and dozed on and off for two hours. When I got back to the recovery room, a Kickapoo deputy was waiting to relieve me. He said he'd be keeping watch on Clyda once she recovered. He offered me his squad car to return to Lake Hope. I thanked him but said I wanted to wait till Clyda woke up. I wanted to interview her. I told the deputy he was welcome to sit in as a witness to the questioning. He declined my offer.

It was 8 p.m. when the ER doc came in to tell me Clyda was conscious and able to answer questions. He warned me not to push too hard. Her condition was stable, but stress could easily change that. I promised to be gentle.

Clyda was awake when I entered her room. She was hooked up to machines and tubes. She forced a smile when she saw me.

"Guess this means you won't be coming to work for me." Her voice sounded dreamy, no doubt the result of the sedatives.

"It doesn't look like it. I'm ready to be put out to pasture."

"You'll never quit, Pat."

"This is my last day of fighting crime."

"I vaguely remember you taking care of me after I was shot."

"Zach Layman, part-time deputy, was the one who saved your life."

"It might've been better if he hadn't."

"Why did you do it? David Swalheim, I mean."

"I actually liked David. Had a sort of fling before I found out he was married."

"Then what? Oh, and I'm going to record this conversation. And, for the record . . ." I recited her Miranda Rights.

"Fine, yes, I understand, but I'll say I was under the influence of sedatives. Not responsible for my answers."

"Might work. But tell me the story."

"I was his lawyer, keeping him out of jail. IRS mostly. He spent a lot more than he earned. Uncle Sam notices those things."

"Gambler, blackmailer, what else?"

"Had a few other business dealings. His pharma sales were not always legit."

"You were both hunters."

"Yes, we had that. I got him into the Kilimanjaro Society. He loved the thrill of hunting his peers. I don't think he ever shot anybody. A lot of guys turn it into a game for money. Put stiff wagers on who'll capture the other guy."

"And you?"

"That is not something we will discuss."

"Okay, so why Swalheim?"

"First, you have to know, Kelly was never involved. She's a victim here."

"The victim was pointing a rifle at me yesterday."

"That was on me, not her." Her focus turned to the table next to her bed. "Can you hand me some chunks of ice? No food or water allowed. Just ice chips to wet my mouth and throat."

"Pain?"

"Not yet. They got me all doped up. But I'll live." Her voice was low and raspy.

"I'm glad."

"You want to see me behind bars, huh?"

"That's not why."

"I suppose you're here to beat a confession out of me."

"I don't think we need one, but the details would be good. You're the lawyer; you understand leniency in sentencing."

"Maybe thirty years instead of fifty? Won't help me much."

"Why did you do it?"

"I told you about my old man. Mean, abusive bastard. Sexually assaulted my sister. I would have been next." She sucked on an ice chip. "David was no better. Abused his own wife. He trapped her into having sex with prominent men. Blackmailed the men then turned it against his wife. Said he'd release recordings if she quit performing. He forced her to become a sex slave. She is innocent in all of this. She was forced to meet his clients, and he threw the money away on gambling, hunting, and women. He was a pig. You know how I feel about pigs."

"So, you gutted him like a hog?"

"I guess that was my thinking. Act like a pig, get treated like a pig."

"Why out at the ridge?"

"I wanted to find the most remote place in the state. You realize it was a fair fight. We stalked each other. He was armed too. It could've been my remains up there."

"Jury might go for that. But why leave the entrails?"

"Like you said, gutted him like a hog. Figured nobody'd ever find them, or at least not recognize them. Feed him to the skunks."

"But a trained army medic found them."

"What are the odds?"

"How did you move the body?"

"That's my little secret."

"You must've had help. Your guide?"

"He was not around the day of the hunt."

"Somebody helped you. Was it Mrs. Swalheim?"

"I prefer not to answer that question."

"Or how about Harley Januss? He helped you, then you killed him?"

"Next question."

"Eventually, the body would've been found."

"Could've been years. Only a few people knew that trail. Animals would've scattered what they didn't eat."

"So, you killed Harley Januss because he knew too much?"

"He found out about the sex files and wanted to keep the golden goose for himself. Planned to take over where David left off."

"So, you shot him?"

"I did. I told him there was a huge buck in the woods near the lodge. He was armed too, but that guy was so stupid. I kept both of their rifles as trophies."

"Anybody else?"

"I've told you enough. What'll happen with the videos?"

"Turned over to Lakeshore County."

"Don't let them release those files. It'll destroy Kelly's life. She's a victim. Don't ruin her life."

"That's out of my control now. The video of Hennie was not coerced by Kelly's husband—seeing as he was dead."

"That one was my fault. I thought I saw an easy way to end the investigation. I talked her into doing that one. Forced her really." Clyda paused, and a pained expression spread across her face. "I'm sorry to say, I told her I'd release her recordings if she didn't do the video with Hennie. Most dreadful thing I've ever done. I love Kelly like a sister."

"So, you made her a sex slave. That sounds hypocritical."

"Sorry. Let's change the subject. We could have made a good team, Pat. If you weren't so damn righteous."

"That is not a word I've ever been called before."

"You act tough, but you're a do-gooder at heart. Such a waste."

"Oh, one more thing. Nice touch planting my notebook at the scene where Januss died. It almost worked."

"We all do what we can."

# / 23 /

AFTER PAT PLAYED HIS RECORDING, THE SHERIFF BREATHED A LOUD SIGH
of relief. "I think we have solved the mystery of David Swalheim. The
confession may not be fully admissible in court, but Clyda certainly
gave us everything we need to build a case. And the Januss case we
leave to Lakeshore County to prove. She'll face two separate trials.
DA can decide what to do about Kelly. Maybe she was a victim. But
she framed Hennie and pointed a gun at you."

"Kelly is no longer my concern," Pat said calmly.

"I got mixed feelings. If it weren't for that sex recording, Hennie
would be alive," I added.

"Tell me about the Hennie video," Phil said.

"Not sure where it is," said Pat. "It wasn't with the ones they found
in the house."

"I know you know more than you're telling, but, what the hell?
I'm not going to press you."

"Let's just say it's lost." Pat said no more.

"Just as well. And speaking of Hennie, I think we should discuss a
memorial ceremony. He died in service."

"May not be my call," Pat said, "but I thought about that, and from
what I know of Hennie, he wouldn't want a ceremony. He was a private guy. I say a plaque at headquarters. I don't think he'd want more."

"I don't often do this," I said. "But I agree with Pat. No hoopla for Hennie."

"I will trust your judgment—at least for now." Phil seemed content to close the case and move on. I agreed.

Zach stood up first. "I'm out of here. The sheriff needs rest before they release him to finish all this paperwork. And I have serious plans to discuss with my wife. What about the rest of you?"

I responded quickly, "My bags are packed. I'm heading back to the real world. Probably a stack of cases waiting in Madison." I paused. "Then I'm going to start planning a real vacation—two weeks, maybe France or Spain."

"You deserve it," Phil chimed in. "How 'bout you, Pat?"

"Going down to Murphy's, order an IPA and two cheeseburgers, and see how high I can raise my cholesterol. Then I'm going buy a bottle of gin, drive back to Raven's, get shit-faced drunk, and try to put this case out of my mind—well, at least till 4 a.m., when I will wake up with screaming headache. But before I do that, I'm going to ask Clancy if he knows of any cabins along the river I could rent. Then I'm going to turn off my computer, throw away my phone, and simply disappear from this world."

The guys in the room chuckled at Pat's crazy plan, but I didn't. I knew he was telling the truth. A realization hit me at that minute that I'd never see Pat Donegal again. He was serious. He was walking away and never coming back. In a way it was a relief, but at the same time it fucking broke my heart.

# / 24 /

CHRISTMAS PASSED UNCEREMONIOUSLY. IT WAS THE FIRST ONE I EVER spent alone. Not that I'm sobbing in my beer. It was my choice. Technically, I wasn't alone. I spent the day with Jack Taylor—though Jack's not a real person. He's a dysfunctional character in a series of Irish crime novels that I had become addicted to. Jack is a literary character I can identify with, not like the Great Gatsby or Atticus Finch. No, this guy I understand.

At the end of the Ibsen Ridge case, I said I was going to turn off my computer and throw away my phone. I didn't exactly keep my word, but I came close. When we left the sheriff's hospital room that day, Shea drove back to Madison, to a world that might actually make sense. Zach Layman went home to contemplate his future as a member of the sheriff's department. Phil Grimes, still nursing a bullet wound in his thigh, went back to his office to figure out a plan to convict Clyda McCabe. That might be easier said than done. She was a good lawyer. Plus, she had the finances to hire other good lawyers. I assured Phil I would testify in court if needed.

When I left the meeting in Phil's room, I did some of what I said I would do. I went back to Raven's house and got drunk. I switched off my phone—and only turn it on when I urgently need to—which isn't often. I've noticed an alert that says I have forty-one voicemail messages and about twice that many texts. So far, I've resisted the temptation to see who's trying to get hold of me. I would probably be disappointed.

When I sobered up the next morning, I drove to Milwaukee and delivered the sex flash drive to Johnnie Sangiovese. I didn't know him well, but his brother helped me solve the case. Johnnie thought I came to extort money, and he couldn't understand when I said he could bust the thumb drive with a hammer in front of me, and there was to my knowledge no backup. He didn't know what to say. Of course, what was I going to do with the file? If I turned it into Lakeshore County, they'd know I'd tampered with evidence. I'd be back in the interrogation room with Chase Norman. No thanks.

On the bright side, when I stopped to say hello to Sammy, he told me that for some reason, unknown to him, his brother Johnnie wanted to make sure I got a really sweet deal on a vehicle—compliments of Johnnie. Sammie knew better than to ask questions. Bottom line, I'm now driving the Toyota Tundra that Sammie tried to sell me earlier. Huh, and Clyda said I was a do-gooder who couldn't take care of himself.


**FOR** two months I've been living in a small, poorly winterized three-room cabin near the Mississippi River a few miles from a town called Thelma. There's a nice diner, a bar, a grocery store, and a library. All the necessities of my new life. I'm alone most days, and that is not a bad thing. I can't hurt anyone or piss anybody off if there's nobody around. What happened with Hennie will haunt me forever. The whole business with Raven seems in the distant past now. That was doomed from day one. I do miss Shea—at least the relationship we had before she saw my real personality. We worked well together on several cases. There was a mystical link between us—not a romantic one, something deeper than that. Too hard for an idiot like me to explain, or even understand. But it was real.

I visited Clancy Lone Owl a few times. We drank beer and fished through the ice. I'm not sure he enjoyed my visits as much as I did, but he invited me back. A woman named Lucy, who works the check-out desk at the local library, talks to me every time I stop. She asks me how I liked the books I'm returning, and then tells me about the books she's reading. My guess is she's lonely and just wants somebody to talk to. The thing she doesn't understand is some people who live alone are lonely and wish they had someone to be with, but other people live alone because they want to be away from people. I fit into that second category—at least I keep telling myself I do.

One thing that keeps me awake at night, maybe it's the reason I'm living alone beside the river, comes from my conversation with Clyda the night we went to her lake house. It was when she told me I was no better than she was. She claimed to get an adrenaline rush out of hunting humans for sport, and she said I did too. I denied it. Denied it to her—and to myself. But sometimes I wonder. I wonder why I had such a hard time breaking away from law enforcement. Was it some noble drive to right wrongs and keep the world safe? Or was it because I enjoyed the thrill of the chase, the showdown, the feeling of conquest?

Clyda is still awaiting trial. Maybe someday she'll be set free—enjoying vodka gimlets, parties, fast cars. Who can say how the process of justice will turn out? But for now, she's experiencing life in a locked cage with a random cellmate. I live in a small cabin by myself, out of touch with everyone—friends and family. I read novels and drink alone every night. I'm not sure who is better off.

So far, no indictments have been filed against Kelly Swalheim. She certainly obstructed our investigation, took part in the extortion scheme, made a video that drove Hennie off a cliff, and pointed a rifle at me on Ibsen Ridge. Chances are the DA will determine an appropriate charge. That is not my decision. Still, considering what she went through, I'm not convinced she wasn't a victim. I've made plenty of mistakes in my life, but the world has given me plenty of do-overs, and most of them I've screwed up. Maybe Kelly will get another chance. It is not my problem.

In my rented cabin, on a bulletin board in the kitchen, I tacked a handwritten poem, a rough draft written in pencil with cross-outs and erasures. I found it on a table at the local library. It hits hauntingly close to home. I read it every morning.

## MEDITATIONS WRITTEN IN EXILE
### by Chanz Loman

I retreat to the woods because I must.
In isolation I confront my true self.
I am not afraid of darkness because it
Shields me from the glare of violence.
I have hunted men—evil scoundrels
Who prey on the weak and defenseless.
And, yes, I have at times become the brute
That I have been praised for crushing out.
Even heroes, when they bathe, stand naked.
In solitude I lose the self that others see
And become a shadow or maybe a ghost
Of the creature I always wanted to be.

# Acknowledgments

I want to thank my family, who many years ago realized I spend part of my life in a fictional world of good guys and bad guys. Sometimes the lines get blurred.

I appreciate the entire crew at University of Wisconsin Press, led by Dennis Lloyd, who stood behind this project through the reviews and revisions. Thanks to Jacqulyn Teoh, who keeps me up-to-date with deadlines and paperwork. Appreciation also to managing editor Adam Mehring, copyeditor Michelle Wing for her insightful suggestions, designer Jennifer Conn, and publicity manager Kaitlin Svabek. A special huge thank you to authors Patricia Skalka and Jim Guhl for their thoughtful and detailed peer reviews and for all the suggestions for improvement that provided my blueprint for revision.

Thank you to Laurie Scheer, University of Wisconsin Continuing Studies, for her coaching in putting together the book proposal for this novel.

Thanks to Roy Dorman and Craig Akey for editing assistance and moral support.

Although these characters are totally fictional and come completely from my imagination, the army medic, Zach Layman, was inspired by John Miller, who was a medic with the Black Horse regiment in Vietnam during the era of the Tet Offensive. Some of Zach's lines come directly from John.

Thanks also to the members of the Waunakee Writers Group for generating ideas for writing experiments and for providing moral support. Thanks to the staff at the Waunakee Public Library, who provide a comfortable place to work and plenty of coffee. Likewise, thanks to the area coffee shops that offer an energetic workspace.